WITHDRAWN

THE QUEEN OF SUSPENSE,
#1 internationally bestselling author
MARY HIGGINS CLARK . . .

"Gets better with every bo~~~ ~~~"

"A master of plot and sus~~~"

"Knows what she's doing ~~~
up with something unexpected."

—*The New York Times Book Review*

**More praise for "GRANDMASTER OF MYSTERY
WRITING"** (*Hartford Courant*) **MARY HIGGINS CLARK
and her heart-pounding novels**

JUST TAKE MY HEART

"Tantalizes readers from the first sentence to the final
paragraph. . . . Mary Higgins Clark rarely misses the mark."
—Bookreporter.com

WHERE ARE YOU NOW?

"Clark stays up to date with the latest technologies and detective
techniques. Her visual, smooth narrative keeps readers hooked."
—*San Antonio Express-News*

Just Take My Heart is also available from
Simon & Schuster Audio and as an eBook

THE SECOND TIME AROUND

"Clark keeps the chase lively throughout."

—*People*

"[Clark] knows how to spin an intriguing tale . . . she's created a convincing heroine in Carley."

—*Booklist*

"There's something special about Clark's thrillers. . . . Grace, charm, and solid storytelling."

—*Publishers Weekly*

DADDY'S LITTLE GIRL

"A fast and fascinating read."

—*Knoxville News-Sentinel* (TN)

"Her best in years . . . a tightly woven, emotionally potent tale of suspense and revenge. . . . This is Clark at her most winning."

—*Publishers Weekly*

"Few stories of obsession will grab readers quite like this one."

—*Ottawa Citizen*

"The plot is classic Clark, except the author tells her story from a first-person perspective. She pulls it off well."

—*Star Ledger* (NJ)

ON THE STREET WHERE YOU LIVE

"Is a reincarnated serial killer at work in a New Jersey resort town more than a century after he first drew blood? That's the catchy premise that supports [this] plot-driven novel."

—*Publishers Weekly*

"A suspenseful page-turner that will delight her many fans."

—*Booklist*

MARY HIGGINS CLARK

JUST TAKE MY HEART

Pocket Books

New York   London   Toronto   Sydney

Pocket Books
A Division of Simon & Schuster, Inc.
1230 Avenue of the Americas
New York, NY 10020

Copyright © 2009 by Mary Higgins Clark

This book is a work of fiction. Names, characters, places, and
incidents either are products of the author's imagination or are
used fictitiously. Any resemblance to actual events or locales or
persons, living or dead, is entirely coincidental.

First Pocket Books paperback edition April 2010

POCKET and colophon are registered trademarks of
Simon & Schuster, Inc.

For information about special discounts for bulk purchases,
please contact Simon & Schuster Special Sales at
1-866-506-1949 or business@simonandschuster.com.

The Simon & Schuster Speakers Bureau can bring authors to
your live event. For more information or to book an event,
contact the Simon & Schuster Speakers Bureau at
1-866-248-3049 or visit our website at www.simonspeakers.com.

Cover design by John Vairo, Jr.

Manufactured in the United States of America

10 9 8 7 6 5 4 3 2 1

ISBN 978-1-4165-7087-5
ISBN 978-1-4391-5924-8 (ebook)

Acknowledgments

We all live in a time of medical miracles. Every day, lives are saved that even a generation ago would have been lost. A number of times I have written novels that touched on this subject and truly enjoyed the process of telling this kind of story.

It is always a joy to begin my acknowledgments by thanking my longtime editor and friend, Michael Korda, who with the assistance of Senior Editor Amanda Murray guides and encourages me from page one to "The End." Many thanks.

Thanks always to Associate Director of Copyediting Gypsy da Silva, my publicist Lisl Cade, and my readers-in-progress Irene Clark, Agnes Newton, and Nadine Petry. What a grand team I have working with me.

Many thanks to Dr. Stuart Geffner, Director of Renal and Pancreas Transplant Surgery at Saint Barnabas Medical Center in Livingston, New Jersey, for his kindness in answering my inquiries about lifesaving heart transplant surgery.

Special thanks to Lucki, the beloved little Maltese who belongs to my daughter Patty and my grandson

Jerry. Lucki was the inspiration in this book for Emily's dog, Bess. I owe her a treat.

And now it's time for you, my friends and readers, to begin to turn these pages. As my Irish ancestors would say, "I hope you have a fine time."

For John Conheeney
Spouse Extraordinaire
and
For our wonderful children and grandchildren
With love

JUST
TAKE
MY HEART

1

It was the persistent sense of impending doom, not the nor'easter, that made Natalie flee from Cape Cod back to New Jersey in the predawn hours of Monday morning. She had expected to find sanctuary in the cozy Cape house that had once been her grandmother's and now was hers, but the icy sleet beating against the windows only increased the terror she was experiencing. Then, when a power failure plunged the house into darkness, she lay awake, sure that every sound was caused by an intruder.

After fifteen years, she was certain that she had accidentally stumbled upon the knowledge of who had strangled her roommate, Jamie, when they were both struggling young actresses. And he *knows* that I know, she thought—I could see it in his eyes.

On Friday night, he had come with a group to the closing night of *A Streetcar Named Desire* at the Omega Playhouse. She had played Blanche DuBois, the most demanding and satisfying role of her career to date. Her reviews had been wonderful, but the role had taken its emotional toll on her. That was why, after the performance, when someone knocked on the door of her dressing room, she had been tempted not to answer. But she had, and they all crowded in to congratulate her, and out of nowhere she recognized him. In his late forties now, his face had filled out, but he was undoubtedly the person whose picture was missing from Jamie's wallet after her body was found. Jamie had been so secretive about him, only referring to him as Jess, "my pet name for him," as she put it.

I was so shocked that when we were introduced, I called him "Jess," Natalie thought. Everyone was talking so much that I am sure no one else noticed. But *he* heard me say his name.

Who do I tell? Who would *believe* me? My word against his? My memory of a small picture that Jamie had hidden in her wallet? I only found it because I had lent her my Visa card and I needed it back. She was in the shower and called to me to get it out of her wallet. That was when I saw the picture, tucked in one of the compartments, behind a couple of business cards.

All Jamie ever told me about him was that he'd tried his hand at acting and wasn't good enough, and that he was in the middle of a divorce. I tried to tell her that was the oldest story in the world, Natalie thought, but she wouldn't listen. She and Jamie had been sharing an apartment on the West Side until that terrible morning when Jamie was strangled while jogging early in Central Park. Her wallet was on the ground, her money and watch were missing. And so was the picture of "Jess." I told the cops that, she thought, but they didn't take it seriously. There had been a number of early-morning muggings in the park and they were sure Jamie just happened to be one of the victims, the only fatal victim, as it turned out.

It had been pouring through Rhode Island and Connecticut, but as Natalie drove down the Palisades Parkway the rain steadily lessened. As she drove farther down, she could see that the roads were already drying.

Would she feel safe at home? She wasn't sure. Twenty years ago, after being widowed, her mother, born and raised in Manhattan, had been happy to sell the house and buy a small apartment near Lincoln Center. Last year, when Natalie and Gregg separated, she heard that the modest house in northern New Jersey where she'd been raised was for sale again.

"Natalie," her mother warned, "you're making a terrible mistake. I think you're crazy not to try to make a go of your marriage. Running back home is never the answer for anyone. You can't re-create the past."

Natalie knew it was impossible to make her mother understand that the kind of wife Gregg wanted and needed was not the person she could ever be for him. "I was unfair to Gregg when I married him," she said. "He needed a wife who would be a real mother to Katie. I can't be. Last year I was away a total of six months in all. It just isn't working. I honestly think that when I move out of Manhattan, he'll understand that the marriage is really over."

"You're still in love with him," her mother insisted. "And he is with you."

"That doesn't mean we're good for each other."

I'm right about that, Natalie thought, as she swallowed the lump in her throat that was always there when she allowed herself to think about Gregg. She wished she could talk to him about what had happened Friday evening. What would she say? "Gregg, what do I do about having the certain knowledge that I know who killed my friend Jamie, without a shred of proof to back me up?" But she couldn't ask him. There was too much of a chance that she'd be unable to resist his begging her to try again. Even though she'd lied and told him she was interested in someone else, it hadn't stopped Gregg's phone calls.

As she turned off the parkway onto Walnut Street, Natalie realized she was longing for a cup of coffee. She had driven straight through and it was quarter of eight. By this time, on a normal day, she would already have had at least two cups.

Most of the houses on Walnut Street in Closter had been torn down to make way for new luxury homes. It was her joke that now she had seven-foot hedges on either side of her house, giving her complete privacy from either neighbor. Years ago, the Keenes had been on one side and the Foleys on the other. Today, she hardly knew who her neighbors were.

The sense of something hostile hit her as she turned in to her driveway and pushed the clicker to open the garage door. As the door began to rise, she shook her head. Gregg had been right when he said that she became every character she played. Even before the stress of meeting Jess, her nerves had been unraveling, like those of Blanche DuBois.

She drove into the garage, stopped, but for some reason did not immediately push the clicker to close the garage door behind her. Instead, she opened the driver's door of the car, pushed open the kitchen door, and stepped inside.

She felt gloved hands dragging her in, twirling her around, and throwing her down. The crack of her head on the hardwood floor sent waves of pain radiating through her skull, but she could still see that he was wearing a plastic raincoat and plastic over his shoes.

"Please," she said, "*please.*" She held up her hands to protect herself from the pistol he was pointing at her chest.

The click as he pushed down the safety catch was his answer to her plea.

2

At ten minutes of eight, punctual as always, Suzie
Walsh turned off Route 9W and drove to the home of
her longtime employer, Catherine Banks. She had been
the seventy-five-year-old widow's housekeeper for thirty
years, arriving at eight A.M. and leaving after lunch at
one P.M. every weekday.

A passionate theatre buff, Suzie loved the fact that
the famous actress Natalie Raines had bought the house
next to Mrs. Banks last year. Natalie was Suzie's absolutely favorite actress. Only two weeks ago, she had seen
her in the limited run of *A Streetcar Named Desire* and
decided no one could ever have played the fragile heroine Blanche DuBois better, not even Vivien Leigh in
the movie. With her delicate features, slender body, and
cascade of pale blond hair, she was the living embodi-
ment of Blanche.

So far Suzie had not met face-to-face with Raines.
She always hoped that she'd run into her someday in the
supermarket, but that hadn't happened yet. Whenever
she was coming to work in the morning, or driving
home in the afternoon, Suzie always made it her business to drive past Raines's house slowly, even though in

the afternoon, it meant driving around the block to get to the highway.

This Monday morning, Suzie almost realized her ambition of seeing Natalie Raines close-up. As she drove past her house, Raines was just stepping out of her car. Suzie sighed. Just that much of a glimpse of her idol was like a bit of magic in her day.

At one o'clock that afternoon, after a cheerful good-bye to Mrs. Banks and armed with a shopping list for the morning, Suzie got into her car and backed out of the driveway. For a moment she hesitated. There wasn't a million to one chance that she would see Natalie Raines twice in one day, and anyway she was tired. But habit prevailed, and she turned the car left, driving slowly as she passed the house next door.

Then she stopped the car abruptly. The door to Raines's garage was open and so was the driver's door of her car, exactly as it had been this morning. She *never* left the garage door open and certainly wouldn't be the kind to leave a car door open all day. Maybe I should mind my own business, Suzie thought, but I can't.

She turned into the driveway, stopped, and got out of her car. Uncertainly, she walked into the garage. It was small and she had to partially close the door of Raines's car to reach the kitchen door. By now she was sure something was wrong. A glance into the car had revealed a pocketbook on the front passenger seat and a suitcase on the floor in the back.

When there was no response to her knock on the kitchen door, she waited, then, unable to go away unsatisfied, turned the knob. The door was unlocked. Worried that she could end up being arrested for trespassing, something still made Suzie open the door and step into the kitchen.

Then she began to scream.

Natalie Raines was crumpled on the kitchen floor, her white cable-knit sweater matted with blood. Her eyes were closed but a soft, hurt cry was coming from her lips.

Suzie knelt beside her as she grabbed the cell phone from her pocket and dialed 911. "80 Walnut Street, Closter," she screamed to the operator. "Natalie Raines. I think she's been shot. Hurry. Hurry. She's dying."

She dropped the phone. Stroking Natalie's head, she said soothingly, "Ms. Raines, you'll be all right. They'll send an ambulance. It will be here any minute, I promise."

The sound from Natalie's lips ended. An instant later her heart stopped.

Her last thought was the sentence Blanche DuBois utters at the end of the play: "I have always depended on the kindness of strangers."

3

She had dreamt of Mark last night, one of those vague, unsatisfying dreams, in which she could hear his voice and was wandering through a dark, cavernous house looking for him. Emily Kelly Wallace woke up with the familiar weight on her mind that often settled in after that kind of dream, but determined that she wouldn't let it grab hold of her today.

She glanced over at Bess, the nine-pound Maltese her brother, Jack, had given her for Christmas. Bess was fast asleep on the other pillow, and the sight of the dog brought immediate comfort. Emily slid out of bed, grabbed the warm robe that was always close at hand in the cold bedroom, picked up a reluctantly awakening Bess, and headed down the stairs of the home in Glen Rock, New Jersey, that she had lived in for most of her thirty-two years.

After a roadside bomb in Iraq had taken Mark's life three years ago, she decided she didn't want to stay in their apartment. About a year later, when she was recovering from her operation, her father, Sean Kelly, had signed over this modest, colonial-style house to her. Long a widower, he was remarrying and moving to Florida. "Em, it makes sense," he had said. "No mortgage. Taxes not too bad. You know most of the neighbors. Give it a try. Then if you'd rather do something else, sell it and you'll have a down payment."

But it *has* worked, Emily thought, as she hurried into the kitchen with Bess under her arm. I love living here. The coffeepot set to a seven A.M. timer was squeaking its announcement that the coffee was ready to pour. Her breakfast consisted of fresh-squeezed orange juice, a toasted English muffin, and two cups of coffee. Carrying the second one, Emily hurried back upstairs to shower and change.

A new bright red turtleneck added a cheery note to last year's charcoal gray pants suit. Suitable for court, she decided, as well as an antidote for this overcast March morning and the dream of Mark. She took a moment to debate about leaving her straight brown hair loose on her shoulders, then decided to pin it up. A quick dash of mascara and lip liner followed. As she snapped on small silver earrings the thought crossed her mind that she never bothered to wear blush anymore. When she had been sick she'd never gone without it.

Downstairs again, she let Bess out in the backyard one more time, then, after an affectionate squeeze, locked her in her crate.

Twenty minutes later she was driving into the parking lot of the Bergen County Courthouse. Although it was only eight fifteen, as usual the lot was almost half full. An assistant prosecutor for the last six years, Emily never felt more at home than when she got out of her car and crossed the tarmac to the courthouse. A tall, slender figure, she was unaware of how many admiring eyes followed her as she moved swiftly past the arriving cars. Her mind was already focused on the decision that should be coming from the grand jury.

For the past several days, the grand jury had been hearing testimony in the case involving the murder of Natalie Raines, the Broadway actress who had been fatally shot in her home nearly two years ago. Although he had always been a suspect, her estranged husband, Gregg Aldrich, had only been formally arrested three weeks ago, when a would-be accomplice had come forward. The grand jury was expected to issue an indictment shortly.

He did it, Emily told herself emphatically as she entered the courthouse, walked through the high-ceilinged lobby, and, scorning the elevator, climbed the steps to the second floor. I'd give my eyeteeth to try that case, she thought.

The Prosecutor's section, in the west wing of the courthouse, was home to forty assistant prosecutors, seventy investigators, and twenty-five secretaries. She punched in the code of the security door with one hand, pushed it open, waved to the switchboard operator, then slipped out of her coat before she reached the tiny windowless cubicle that was her office. A coatrack, two gray steel filing cabinets, two mismatched chairs for witness interviews, a fifty-year-old desk, and her own swivel chair comprised the furnishings. Plants on top of the files and on the corner of her desk were, as Emily put it, her attempt to green America.

She tossed her coat on the unsteady coatrack, settled in her chair, and reached for the file that she had been studying the night before. The Lopez case, a domestic dispute that had escalated into homicide. Two young children, now motherless, and a father in the county jail. And my job is to put him in prison, Emily thought, as she opened the file. The trial was scheduled to begin next week.

At eleven fifteen her phone rang. It was Ted Wesley, the prosecutor. "Emily, can I see you for a minute?" he asked. He hung up without waiting for an answer.

Fifty-year-old Edward "Ted" Scott Wesley, the Bergen County Prosecutor, was by any standards a handsome man. Six feet two, he had impeccable carriage that not only made him seem taller but gave him an air of authority that, as a reporter once wrote, "was comforting to the good guys and disconcerting to anyone who had reason not to sleep at night." His midnight blue eyes and full head of dark hair, now showing light traces of gray, completed the image of an imposing leader.

To Emily's surprise, after knocking on the partially open door and stepping inside his office, she realized her boss was scrutinizing her carefully.

Finally he said, crisply, "Hi, Emily, you look great. Feeling good?"

It was not a casual question. "Never better." She tried to sound offhand, even dismissive, as though she was wondering why he had bothered to ask.

"It's important that you feel good. The grand jury indicted Gregg Aldrich."

"They *did*!" She felt a shot of adrenaline. Even though she had been sure it would happen, Emily also knew that the case was largely based on circumstantial evidence and would certainly not be a slam dunk at trial. "It's been driving me crazy to see that creep plastered all over the gossip columns, running around with the flavor of the month when you know he left his wife bleeding to death. Natalie Raines was such a great actress. God, when she walked onstage, it was magic."

"Don't let Aldrich's social life drive you crazy," Wesley said mildly. "Just put him away for good. It's your case."

It was what she had been hoping to hear. Even so, it took a long moment to sink in. This was the kind of trial a prosecutor like Ted Wesley reserved for himself. It was sure to stay in the headlines, and Ted Wesley loved headlines.

He smiled at her astonishment. "Emily, strictly and totally between us, I'm getting feelers about a high-level job that's coming up in the fall with the new administration. I'd be interested, and Nan would love to live in Washington. As you know, she was raised there. I wouldn't want to be in the middle of a trial if that situation does work out. So Aldrich is yours."

Aldrich is mine. Aldrich is mine. It was the gut-level-satisfying case that she'd been waiting for before she was derailed two years ago. Back in her office, Emily debated calling her father, then vetoed that idea. He'd only caution her not to work too hard. And that's exactly what her brother, Jack, a computer designer who worked in Silicon Valley, would say, she thought, and anyhow, Jack's probably on his way to work. It's only eight thirty in California.

Mark, Mark, I know you'd be so proud of me . . .

She closed her eyes for a moment, a tidal wave of pure longing washing through her, then shook her head and reached for the Lopez file. Once again, she read every line of it. Both of them twenty-four years old; two kids; separated; he went back pleading for a reunion; she stormed out of the apartment, then tried to pass him on the worn marble staircase of the old apartment building. He claimed she fell. The babysitter who had followed them from the apartment swore that he'd pushed her. But her view was obstructed, Emily thought, as she studied the pictures of the stairway.

The phone rang. It was Joe Lyons, the public defender assigned to Lopez. "Emily, I want to come over and talk about the Lopez case. Your office has it all wrong. He didn't push her. She tripped. This was an accident."

"Well, not according to the babysitter," Emily replied. "But let's talk. Three o'clock would be good."

As she hung up, Emily looked at the file picture of the weeping defendant at his arraignment. An unwelcome feeling of uncertainty nagged at her. She admitted to herself that she had doubts about this one. Maybe his wife really did fall. Maybe it *was* an accident.

I used to be so tough, she sighed.

I'm beginning to think that maybe I should have been a defense attorney.

4

Earlier that morning, through the tilted slats of the old-fashioned blinds in the kitchen of his house, Zachary Lanning had watched Emily having her quick breakfast in her kitchen. The microphone he had managed to secretly install in the cabinet over the refrigerator when her contractor left the door unlocked had picked up her random comments to her puppy, who sat on her lap while she was eating.

It's as though she was talking to me, Zach thought happily, as he stacked boxes in the warehouse where he worked on Route 46. It was only a twenty-minute drive from the rented house where he had been living under a new identity since he fled from Iowa. His hours were eight thirty to five thirty, a shift that was perfect for his needs. He could watch Emily early in the morning, then go to work. When she came home in the evening, as she prepared dinner, he could visit with her again. Sometimes she had company, and that would make him angry. She belonged to *him*.

He was sure of one thing: There was no special man in her life. He knew she was a widow. If they happened to see each other outside, she was pleasant but distant. He had told her he was very handy if ever she needed any quick repairs, but he had been able to tell right away that she would never call him. Like all the others during his whole life, she just dismissed him with a glance. She simply didn't understand that he was watching her, *protecting* her. She simply didn't understand that they were meant to be together.

But that would change.

With his slight build, average height, thinning, sandy hair and small brown eyes, in his late-forties, Zach was the kind of nondescript person whom most people would never remember having met.

Certainly most people would never imagine that he was the target of a nationwide manhunt after coldly murdering his wife, her children, and her mother a year and a half ago in Iowa.

5

Gregg, I've said it before and I'll be saying it again over the next six months because you'll need to hear it." Attorney Richard Moore did not look at the client sitting next to him as his driver slowly managed to work the car through the throng of media that was still shouting questions and aiming cameras at them in the Bergen County Courthouse parking lot. "This case hangs on the testimony of a liar who's a career criminal," Moore continued. "It's pathetic." It was the day after the grand jury had handed up the indictment. The prosecutor's office had notified Moore and it had been agreed that Aldrich would surrender this morning.

They had just left the courtroom of Judge Calvin Stevens, who had arraigned Gregg on the murder indictment and had set bail at one million dollars which had been immediately posted.

"Then why did the grand jury vote an indictment?" Gregg Aldrich asked, his voice a monotone.

"There's a saying among lawyers. The prosecutor could indict a ham sandwich if he's so inclined. It's very easy to get an indictment, especially in a high-profile case. All the indictment means is that there's enough evidence to allow the prosecutor to go forward. The press has kept this case front and center. Natalie was a star and any mention of her sells papers. Now this long-time crook Jimmy Easton, caught red-handed in a burglary, claims you paid him to kill his wife. Once there is a trial and you're acquitted, the public will lose interest in it quickly."

"Just the way they lost interest in O.J. after he was acquitted of his wife's murder?" Aldrich asked, a note of derision in his voice. "Richard, you know and I know that even if a jury finds me not guilty—and you're a lot more optimistic than I am about that outcome—this case will never be over unless and until the guy who killed Natalie knocks on the prosecutor's door and spills his guts. In the meantime, I'm out on bail and I have surrendered my passport, which means I can't leave the country, which is terrific for someone in my business. Of course, that is to say nothing of the fact that I have a fourteen-year-old daughter whose father is going to be front and center in newspapers, on television, and online for the indefinite future."

Richard Moore let further reassurances die on his lips. Gregg Aldrich, a very intelligent realist, was not the kind of client to accept them. On one hand, Moore knew the state's case had serious problems and depended on a witness he knew he could skewer during cross-examination. On the other hand, Aldrich was right that having been formally accused of the murder of his estranged wife, no matter what the verdict, in some people's minds he would never be free of the suspicion that he was a killer. But, Moore thought wryly, I'd much rather have him dealing with that situation than sitting in prison for life after a conviction.

And *was* he the killer? There was something that Gregg Aldrich was not telling him. Moore was sure of it. He didn't expect anything resembling a confession from Aldrich, but with the indictment only a day old, he was already beginning to wonder if whatever information Aldrich was withholding would come back to haunt him at the trial.

Moore glanced out the window. It was a miserable March day, totally in keeping with the mood inside the car. Ben Smith, the private investigator and sometime chauffeur, who had worked for him for twenty-five years, was at the wheel. From the slight tilt of his head, Moore knew that Ben was catching every word of what he and Aldrich were saying. Ben's keen hearing was a plus in his line of work, and Moore often used him as a sounding board after his conversations with clients in the car.

Forty minutes of silence followed. Then they were stopping in front of the Park Avenue apartment building in Manhattan where Gregg Aldrich lived. "This is it, at least for the present," Aldrich said as he opened the car door. "Richard, it was good of you to pick me up and deliver me back. As I told you before, I could have met you somewhere and saved you the trouble of a round trip over the bridge."

"It was no trouble and I'm spending the rest of the day at the New York office," Moore said matter-of-factly.

He extended his hand. "Gregg, remember what I told you."

"It's burned in my mind," Aldrich said, his voice still totally flat.

The doorman hurried across the sidewalk to hold open the car door. As Gregg Aldrich murmured his thanks he looked into the man's eyes and saw the expression of barely concealed excitement that he knew some people experience when they are close spectators to a sensational crime story. I hope you're enjoying yourself, he thought bitterly.

On the elevator to his fifteenth-floor apartment, he asked himself: How could this all have happened? And why did he follow Natalie to Cape Cod? And did he in fact drive to New Jersey that Monday morning? He knew that he had been so distraught, tired, and angry that when he got home he had gone out for his usual run in Central Park, and later was shocked to realize he had been jogging for nearly two and a half hours.

Or had he been?

He was terrified to realize that he was not sure now.

6

Emily admitted to herself that the combination of Mark's death and her own sudden illness had devastated her. Added to that was her father's marriage, his decision to move permanently to Florida, and the fact that her brother, Jack, had accepted a job offer in California—all emotional blows that had left her reeling.

She knew she had kept up a good front when both her father and brother worried about leaving her at this time in her life. She also knew that her father signing over the house to her, with Jack's heartfelt consent, was a certain salve to their consciences.

And it's not as if they should feel guilty, she thought. Mom's been dead twelve years. Dad and Joan were seeing each other for five years. They're both pushing seventy. They love sailing and have the right to enjoy being able to do it year round. And certainly Jack couldn't pass up that job. He's got Helen and two little kids to think about.

All that having been said, Emily knew that not being able to see her father, her brother, and his family regularly had made the adjustment to losing Mark even more difficult. Certainly it was wonderful to be back in the house—it had a "return to the womb" aspect that brought with it a healing quality. On the other hand,

the neighbors who were still there from when she was
growing up were the age of her parents. The ones who
had sold their homes had been replaced by families with
young children. The sole exception was the quiet little
guy who rented next door to her and who had shyly told
her he was very handy in case she ever needed anything
fixed.

Her immediate inclination had been to turn him
down flat. The last thing she wanted or needed was a
close neighbor who might try to latch onto her under
the guise of helpfulness. But as the months passed, and
the little she got to see of Zach Lanning was if they happened to arrive or depart their homes at the same time,
Emily's guard began to drop.

In the first weeks after she was assigned the Aldrich
trial, she spent long hours reviewing and absorbing the
file. It immediately became necessary for her to leave
the office at five o'clock, race home to walk and feed
Bess, then return to the office until nine or ten o'clock
at night.

She liked the demands of her job. It gave her less
time to dwell on her own sorrow. And the more she
learned about Natalie, the more she felt a kinship with
her. They had both returned to their childhood homes,
Natalie because of a broken marriage, Emily because of
a broken heart. Emily had reams of information she had
downloaded on the subject of Natalie's life and career.
She had thought of Natalie as being a natural blond, but
the background material revealed that she had changed
her hair color from brunette when she was in her early

twenties. Seeing her early pictures, Emily was struck by the realization that there was a genuine resemblance between the two of them. The fact that Natalie's grandparents came from the same county in Ireland where her grandparents had been born made her wonder if four or five generations back, they would have been considered "kissing cousins," the Irish term for extended family.

Even though she loved the process of preparing a new case and truly didn't mind the hours, Emily soon began to realize that running back and forth from the office to the house to take care of Bess was just too time-consuming. She also felt guilty that Bess was alone so long every day and now late into the evening.

Someone else had noticed it, too. Zach Lanning had begun to prepare his yard for spring planting. Early one evening he was waiting after she had deposited Bess back into the house. "Miss Wallace," he began, his eyes slightly averted, "I can't help but notice that you seem to be hurrying home because of the dog. And I see you rush right out again. I read about that big case that you're involved in. I bet it's a lot of work. What I mean to say is that I love dogs, but the owner is allergic and won't let me have one in this house. I'd really enjoy having your dog—I heard you call her Bess—as company when I get home. If your house is just like this one, your back porch is enclosed and heated. So if you wanted to leave the cage out there and give me a key to just the porch, I could let her out, then feed her, then take her for a nice long walk. My backyard is enclosed and she can run around a bit while I'm working in the garden.

Then I'll put her back and lock the door behind me. That way you don't have to worry about her. I bet that she and I would get along great."

"That's really nice of you, Zach. Let me just give it some thought. I'm really rushed right now. I'll call you in the next day or so. Is your number listed?"

"I just have a cell phone," he responded. "Let me jot down the number for you."

As Emily pulled the car out of her driveway to head back to the office, Zach could barely contain his excitement. Once he had a key to her porch, it would be easy to take a wax impression of the lock on the door that led into the rest of the house. He was sure she was going to take him up on his offer. She really loves that useless hunk of fur, he thought. And once I'm inside, I'll go up to her bedroom and go through her drawers.

I want to touch everything that she wears.

7

Alice Mills dreaded the thought of being called as a witness at the trial. The loss of her only child, Natalie Raines, had left her more bewildered than bitter. How *could* he do that to her? was the question she asked herself over and over again during the day, and haunted her at night. In her recurring dream, she was always trying to reach Natalie. She had to warn her. Something terrible was going to happen to her.

But then the dream became a nightmare. As Alice ran blindly in the dark, she felt herself stumble and fall. The faint scent of Natalie's perfume filled her nostrils. Without seeing it, she knew she had tripped over Natalie's body.

And that was when she would wake and scream, "How *could* he do that to her?" as she bolted up from the pillow.

After the first year, the nightmare had come less frequently but then increased again after Gregg was indicted and the media frenzy began. That was why, when Alice received a call in mid-April from Assistant Prosecutor Emily Wallace asking her to come in for an interview the following morning, she sat up the night before in the comfortable chair where she often dozed off while watching television. It was her hope that if she did fall asleep, it would be a light slumber that wouldn't let her sink into the nightmare.

Her plan didn't work. Only this time she called out Natalie's name as she woke. For the rest of the night, Alice was awake thinking of her lost daughter, musing over the memory that Natalie had been born three weeks early, arriving on her thirtieth birthday. Of course, after a marriage that had been, to her sorrow, childless for eight years, that had made Natalie a true gift from heaven.

Then Alice thought about the evening a few weeks ago when her sisters had insisted on taking her to dinner for her seventieth birthday and toasted her at the table. They were afraid to mention Natalie's name but I insisted we toast her, too, Alice remembered. We even managed to joke about it. "Trust me, Natalie wouldn't have allowed a fortieth birthday party," she'd said. "Remember, she always told us that in show business it's a good idea to be eternally young."

She *is* eternally young, Alice thought, sighing, as she got up from the easy chair at seven A.M. and reached down to pull on her slippers. Her arthritic knees were always worse in the morning. Wincing as she got to her feet, she walked across the living room of her small apartment on West Sixty-fifth Street, closed the windows, and pulled up the shades. As always, the sight of the Hudson River in Manhattan lifted her spirits.

Natalie had inherited her love of the water. That was

why she had so often driven up to Cape Cod, even for just a few days.

Alice tightened the sash on her soft cotton bathrobe. She loved fresh air, but it had become colder during the night and now the living room was chilly. She adjusted the thermostat upward, went into the galley kitchen, and reached for the coffeepot. It had been set to go on at 6:55. The coffee had brewed and her cup was on the sideboard next to it.

She knew she should eat at least a slice of toast, but she simply didn't want it. What would the prosecutor ask her? she wondered as she carried the cup into the dinette and sat at the table in the chair that gave the best view of the river. And what can I add to what I already told the detectives more than two years ago? That Gregg wanted a reconciliation and that I urged my daughter to go back to him?

That I loved Gregg?

That I now despise him?

That I will never understand how he could have done this to her?

For the interview, Alice decided to wear a black pants suit with a white blouse. Her sister had bought it for her to wear to Natalie's funeral. In these two years, she had lost a little weight and knew the suit hung loosely on her. But what difference does that make? she asked herself. She had stopped touching up her hair and now it was pure white, with a natural wave that saved her many trips to the beauty salon. The weight loss had caused the wrinkles on her face to deepen, and she had no energy to keep up with facials, as Natalie had always reminded her to do.

The meeting was scheduled for ten o'clock. At eight, Alice went downstairs, walked a block past Lincoln Center, went into the subway, and took the train that stopped at the Port Authority Bus Terminal. On the brief ride, she found herself thinking about the house in Closter. A real estate agent had urged her not to try to sell it while the newspapers were writing daily about Natalie. "Wait awhile," he'd suggested. "Then paint the whole interior white. That will give it a nice clean and fresh feeling. *Then* we'll put it on the market."

Alice knew the man hadn't meant to be rude or insensitive. It was just that the idea of somehow whitewashing Natalie's death hurt so much. When his exclusive on the listing of the house ended, she did not renew it.

When she got to the Port Authority, it was, as usual, teeming with people rushing in and out of the building, hurrying to and from platforms to catch their buses or to flag down a cab. For Alice, like everywhere she went, it was a reminder. She could see herself rushing Natalie through here after school for television commercial auditions as early as when she was still in kindergarten.

Even then, people stopped to look at her, Alice thought, as she waited on line to buy a round-trip ticket to and from Hackensack, New Jersey, where the courthouse was located. When all the other kids had long hair Natalie had the pageboy cut and bangs. She was a beautiful child and she stood out.

But it was more than that. She had stardust clinging to her.

After all these years, it would have felt natural to go to Gate 210 where the bus to Closter was located, but Alice, her feet leaden now, went to Gate 232 and waited for the bus to Hackensack.

An hour later she was walking up the steps of the Bergen County Courthouse and, as she placed her bag on the electronic security monitor, timidly inquired as to the location of the elevator that would take her to the second-floor prosecutor's office.

8

As Alice Mills was getting off the bus down the block from the courthouse, Emily was reviewing her notes for the interview with Billy Tryon and Jake Rosen, the two homicide detectives who had worked on the Natalie Raines case from its inception. They had been among the prosecutor's team which responded to the call from the Closter police after they had arrived at Natalie's home and found her body.

Tryon and Rosen had settled in chairs opposite her desk. As usual, when Emily looked at them, she couldn't help but feel the stark contrast in her reaction to the two men. Jake Rosen, age thirty-one, six feet tall, with a trim body, close-cropped blond hair, and an intelligent demeanor, was a smart, diligent investigator. She had worked with him several years before, when they both had been assigned to the juvenile division, and they had gotten along well. Unlike a couple of his colleagues, including Billy Tryon, he had never seemed to resent having a woman as his supervisor.

Tryon, however, had been cut from a different cloth. Emily and other women in the office had always felt his thinly veiled hostility. They all resented the fact that because he was Prosecutor Ted Wesley's cousin, no complaints, however justified, had ever been filed against him.

He was a good investigator, Emily didn't dispute that. But it was common knowledge that in the methods that he sometimes used to obtain convictions, he walked the line. There had been numerous accusations over the years by defendants who angrily denied that they had made the incriminating verbal statements he described in his sworn testimony at trials. While she understood that all detectives receive that kind of complaint at some point, there was no doubt that Tryon had much more than his share of them.

He was also the detective who had been the first to respond to Easton's request to talk to someone from the prosecutor's office after his arrest for the burglary.

Emily hoped the distaste she felt for Tryon did not show in her expression as she looked at him, slouched in his chair. With his weather-beaten face, shaggy haircut, and eyes perpetually half closed, he looked older than his fifty-two years. Divorced, and known to consider himself a ladies' man, she knew that some women outside the office found him appealing. Her distaste was magnified when she heard that he was telling people she wasn't tough enough to try this case. But after studying the file she had to admit that he and Rosen had done a thorough job of investigating the crime scene and of interviewing the witnesses.

She did not waste time on pleasantries. She opened the manila folder on top of the file on her desk. "Natalie Raines's mother will be here in a little while," she said crisply. "I've been going over your reports and her initial statement to you the night Natalie died and her written statement a few days later."

She looked up at the two of them. "From what I see here, the mother's first reaction was that she absolutely refused to believe that Gregg Aldrich could have anything to do with this."

"That's right," Rosen confirmed quietly. "Mrs. Mills said she loved Gregg like a son and had begged Natalie to go back to him. She thought Natalie worked much too hard and wanted to see her give more time to her personal life."

"You'd think she'd want to kill him," Tryon said sarcastically. "Instead she's all worried and upset about him and his kid."

"I think she understood Aldrich's frustration," Rosen said, turning to Emily. "The friends we interviewed all agreed that Natalie was a workaholic. The irony of it is that what drove him to murder could make the jurors feel sorry for him. Even his own mother-in-law felt sorry for him. She didn't even believe he did it."

"When was the last time either one of you spoke to her?" Emily asked.

"We called her just before Easton's statement hit the papers. We didn't want her to read about it. She was really shocked. Before that, she called a few times to see if anything had developed in the investigation," Rosen said.

"The old lady wanted someone to talk to," Tryon interjected, his voice indifferent, "so we talked to her."

"How nice of you," Emily snapped. "I see in her statement that Mrs. Mills talked about Natalie's roommate, Jamie Evans, being murdered in Central Park fifteen years before Natalie died. You asked her if she thought there could be any connection to this?"

"She said that would be impossible," Tryon replied. "She told us Natalie never met the roommate's boyfriend. She did know that he was married and supposedly getting a divorce. Natalie had urged her roommate to break it off because she knew he was conning her. Natalie said she did see his picture once, and when it was missing from the roommate's wallet after the murder, she thought there could be a connection, but the detectives on the case didn't buy it. There had been a series of muggings in the park about that time. Jamie Evans's wallet was on the ground with her credit cards and money gone, and her watch and earrings were missing, too. The cops believe she resisted the robbery and ended up dead. Anyway, they never did figure out who the boyfriend was, but the bottom line is they thought it was a robbery gone bad."

The phone rang. Emily picked it up. "Emily, Mrs. Mills is here," the receptionist said.

"Okay. We'll be right there."

Rosen stood up. "Why don't I get her, Emily?"

Tryon did not move.

Emily looked at him. "We'll need another chair," she said. "Would you mind pulling one in?"

Tryon ambled to his feet. "Do you really need both of us here for this? I'm finishing my report on the Gannon case. I don't think Momma is going to come up with any surprises."

"Her name is Mrs. Alice Mills." Emily made no effort to hide her irritation. "I would appreciate it if you would be a little more sensitive."

"Lighten up, Emily. I don't need any instructions." He looked her in the eye. "And keep in mind I was working on cases in this office when you were in the third grade."

As Tryon left, Rosen walked in with Alice Mills. In a quick moment, Emily observed the sorrow etched in the older woman's face, the slight tremor in her neck, the fact that the suit she was wearing seemed too big for her. Still standing, Emily introduced herself, expressed her condolences, and invited her to sit down. When she sat back in her own chair, Emily explained to Natalie Raines's mother that she would be handling the trial and would do her best to convict Gregg Aldrich and obtain justice for Natalie.

"And please call me Emily," she concluded.

"Thank you," Alice Mills said softly. "I must tell you that the people from your office have been very kind. I only wish they could bring my daughter back."

An image of Mark saying good-bye to her that last time flashed through Emily's mind. "I wish I could bring her back," Emily replied, hoping that the catch in her throat was not apparent.

For the next hour, her voice conversational, her manner unhurried, Emily reviewed the statements that Mills had given two years before. To her dismay, it soon became clear that Natalie's mother still was torn about whether Gregg Aldrich could have committed the crime. "When they told me about Easton, I was stunned and devastated, but at least it was a relief to know the truth. But the more I read about this fellow Easton, the more I wonder."

If the jury thinks like that, I'm cooked, Emily thought, and moved on to the next area she wanted to discuss. "Mrs. Mills, Natalie's roommate, Jamie Evans, was killed in Central Park many years ago. I understand that Natalie thought that the mystery guy she was seeing might be responsible?"

"Jamie and Natalie both gone," Alice Mills said, shaking her head as she tried to blink back tears. "And both murdered . . . Who could possibly have imagined such unspeakable tragedy?" She dabbed at her eyes with a tissue and then continued. "Natalie was wrong," she said. "She saw that man's picture in Jamie's wallet once, but that was at least a month before Jamie was killed. For all Natalie knew, Jamie might have thrown it out herself. I think Natalie's reaction was like what I feel right now. She and Jamie were so close. She needed to blame someone, to punish someone for her death."

"As you want to punish Gregg Aldrich?" Emily asked.

"I want to punish her murderer, whoever he is."

Emily averted her eyes from the naked pain on the other woman's face. This was the part of her job that she dreaded. She realized that the empathy she felt when she saw the anguish of a victim's family was what drove her to present the best possible case in court. But today, for some reason, more than ever before, the grief she was witnessing touched her to her very soul. She knew it was useless to try to assuage this mother's grief with words.

But I can help her by proving not only to a jury but to *her* that Gregg Aldrich was responsible for Natalie's death and deserves the harshest sentence the judge can give him—life in prison without parole.

Then she did something she had not expected to do. As Alice Mills got up to leave, Emily stood up, hurried around her desk, and put her arms around the heartbroken mother.

9

Michael Gordon's desk in his office on the thirtieth floor of Rockefeller Center was heaped with newspapers from all over the country, a usual sight in the morning. Before the end of the day, he would have scanned all of them looking for interesting crimes to cover on his nightly program, *Courtside*, on channel 8.

A former defense attorney, Michael's life had changed dramatically at age thirty-four, when he had been invited to be on that same program, one of a panel of experts analyzing ongoing criminal trials in Manhattan. His perceptive comments, quick wit, and black Irish good looks had ensured his frequent invitations to be a guest on the show. Then when the long-time host retired, he was asked to take over, and now, two years later, it was one of the most popular programs in the country.

A native of Manhattan, Mike lived in an apartment on Central Park West. Though a sought-after bachelor, and despite the many invitations that were showered on him, he spent many nights quietly at home working on the book he had contracted to write, an analysis of great crimes of the twentieth century. He planned to open it with Harry Thaw's killing of the architect Stanford

White in 1906 and end with the first O. J. Simpson trial in 1995.

It was a project that fascinated him. He had come to believe that most domestic crimes were rooted in jealousy. Thaw was jealous that White had been intimate with his wife when she was a very young woman. Simpson was jealous that his wife was being seen with someone else.

What about Gregg Aldrich, a man he had admired and liked? Michael had been a close friend of both Gregg and Natalie even before they were married. He had spoken eloquently at Natalie's memorial service and had frequently invited Gregg and his daughter, Katie, to his skiing lodge in Vermont on weekends during the two winters since Natalie's death.

I always believed that the cops rushed to judgment by publicly referring to Gregg as "a person of interest," Michael thought, as he absentmindedly glanced at and pushed aside the newspapers on his desk. *What do I believe now? I just don't know.*

Gregg had called the same day he was indicted. "Mike, I assume you'll be covering the trial on your program?"

"Yes."

"I'm going to make it easy for you. I'm not going to ask you if you believe Easton's story. But I think it best if we avoid each other until after the trial."

"I think you're right, Gregg." An uncomfortable silence settled between them.

They had not seen each other much in these past six

months. Occasionally they'd been in the theatre or at a cocktail party and had only nodded in passing. Now the trial was scheduled to start on September 15th, next Monday. Mike knew he would cover it the usual way, highlights of the day's testimony every evening, followed by discussion with his panel of legal experts. It was a real break that the judge was allowing cameras inside the courtroom. Clips of the actual proceedings made for good viewing.

Knowing Gregg, he was sure that on the surface he would be composed no matter what accusations the prosecutor threw at him. But Gregg's emotions ran deep. At the memorial service he had been composed. Later that evening in his apartment, with only Natalie's mother and Katie and Mike present, he had suddenly started sobbing inconsolably, then, embarrassed, had rushed from the room.

There was no question he had been crazy about Natalie. But had that outburst been pure grief, or had it been remorse? Or was it terror at the prospect of spending the rest of his life in prison? Mike wasn't sure anymore. For some reason the image of Scott Peterson tacking up posters with pictures of his missing wife when he had in fact murdered her and tossed her body in the Pacific Ocean surfaced whenever he thought of the evening that Gregg had broken down.

"Mike."

His secretary was on the intercom. Startled out of his reverie, Michael said, "Oh, uh, yes, Liz."

"Katie Aldrich is here. She'd like to see you."

"Katie! Of course. Send her in."

Mike rushed to get up and around his desk. As the door opened, he greeted the slender, golden-haired fourteen-year-old with open arms. "Katie, I've missed you." He could feel her trembling as he embraced her.

"Mike, I'm so scared. Tell me there's no way they'll find Daddy guilty."

"Katie, your dad has a good lawyer, the best. Everything rests on the testimony of a convicted crook."

"Why haven't we seen you in six months?" She searched his face carefully.

Mike led her over to the comfortable chairs in front of the windows that overlooked the Rockefeller Center skating rink. After they were both seated, he reached over and took her hand. "Katie, that was your dad's idea, not mine."

"No, Mike. When he called you with that suggestion, it was his way of testing you. He said that if you were convinced he was innocent, you wouldn't have taken him up on that offer."

Mike realized he was ashamed to see the anger and hurt now in her eyes. Was she right? "Katie, I'm a journalist. I should not be privy to your dad's defense and if I were in and out of your apartment, it might be inevitable that I hear things that I shouldn't know. As it is, I will have to tell my audience repeatedly that I am and have been a close friend of your dad, but will not speak to him until the proceedings are over."

"Can you help influence public opinion so that if he is acquitted"—Katie hesitated—"*when* he is acquitted, people will understand he is an innocent man who was unfairly accused?"

"Katie, the public will have to make that decision for themselves."

Katie Aldrich pulled her hand from his and stood up. "I'm supposed to go back to Choate for the fall semester, but I'm not going. I'll get a tutor to keep up with the schoolwork. I'm going to be at that trial every day. Dad needs someone rock solid in his corner. I'd hoped you'd be there, too. Dad always said that you were an awesome defense attorney."

Without waiting for his answer she hurried to the door. As she put her hand on the knob she turned back to him. "Hope you have a big audience, Mike," she said. "If you do, I'm sure they'll give you a big bonus."

10

By the end of the week before the trial was to begin, Emily was cautiously optimistic that the case preparation had gone well. The summer had disappeared in a blur. In July, she had managed to take a week's vacation to visit her father and his wife, Joan, in Florida and then had spent five days in August with her brother, Jack, and his family in California.

It had been wonderful to see all of them, but always in the back of her mind her thoughts had been pulling her back to the case. During July and August she had meticulously interviewed the eighteen witnesses she would call and had their testimony virtually committed to memory.

The intensity of the preparation had also been a turning point in her adjustment to Mark's death. Though she still very much missed him, she no longer tortured herself a dozen times a day with the phrase that had been consuming so much of her energy, "If only he had lived, if only he had lived . . ."

Instead, as she met with the prospective witnesses, the face of Gregg Aldrich permeated her consciousness now. It was especially present when Natalie's friends related how distressed Natalie would become when, after a lunch or dinner, she would check her cell phone messages and invariably find at least one call or text from Gregg beseeching her to give their marriage another chance.

"I saw her burst into tears on a number of occasions," Lisa Kent, a longtime close friend, said angrily. "She cared very much for him, more than that, I'm sure she loved him. It was the marriage that just didn't work. She had hoped that she could keep him as her agent, but she realized pretty quickly that he was much too emotional about her for them to see each other and be in touch all the time, even if it was only on a business basis."

Emily knew that Kent would make a good witness.

Late Friday afternoon, three days before the trial was to start, Ted Wesley called her to his office. From the moment she saw him, she could tell that he was elated.

"Close the door," he said. "I have something to tell you."

"Let me guess," Emily said, "you've heard from Washington!"

"About fifteen minutes ago. You're the first one in the office that I'm telling. The president is going to announce tomorrow that he is nominating me to be the new attorney general."

"Ted, that's wonderful. What an honor! And no one deserves it more than you do." She felt genuinely happy for him.

"I'm not going anywhere too fast. The Senate confirmation hearings will be scheduled in the next few weeks. I'm kind of glad it's working out that way. I want to be around for the Aldrich trial. I want to see this guy go down."

"So do I. It's a stroke of luck that Easton can remember so many details from Gregg Aldrich's living room. Even with Easton's background, I don't see how Moore can explain that away."

"And you have that call from Aldrich's cell phone to Easton's cell phone. I don't know how Moore is going to get around that, either." Wesley leaned back in his chair. "Emily, you must know there was some unhappiness in this office when I gave you this case. I did it because I think you're ready for it and I know you can pull this case together for the jury."

Emily's smile was rueful. "If you can only tell me how I can transform Jimmy Easton from looking like the creep that he is to a credible witness, I'd be eternally grateful. We bought a dark blue suit for him to wear when he testifies, but we both know he's going to look like a fish out of water in it. I told you that when I spoke to Jimmy at the jail, I realized that, mercifully, the shoe polish color in his hair was fading, but it didn't improve his appearance one bit."

Wesley was frowning thoughtfully. "Emily, I don't care what Easton looks like. You have Aldrich's cell phone call to him, and you have his description of the living room. Even if he comes across lousy, they can't change those two facts."

"Then why is Moore taking this to trial? They have never wanted to negotiate any kind of plea, even after

Easton came into the picture. I just don't know where they're going with this, and whether or not Easton can stand up to Moore's cross-examination."

"We'll soon find out," Wesley said, his tone now mild.

Emily perceived the difference in his voice and felt that she could read his mind. He's getting nervous that Aldrich will be acquitted, she thought. That won't be just a failure for me. It will be considered a failure in judgment on his part that he gave me this case. That won't be the greatest way to start off his Senate confirmation hearings.

After once again congratulating Wesley on his nomination, Emily went home. But early in the morning she was back in her office reviewing her trial notes and ended up spending most of her waking hours there over the weekend.

Thank God for Zach, she thought several times during those days. She recalled how reluctant she had initially been to have any more than a passing acquaintance with him and how relieved and grateful she was now that he had been feeding and walking Bess. He'd even done it while she was on her brief vacations, insisting there was no need to put Bess in a kennel.

"We've become pals," Zach had said in his shy, diffident manner. "She'll be safe on my watch."

But, on Sunday night, when Emily returned home at ten P.M., she found it disturbing that Zach was sitting in the porch room with Bess on his lap and watching television.

"Just keeping each other company," Zach explained, smiling. "Guess you went out to dinner with some friends."

Emily was about to reply that knowing that she would be working late, she had brought a sandwich and fruit to the office, but then she stopped herself. She did not owe Zach any explanations. At that moment, she became acutely aware that Zach, in his isolation, though he probably didn't realize it, was becoming focused not only on Bess, but on *her*.

It was a creepy feeling, and for a moment it made her shudder.

11

On the Sunday night before the trial, Richard Moore and his son Cole, who had assisted in preparing the defense, had dinner with Gregg Aldrich and Katie in the dining club in Gregg's apartment building. They had arranged for one of the small private rooms so they could speak openly, and at the same time shield Gregg from the curious gaze of other diners.

Moore, an adept raconteur, was able to coax smiles and even a few chuckles from Gregg and Katie as the salads and entrées were being served. It was a visibly relaxed Katie who stood up and excused herself before dessert. "I promised Dad that if he let me stay here during the trial I would keep up with the assignments they sent me. I'm starting right now."

"What a strong and mature kid she is," Moore said to Aldrich after Katie left. "You've done a great job with her."

"She continues to amaze me," Aldrich said quietly. "She told me that she wouldn't stay for dessert because she was sure we'd want to have some last-minute discussions. I assume that she was correct?"

Richard Moore looked across the table at his client. In the six months since he had been indicted, Gregg had aged ten years. He had lost weight and even though his face was still handsome, he looked weary and there were deep circles under his eyes.

Cole, a younger version of Richard, had immersed himself in this case, and had expressed to his father how concerned he was about the outcome of the case. "Dad, he's got to understand that it's in his best interest to consider a plea. Why do you think he's never allowed us to negotiate with the prosecutor?"

That was a question that Richard Moore had pondered frequently, and he thought he might have the answer. Gregg Aldrich needed to convince not only the jury, but *himself* that he was innocent. Only once had Gregg referred to the fact that he was surprised, even shocked, to have come home on the morning of Natalie's death and realize he had been jogging for over two hours. It was almost as if he was questioning himself, Moore recalled. Was it because he was in such denial that he had killed her that his mind had shielded him from the memory? It wouldn't be the first time I've seen that, he thought. And Cole and I have privately agreed that he very probably *did* kill Natalie . . .

The waiter came to the table. All three ordered espresso and skipped dessert. Then Richard Moore cleared his throat. "Gregg," he said softly, "I wouldn't be doing my best for you if I didn't raise this topic again. I know that you have never wanted us to have any plea discussions with the prosecutor's office, but it's probably not too late to ask them to consider it. You are facing the rest of your life in prison. But I honestly think that they're nervous about this case, too. I really believe that I could get them to consider a twenty-year sentence. It's a long time, but you would be out in your early sixties and still have a lot of years left."

"Twenty years!" Gregg Aldrich snapped. "*Only* twenty years. Why don't we call them right now? If we wait they might not offer such a good deal."

His voice was rising. He slammed down his napkin, and then as the waiter came back into the room, made a visible effort to calm himself. When the waiter was gone again, he looked from Richard to Cole and then back to Richard. "Here the three of us sit in our designer suits, in a private dining room of a Park Avenue apartment building, and you are suggesting to me that to save myself from dying in prison, I spend the next twenty years of my life there. And that's if they're bighearted enough to agree to that."

He picked up his cup and drank the espresso in one gulp. "Richard, I am going to trial. I am not going to abandon my daughter. And there's one other little fact that I should mention: I *loved* Natalie! There is no way on God's earth that I could ever have done this to her. And as I have made clear to you, I intend to testify. Now, if both of you will excuse me, I'm going to try to get some sleep. I'll be at your office at eight o'clock tomorrow morning, then we'll present ourselves in court. As a team, I hope."

The Moores looked at each other, then Richard spoke. "Gregg, I will not raise this topic again. We will give them hell. And I promise you, I will savage Easton."

12

On September 15th, the trial of the State of New Jersey versus Gregg Aldrich began. Presiding was the Honorable Calvin Stevens, a longtime veteran of the criminal bench, the first African-American appointed to the Bergen County Superior Court, and considered to be a tough but fair jurist.

As the jury selection was about to begin, Emily looked over at Aldrich and his attorney Richard Moore. As she had thought many times during the preparation of this case, Aldrich had picked the right guy to represent him. Moore was a lean, handsome man in his midsixties with a full head of salt-and-pepper hair. Impeccably dressed in a dark blue suit, light blue shirt, and patterned blue tie, he exuded an air of quiet confidence. Emily knew he was the kind of attorney who would exhibit a friendly and respectful demeanor toward the jurors, and that they would like him.

She also knew that he would exhibit the same demeanor toward the witnesses who really didn't hurt his client, and save his rapier attacks for the ones who did. She was fully aware of his record of success in cases where the state had been forced, as she would be shortly, to call as a witness a career criminal like Jimmy Easton, who would claim that the defendant had solicited him to commit the crime.

Sitting next to Moore was his son and associate Cole Moore, whom she knew well and liked. Cole had spent four years as an assistant prosecutor in her office before going to work for his father five years ago. He was a good lawyer and, together with his father, would present a formidable defense team.

Aldrich was sitting on the other side of Richard Moore. Facing life in prison, he had to be terrified, but outwardly he appeared calm and poised. At forty-two, he was one of the top theatrical agents in the business. Noted for his quick wit and charm, it was easy to see why Natalie Raines had fallen in love with him initially. Emily knew he had a fourteen-year-old daughter from his first marriage, who lived with him in New York City. The girl's mother had died young and their investigation had shown that he had hoped and expected that Natalie would be a second mother to her. That had been one of the reasons for the breakup, according to Natalie's friends. Even they had admitted that for Natalie, *nothing* was more important than her career.

They'll make good witnesses, Emily thought. They'll show the jury how angry and frustrated Aldrich was before he snapped and killed her.

Jimmy Easton. He was going to make or break her case. Fortunately there would be some corroboration of his testimony. Several credible witnesses would be called to testify that they had seen him with Aldrich at a bar two weeks before Natalie Raines was murdered.

Even better than that, Emily reflected again, Easton had accurately described the living room of Aldrich's New York apartment. Let Moore get around that, Emily reassured herself again.

But it was still going to be a tough road to a conviction. The judge had addressed the jurors and informed them that the case involved a murder charge and that including jury selection and allowing for jury deliberation, the trial would probably take about four weeks.

Emily looked over her right shoulder. There were several reporters in the front row of the courtroom, and she was aware that there had been television cameras and photographers filming Aldrich and his attorneys as they entered the courthouse. She also knew that once the jury was impaneled and she and Moore were giving their opening statements, the courtroom would be packed. The judge had ruled that the trial could be televised, and Michael Gordon, the anchor of the cable show *Courtside*, was planning to cover it.

She swallowed to combat the sudden dryness in her throat. She had over twenty jury trials under her belt and had won most of them, but this was by far the highest-profile case in which she had ever been involved. Again she warned herself: This is no slam dunk.

The first potential juror, a grandmotherly lady in her late sixties, was being questioned at the bench. The judge asked her out of the hearing of the rest of the panel if she had formed any opinion about the defendant.

"Well, Your Honor, since you're asking me, and since I'm an honest person, I think he's guilty as sin."

Moore didn't have to say anything. Judge Stevens did it for him. Politely but firmly, he told the obviously disappointed juror that she was dismissed.

13

The tedious task of selecting and swearing a jury took three days. At nine A.M. on the fourth day, the judge, the jury, the attorneys, and the defendant were assembled. Judge Stevens told the jurors that the attorneys would now be presenting their opening statements. He gave them general instructions and explained that since the prosecutor had the burden of proof, she would proceed first.

Taking a deep breath, Emily rose from her chair and walked over toward the jurors. "Good morning, ladies and gentlemen. As Judge Stevens has told you, my name is Emily Wallace and I am an assistant prosecutor in the office of the Bergen County Prosecutor. I have been given the responsibility of presenting to you, for your review and your consideration, the evidence that the state has gathered in the matter of State versus Gregg Aldrich. As Judge Stevens has also told you, what I say now and what Mr. Moore may say in his opening statement is not evidence. The evidence will come from the witnesses who will testify and from the exhibits that are marked into evidence. The purpose of my opening statement is to give you an overview of the state's case so that as each witness testifies, you will have a better understanding of where that testimony fits within the total scheme of the state's case.

"After all of the testimony is completed, I will have another opportunity to speak to you—in my summation—and, at that time, I respectfully submit to you, I will be able to say to you that the state's witnesses and the physical exhibits have demonstrated beyond any reasonable doubt that Gregg Aldrich brutally murdered his wife."

For the next forty-five minutes, Emily meticulously detailed the investigation and the circumstances that had led to Aldrich's indictment. She told them that by all accounts Natalie Raines and Gregg Aldrich had been very happy early on in their five-year marriage. She spoke of Natalie's success as an actress and of Aldrich's prominence as her theatrical agent. She explained to them that the evidence would show that as time passed, the demands of Natalie's career, including long separations when her shows took her on the road, began to cause substantial strain.

Her voice lowered, she sketched Aldrich's growing frustration at these circumstances and his disappointment, which evolved into deep anger, that Natalie was not home much more often with him and his young daughter. With a tone of sympathy, she related that Aldrich's first wife had died when his little girl, Katie, had been only three years old and that he had hoped and expected that Natalie would be a second mother to her. Katie had been seven years old at the time that they married. Emily indicated that she would produce witnesses who had been friends of the couple who would testify to Gregg's repeated statements of anger and frustration that Natalie was consumed by her career, and was not there emotionally for either one of them.

She then informed the jury that Natalie and Aldrich had a prenuptial agreement which kept their finances generally separate. However, she stated, much of Gregg Aldrich's income was earned as Natalie's agent. When, a year before her death, she had separated from him, she told him that she still cared deeply for him and wanted him to continue as her agent. But as the months went by, and Natalie became convinced that because of Aldrich's resentment a total break would be necessary, he faced the loss of the substantial income from his most successful client.

Emily related that the evidence would show that Gregg made repeated requests to Natalie to reconcile but was rebuffed. She told the jurors that after the separation, Natalie had bought her childhood home in Closter, New Jersey, a thirty-minute drive from the midtown Manhattan apartment where Gregg continued to reside with his daughter. Emily explained that Natalie was comfortable and happy in her home, which provided close proximity to the New York theatre, but both emotional and physical distance from Gregg. Shortly after this move, and sure of her decision, Natalie filed for divorce. Witnesses would testify that Gregg had been devastated, but still not convinced that the marriage was over.

Emily continued. The evidence would demonstrate

that Gregg Aldrich, growing more desperate, began to stalk Natalie. On the Friday night prior to the early Monday morning death of Natalie, he attended the final Broadway performance of *A Streetcar Named Desire*, sitting in the last row so that she could not see him. He was observed by others who would testify that he had appeared stone-faced throughout the performance and had been the only person in the audience not to rise for a standing ovation at the end.

As the jurors listened intently, their eyes shifting between Emily and the defense table, Emily continued. "Telephone records reveal that on the following morning, Saturday, March 14th, Gregg received what would be his last phone call from Natalie. According to his own statement to the police after her body was found, Natalie left a message for Gregg that she had gone to her Cape Cod home for the weekend. She told him that she still intended to be present at the scheduled three o'clock transition meeting on Monday in her new agent's Manhattan office."

Emily related that Aldrich explained to the police that this meeting had been scheduled so that he and the new agent could review her contracts and pending offers in Natalie's presence. Gregg admitted to the police that in the message Natalie told him she needed to be alone, and implored him not to contact her for any reason during the weekend.

Emily then turned toward Gregg, as if to confront him. "Gregg Aldrich responded to that request," she said, her voice rising. "Although he initially denied that he had any further contact with Natalie prior to her death, the police challenged him with the records they quickly obtained. Within a half hour of that phone call, his credit card was used to rent a vehicle, a dark green Toyota sedan, which he kept for two days and drove a total of 680 miles. The rental itself was particularly important because the defendant already owned a car, which remained in the garage of the apartment building where he lived."

Turning back toward the jurors, Emily argued that the mileage was extremely significant because the round trip to Natalie's Cape Cod home from Manhattan was five hundred and forty miles. Only after being confronted by the police with the fact that a Cape Cod neighbor, who lived around the corner from Natalie, had seen him driving a dark green Toyota past his home on the Saturday night prior to Natalie's death, did Gregg Aldrich admit that he had been there.

"And what did he say about why he had gone there? He would have this jury believe," Emily argued, "that his sole purpose in making the trip was to see if his estranged wife was with another man that weekend. Aldrich would also have you believe that if he *had* seen anyone else with her, he would have given up his efforts to reconcile and accept the divorce."

Emily rolled her eyes and shrugged her shoulders. "Just like that," she said. "After begging her to come back to him, the same man who was literally stalking her in a rented vehicle that gave him cover, was going to pick up his marbles and go home. But he didn't count on a neighbor seeing him behind the wheel of that rented car.

"Gregg Aldrich lives very well. There are fine inns on Cape Cod, but he stayed in a cheap motel in Hyannis. He admitted that he drove past Natalie's house twice on Saturday and did not observe any other car or person there. He further admitted that on Sunday he drove by her house three times, the last time at eight o'clock that evening, and that it appeared to him Natalie was alone. He claimed that he drove five hours back to New York and immediately went to bed. He stated that he awoke at seven A.M. on Monday morning, left about seven twenty for a jog in Central Park, jogged or walked for well over two hours, and returned the Toyota to the rental office six blocks from his apartment at ten A.M."

Emily's voice grew increasingly sarcastic. "And what did he tell the police about why he rented a car, as opposed to driving his own luxury vehicle? He stated that his own car was past due for servicing and he didn't want to put this much more mileage on it at that time." She shook her head. "What a pathetic story. I submit to you that Gregg Aldrich rented a vehicle that would not be recognized by Natalie if she had happened to look out her window. He did not want Natalie to know that he was stalking her."

Emily took a deep breath. "But he *did* know her habits. Natalie hated to drive in traffic. She didn't mind driving late at night or very early in the morning. I submit to you that Gregg Aldrich knew Natalie would be back home in Closter sometime early- to mid-morning

Monday, and he went there to confront her. He arrived before her. You will hear from a neighbor's housekeeper, Suzie Walsh, that she saw Natalie getting out of her car in her garage at a few minutes before eight. She will tell you that five hours later, at one o'clock, when she drove past Natalie's home, she saw that the car door was still open, and sensed something was wrong. You will hear that she decided to enter the home and found Natalie dying on the kitchen floor. You will hear from the detectives that there was no sign of forced entry, but Natalie's mother will tell you that Natalie had kept a key to the back door, which had a separate lock, in an imitation rock in the backyard. That key was missing. And very significantly, Gregg Aldrich knew where to look for that key since he had bought that imitation rock for Natalie."

Emily continued, "The state acknowledges to you that no evidence physically connecting Gregg Aldrich to the murder scene was recovered. Hence, in the first two years of this investigation, though substantial circumstantial evidence existed regarding Gregg Aldrich, the Bergen County Prosecutor's Office recognized that even great suspicion is not enough. Gregg Aldrich was not arrested until six months ago. He was arrested after the break that was needed occurred. That break came in the person of Jimmy Easton."

This is the toughest part, Emily thought, as she took a sip of water. "I will begin my reference to Mr. Easton by telling you immediately that he is a career criminal. He has numerous felony convictions over a twenty-year span and he has served several terms in prison. Six months ago he did again what he has done most of his adult life—he committed another crime. He broke into a home in Old Tappan, but was caught running from it with money and jewelry. The police were alerted to this burglary by a silent alarm that had been tripped. When he was being processed at the local police department, no doubt he knew he was facing a long prison term. He told the police that he had important information regarding the murder of Natalie Raines. Detectives from the prosecutor's office immediately responded and spoke to him."

The jurors were all listening intently. She sensed their negative reaction when she detailed Easton's prior record of burglary, theft, forgery, and sale of illegal drugs. Before going into all of what Easton had told the detectives, she prefaced it by saying that she would never expect a jury to believe him unless there was substantial corroboration to what he was saying. She stated that there was.

Emily bluntly told the jury that, as they might expect, Mr. Easton was not cooperating simply out of the goodness of his heart. In exchange for his testimony, the prosecutor's office had agreed to limit his prison term on his plea to burglary to four years in prison, which was six years less than the ten-year term he could have received as a habitual offender. She told them that sometimes plea agreements like this were necessary to obtain information in a more serious case. She emphasized that Easton would still receive a prison term, but also would benefit from his cooperation.

Emily drew in a deep breath. She was well aware that the jurors were totally engaged and listening to every word. She told them that Easton had informed the detectives that he had had a chance meeting in a bar in Manhattan with Gregg Aldrich two weeks before Natalie Raines was murdered. Easton said that Aldrich was drinking heavily and appeared very depressed. He stated that Aldrich started talking to him as they sat at the bar and indicated that he wanted to get rid of his wife. Easton explained to the police that he had recently been paroled and could not get a job because of his criminal record. He was living in a rented room in Greenwich Village and picking up odd jobs.

"Ladies and gentlemen of this jury, Jimmy Easton told Aldrich about his criminal record and he further told him that he would be happy, for the right price, to take care of his problem. Aldrich offered him five thousand dollars up front and twenty thousand dollars after the crime was committed. You will hear Mr. Easton testify that the agreement was made and that Aldrich gave Easton many details about Natalie's schedule and where she lived. You will also hear, ladies and gentlemen, that telephone records indicate a call was placed from Aldrich's cell phone to Easton's cell phone. You will learn that Jimmy Easton went to Gregg Aldrich's apartment, the interior of which he will describe in detail, and accepted the five thousand dollar down payment. Mr. Easton will tell you, however, that he thereafter became very afraid of getting caught and spending the rest of his life in prison. He will also tell you that he then wrote a letter to Mr. Aldrich informing him that he couldn't go through with it. Ladies and Gentlemen, I submit to you that, tragically for Natalie Raines, it was at that point that Gregg Aldrich decided to kill her himself."

Emily concluded by thanking the jurors for their attention. As the judge was telling them that Mr. Moore would now speak, she walked slowly back to her chair. She nodded almost imperceptibly to Ted Wesley, who was seated in the front row. I'm glad that's over, she thought. I think it went pretty well. Now let's hear what Moore has to say about our star witness.

Moore stood up, theatrically shaking his head as if to clear away the nonsense he had just been forced to endure. He thanked the judge, walked toward the jury box with measured steps, and leaned slightly on the rail.

Good neighbors chatting over the fence, Emily thought sarcastically. He does this all the time. He wants to be their new best friend.

"Ladies and gentlemen, my name is Richard Moore. My son Cole Moore and I represent Gregg Aldrich. We want to start off by saying thank you for the several weeks that you have taken from your personal lives to serve on this panel. It is most appreciated by both of us. It is also most important. You literally have the life and future of Gregg in your hands. We spent a long time picking this jury, and when I said that the jury was 'satisfactory,' I was saying that Gregg and I knew that the people seated here were going to be fair. And that's all we ask of you.

"The prosecutor just spent nearly an hour going

through what she represents as the evidence in the case. You heard it the same way I did. There was no arrest in this case for nearly two years. Up until that time, all the police knew was that Gregg and Natalie, like so many other couples, were in the midst of a divorce. Like so many other people involved in a divorce, Gregg was heartbroken. I promise you that he will testify in this case. He will tell you, as he told the police long before he was arrested, that he went to Cape Cod because he wanted to know if she was involved with anyone else. He did that because he wanted to see if there was any point in continuing to seek reconciliation.

"You will hear that he saw that she was alone, then left Cape Cod and returned to New York. He never even spoke to her.

"Assistant Prosecutor Wallace told you with emphasis about the two hours that Gregg Aldrich was out of his apartment the morning that Natalie was killed. You will hear, however, that his morning jog was a matter of longtime daily routine. The prosecutor's office would have you believe that on that morning, he managed to drive in rush hour traffic to New Jersey, kill Natalie, and then return in rush hour traffic to New York all within these two hours. They would have you believe that he murdered the woman whom he knew was not involved with anyone else, and with whom he still desperately wanted to reconcile. That was pretty much the totality of the evidence until Jimmy Easton came along. This model citizen, this savior of their case—a man who has spent half of his adult life in prison and much of the rest of it on parole."

Moore shook his head and continued, his voice dripping with sarcasm. "Jimmy Easton was arrested yet again while fleeing from the burglary of a house in this county. Once again he had invaded the sanctity of a family's home and ransacked it. Fortunately the silent alarm alerted the police and he was captured. But all was not lost for Jimmy Easton. His ticket out of a lengthy habitual-offender prison term was Gregg Aldrich. You will hear how this pathological liar, this sociopath, transformed a casual chance encounter in a bar with Gregg Aldrich, where the brief conversation was about baseball, into a sinister plot to murder the woman Gregg loved. You will hear how Gregg supposedly offered this total stranger twenty-five thousand dollars to commit this crime. You will hear how Easton accepted this proposal, then you will hear how Easton was shortly thereafter stricken with a guilty conscience, apparently for the first time in his useless life, and then backed out of the deal.

"This is the garbage the state is asking you to swallow. This is the evidence on which they ask you to destroy Gregg Aldrich's life. Ladies and gentlemen, I represent to you that Gregg Aldrich will testify and he will explain to you, and to your satisfaction, how Easton could describe his living room and why there was a phone call to him."

Turning and pointing his finger at Emily, Moore

thundered, "For the first time in over twenty encounters with the criminal justice system, Easton is testifying *for* the state instead of being prosecuted by them."

As Moore strode back to his chair, the judge addressed Emily. "Prosecutor, call your first witness."

14

From the moment she found Natalie, Suzie Walsh had been a celebrity among her friends. She had told and retold the story of how she'd been sure something was wrong when she had seen both Natalie's car door and garage door still open after she left work, exactly as they had been five hours earlier.

"Something made me investigate, even though I was worried that I could be arrested for trespassing," she would relate breathlessly, "and then when I went in and saw that beautiful woman, crumpled on the floor, blood all over her white sweater, and moaning, I tell you, I almost died myself. My fingers were trembling so much that when I dialed 911, I didn't think the call would go through. And then . . ."

Knowing that the police called Natalie's husband, Gregg Aldrich, a "person of interest" in the homicide and that someday he might be indicted, Suzie had gone a half dozen times to the Bergen County Courthouse when a criminal trial was in session, just to familiarize herself with what it would be like if she was ever called as a witness. She found the proceedings exciting and took note of the fact that some witnesses talked too much and were directed by the judge to answer the questions without giving their opinions. Suzie knew that would be hard for her to do.

When after two years, Gregg Aldrich was formally accused of Natalie's murder and Suzie knew she would definitely be a witness at the trial, she and her friends had a long discussion about what she should wear to court. "You may be on the front page of the newspapers," one of them cautioned. "If I were you I'd get a nice, new black or brown pants suit. I know you love red, but red seems too cheerful for someone describing what you saw that day."

Suzie had found exactly what she was looking for on sale in her favorite outlet. It was a brown tweed pants suit with a thread of dark red running through it. Red was not only her favorite color but it always brought her luck. Just having a little of it in the pattern, and the fact that the lines of the suit also made her size fourteen body look slimmer, gave her confidence.

Even so, and even though she'd had her hair colored and blown dry the day before, Suzie felt a flutter in her stomach when she was summoned to the witness stand. She placed her hand on the Bible, swore to tell the whole truth and nothing but the truth, and sat down in the witness chair.

The prosecutor, Emily Wallace, is really attractive, Suzie thought, and she looked so young to be trying an important case like this. She had a nice way about her, too, and after the first few questions, Suzie began to relax. She had talked about what happened so much to her friends that it was easy to answer everything without hesitation.

In response to Emily's questions, Suzie explained that she had gone into the garage, seen Natalie Raines's pocketbook and suitcase in her car, then knocked on the door. Realizing it was unlocked, she then opened it and went into the kitchen. Suzie was about to explain that it wasn't her habit to walk into people's homes uninvited but this time, because of what she had seen, it was different. But she stopped herself. Just answer the questions, she thought.

Then Emily Wallace asked her to describe in her own words what she found in the kitchen.

"I saw her right away. If I'd taken two more steps, I'd have tripped over her."

"Who did you see, Ms. Walsh?"

"I saw Natalie Raines."

"Was she alive?"

"Yes. She was moaning like a hurt kitten."

Suzie heard someone begin to sob. Her eyes flew to the third row, where a woman, whom she recognized from newspaper pictures as Natalie Raines's aunt, grabbed a handkerchief from her purse and pressed it against her lips. As Suzie watched, the expression on the elderly woman's face became agonized, but she did not utter another sound.

Suzie described calling 911 and then kneeling beside Natalie. "There was blood all over her sweater. I didn't know if she could hear me but I know sometimes people who seem to be unconscious really aren't and are aware if someone talks to them, so I told her she'd be all right and that an ambulance was coming. And then she just stopped breathing."

"Did you touch her?"

"I put my hand on her forehead and stroked it. I wanted her to feel that she wasn't alone. She must have been so frightened, I mean lying there, hurting so much, and knowing she was probably dying. I tell you, I'd be scared."

"Objection." Richard Moore jumped from his seat.

"Sustained," the judge ordered. "Ms. Walsh, please just answer the question without additional comment. Prosecutor, repeat the question."

"Did you touch her?" Emily asked again.

"I put my hand on her forehead and stroked it," Suzie said carefully now, frightened by the defense attorney. But then when it was Moore's turn, he only asked her a few more questions and acted very friendly. It was a little embarrassing to admit to him that she almost always drove by Natalie Raines's house in the afternoon when she left work even though it meant going all around the block to get to the parkway. But then she noticed that some people in the courtroom smiled when she said she was such a fan of Natalie's that she loved to catch any possible glimpse of her.

"When was the last time you saw Natalie Raines before you entered her house?" Moore asked.

"Like I said. I saw her getting out of the car that morning."

"No more questions," Moore said crisply.

It was almost disappointing to be finished. As she left the stand Suzie made it her business to get a good look at Gregg Aldrich. He's a fine-looking man, she thought. I can understand why even someone as beautiful as Natalie Raines could fall in love with him. His eyes have such a sad expression. What a phony he is. It's enough to make a person sick.

She hoped he caught the contemptuous glance she shot at him as she exited the courtroom.

15

Because of his long friendship with Gregg, and because Katie's comments had stung him, Michael Gordon had expected to be drawn emotionally into the trial of the State of New Jersey versus Gregg Aldrich. However, he had not expected to feel an almost fatalistic sense that Gregg was not only guilty, but that he was going to be convicted of Natalie's murder.

As he had expected, the trial attracted national attention. Natalie had been a major Broadway star and an Academy Award nominee. Gregg, a regular at star-studded events, was a familiar figure to the avid tabloid readers whose lives revolved around those of celebrities. After Natalie's death, Gregg had been a particular target of the paparazzi. Every time he escorted an actress to an event, it was rumored that he was involved with her.

The headlines in the gossip magazines had also kept front and center the fact that he was a "person of interest" in Natalie's death.

Michael knew Gregg was carrying a lot of baggage into the trial. But added to that was an unexpected element: The news stories were also focusing on the young, beautiful prosecutor Emily Wallace, and the skillful manner in which she was building up the case against Aldrich.

As a former defense attorney, Michael recognized that Emily was closing the doors to the possibility that Natalie's death had been a random crime. The detectives from her office, Billy Tryon and Jake Rosen, were good witnesses, articulate and prompt in their answers to her questions.

They testified that there had been no break-in at the home of Natalie Raines. The security system had not been tampered with. A professional thief could have opened the small safe in Natalie's bedroom closet with a can opener, but there was no sign it had been touched. Evidence seemed to indicate that the perpetrator had exited by the back door and run through the yard and the wooded area behind it to the next street. It had rained during the night and they believed he might have had some kind of plastic covering over his shoes since it was impossible to get a useful cast of a footprint, even though there were two specific indentations where the grass was particularly soft. The shoe size ranged between a ten and a twelve.

Gregg Aldrich wore a size eleven shoe.

The security system log was entered into evidence. The last time it was turned on was at four o'clock Friday afternoon, March 13th. It was disengaged at eleven thirty that same evening, the security installer testified, and was never reset, indicating the house was not armed over the weekend nor on the Monday morning Natalie Raines was murdered.

When she was on the stand, Natalie's mother, Alice Mills, testified that Natalie kept a spare key inside a fake rock in the backyard of the Closter house. "Gregg knew about that rock," she swore. "He bought it for Natalie. When she lived with him, she was always losing or forgetting her apartment key. That was why when she moved to Closter, he told her she'd better have a spare key around, or she'd find herself locked out on a cold night."

Alice Mills's next remark was stricken from the record but it had been heard by everyone in the courtroom. She had started sobbing and, looking at Gregg, had cried: "You were always so protective of Natalie! How could you have changed so much? How could you have hated her enough to do that to her?"

The next witness was a clerk from Brookstone with a copy of the sales slip showing that Gregg had paid for the rock with his credit card.

The medical examiner's testimony was unemotional and specific. From the position of the body, he believed that Natalie Raines was attacked as soon as she walked in the door. A lump on the back of her head suggested she had been grabbed and thrown down on the floor, then shot at close range. The bullet just missed her heart. The cause of the death was internal bleeding.

"If she had received immediate help after she was shot, could she have been saved?" Wallace asked.

"Absolutely."

That night the panel discussion on *Courtside* centered on Emily Wallace.

"The look she gave Aldrich after that last question to the medical examiner was pure theatre," Peter Knowles, a retired prosecutor, commented. "What she was telling the jury was that after Aldrich shot Natalie, he could still have saved her life. Instead he left her to bleed to death."

"I don't buy that," Brett Long, a criminal psychologist, said forcefully. "Why would he take a chance that somebody else might happen to come in after he left and get help for her? Aldrich or whoever shot her thought she was finished."

That was exactly what Michael had been thinking. Why didn't I say it first? he asked himself. Was it because I don't want to offer Gregg even the slightest support? Am I that sure he's guilty? Instead of agreeing with Brett Long, he said: "Emily Wallace has the gift of making every juror feel as though she's in an intimate conversation with him or her. We all know how effective that is."

At the end of the second week of the trial, viewers were invited to register their opinions of Gregg's guilt or innocence on the *Courtside* Web site. The number of hits was overwhelming and seventy-five percent of them voted for a guilty verdict. When a panelist on the show congratulated him on the response, Michael remembered Katie's bitter comment that he would probably get a bonus for his coverage of the trial.

As each day seemed to tighten the web around Gregg, Michael felt a deepening sense of having abandoned his friend and even helping to sway public opinion against him. How about the jurors? he asked himself. Members of the jury were supposed to avoid news coverage of the trial. Michael wondered how many of them watched his show every night and if they would be influenced by the polls.

Was Gregg watching *Courtside* after he got back to his apartment? Somehow Michael was sure that he was. And he also wondered if by any wild chance Gregg was having the same reaction he was to Emily Wallace — that in an unsettling way, there was something about her that reminded him of Natalie.

16

Zach knew he had made a mistake. He should never have been sitting on Emily's porch watching television when she got home that night. Immediately, a worried look had come into her eyes, and she'd been very cool when she thanked him for taking care of Bess.

He knew that the only reason she hadn't changed their arrangement yet was because of her trial, but he was certain that very soon she would find some excuse to get rid of him. Even worse, would she run some kind of check on him? She was a prosecutor after all. She must not get suspicious.

Zachary Lanning had been the name he'd picked for his new identity in the months that he planned his revenge on Charlotte, her mother, and her kids. He tried never to think about his other names, even though sometimes they bubbled to the surface in his sleep.

In Des Moines he'd been Charley Muir, and in that life he had been an electrician and volunteer fireman. Charlotte was his third wife, but he didn't tell her that. He used his savings to buy her a house. Charley and Charlotte, it sounded so warm and cozy. Then in two years, she kicked him out. Her mother moved in with her and the kids. She camped in my house, he thought, even though when I lived there, she never even came to visit. Charlotte sued him for divorce and the judge awarded her the house and alimony because she claimed she had given up her good job to stay home and cook meals for him. Charlotte was a liar. She had hated that job.

Then he found out that she was dating one of the other guys in the firehouse, Rick Morgan. He overheard Rick tell someone that Charlotte had split because she was afraid of him, that he was creepy . . .

It had been a treat watching Emily Wallace spend her whole summer pulling a case together to convict a guy for killing his wife. And she's going to do it, too, Zach thought, that's how smart she is. But she's not smart enough to know I killed five people at once! He took pride in the fact that Emily's name and face were all over the media—it was almost as though they were complimenting him, too.

No one is closer to her than I am, he thought. I check her e-mails. I go through her desk. I touch her clothes. I read the letters her husband wrote to her from Iraq. I know Emily better than she knows herself.

For now he had to do something to quell her suspicions, however. He scouted around the neighborhood and found a high school kid who wanted some kind of after-school job. Then Friday evening of the second week of the trial, he watched for Emily coming home and stopped her as she was getting out of the car.

"Emily, I'm so sorry, I've been switched to working the four-to-eleven shift in the warehouse for a while," he lied. "That doesn't do you much good with Bess."

He really resented seeing that this time the expression in Emily's eyes was one of pure relief. Then he told her about the kid down the block who was willing to take over walking and feeding Bess at least until Thanksgiving, when she'd start rehearsals for the school play.

"Zach, that is *very* sweet of you," Emily told him. "Actually, I'll be keeping more reasonable hours, so I won't need any help."

She might as well have added the word "ever." Zach could tell that Emily wouldn't be letting anyone in and out of her house again.

"Well, here's her number, just in case, and here's your key," Zach said, then not looking at her, his tone shy, added, "I watch that *Courtside* program every night. You're doing a great job. I can't wait to see how you treat that guy Aldrich when he gets on the stand. He must be a terrible person."

Emily smiled her thanks and tucked the key in her pocket. That's a happy ending, she thought as she walked up the steps to the front door. I was trying to figure out how to cut off this situation and the poor guy did it for me.

Zach watched her go with narrowed eyes. As surely as Charlotte had put him out of his house, Emily had put him out of her life. It wouldn't be the way he had hoped, that she'd let the kid down the block help out with that dog of hers, then be glad to have him take over again. That wasn't going to happen.

The fury that had washed over him at other times in his life engulfed him again. He made his decision.

You're next, Emily, he thought. I don't take rejection. I never have and I never will.

When she was in the house, for some inexplicable reason, Emily felt uneasy and double-locked the door behind her. Then, when she was on the back porch, letting Bess out of her crate, the thought crossed her mind that it wouldn't be a bad idea to get a bolt for the porch door.

Why am I getting all these feelings of apprehension? she asked herself. It has to be the trial.

I've talked so much about Natalie that I feel as though I've become her.

17

Since the trial began it had become a pattern for Gregg Aldrich to go directly to his lawyer's office from the courthouse and spend a couple of hours going over the testimony of the prosecutor's witnesses who had been on the stand that day. Then a car would drive him home. Katie, adamant in her need to be with him in the courtroom, had agreed that she would go home when the court recessed around four P.M. and meet her tutor there.

She had also agreed, at her father's insistence, that at least some evenings would be spent with friends who attended school with her in Manhattan before she became a boarder at Choate in Connecticut.

The nights she was home they watched *Courtside* together. The inevitable result was that seeing the highlights of the trial and hearing the panel discussion brought Katie to a state of anger and tears.

"Daddy, why doesn't Michael *ever* stand up for you?" she would demand. "He was so nice when we used to go skiing with him, and he was always saying how much you helped Natalie's career. Why doesn't he say it now, when he could do you some good?"

"We'll show *him*," was typical of Gregg's replies to

his daughter. "We'll never go skiing with him again." He would shake his fist at the television in mock indignation.

"Oh, Daddy!" Katie would laugh. "I *mean* it."

"So do I," Gregg would say, quietly now.

Gregg admitted to himself that the evenings Katie went out for a few hours with friends gave him a needed break. During the day, the love he felt emanating from her as she sat a few rows behind him in court was as welcome as a warm blanket would be to someone in the throes of hypothermia. But sometimes he simply needed to be alone.

This was one of the evenings Katie had gone out to dinner. Gregg had promised her that he would order room service from the club in the building, but after she left, he poured himself a double scotch over ice and settled down in the den, the remote television clicker in his hand. He intended to watch *Courtside*, but before then he needed to search his memory.

At their meeting a few hours earlier, Richard and Cole Moore had warned him that Jimmy Easton would be on the witness stand tomorrow and that the whole case hung on his credibility as a witness. "Gregg, the crucial, absolutely crucial statement he'll make is when he talks about meeting with you in the apartment," Richard had warned. "I'll ask you again. Is there *any* chance he was ever there?"

Gregg knew his response had been heated. "I never had a meeting with that liar in my apartment and don't ask me about it again." But he was haunted by the question. How could Easton possibly claim he was here? Or am I going crazy?

Now, as he took a sip of the scotch, Gregg found himself bracing for his nightly viewing of *Courtside*, but when it came on, the soothing effect that the fine single-malt scotch had offered vanished. Seventy-five percent of the viewers who had responded to the *Courtside* Web site poll thought he was guilty.

Seventy-five percent! Gregg thought incredulously. Seventy-five percent!

A clip from the trial showing Emily Wallace looking directly at him came onto the screen. The expression of disdain and contempt she conveyed made him cringe now as it had in the courtroom. Everyone watching this program was seeing it, too. "Innocent until proven guilty," he thought bitterly. She's doing a mighty good job of proving I'm guilty.

Aside from the obvious, there was something about Emily Wallace that was unsettling him. One of the panelists on *Courtside* had called her performance "pure theatre." He's right, Gregg thought, as he closed his eyes and lowered the volume of the television. He reached into his pocket and pulled out the folded sheet of paper that was like so many others he had scribbled on during the day in court. He had been doing some calculation. The rental car had 15,200 miles on it when he picked it up, and when he returned it 680 miles had been added. Five hundred and forty would account for the round trip from Manhattan to the Cape. He'd driven back and forth between the motel in Hyannis and Natalie's home

in Dennis five times between Saturday afternoon and
Sunday evening. About 20 miles each round trip. At the
most that would use up another 100 miles or so.

Just enough mileage left for me to have driven to
Natalie's house that Monday morning, killed her, and
been back in Manhattan on schedule, Gregg thought.
Could I have done that? When did I *ever* jog for over
two hours? Was I so out of it that I don't remember
going there?

Could I have left her bleeding to death?

He opened his eyes and turned up the volume with
the remote. His former close friend Michael Gordon
was saying: "Tomorrow there should be fireworks in
court when the state's star witness, Jimmy Easton, testifies that he was hired by Gregg Aldrich to murder his
estranged wife, acclaimed actress Natalie Raines."

Gregg pushed the OFF button on the remote and finished his drink.

18

Your Honor, the state calls James Easton."

The door leading from the holding cell opened. Easton emerged, walking slowly toward the witness chair, escorted by sheriff's officers on either side of him. As she looked at him, an expression that had been a favorite of her grandmother's rushed through Emily's mind: "You can't make a silk purse out of a sow's ear."

Jimmy was wearing the dark blue suit, white shirt, and patterned blue tie that Emily had personally selected for his appearance in court. Under protest, he had gotten a haircut from the jailhouse barber, but even so, as Emily had remarked to Ted Wesley, he still looked like the con man he was.

From long prior experience before criminal judges, he knew what came next. He paused as he reached the area directly in front of the bench. Judge Stevens directed him to first state his full name and then spell his last name.

"James Easton, E-A-S-T-O-N."

"Sir, please raise your right hand to be sworn," the judge instructed.

The pious look on Jimmy's face when he swore to tell the truth, the whole truth, and nothing but the truth caused a ripple of snickering among a number of the spectators in the courtroom.

Terrific, Emily thought, dismayed. Pray God, the jury will keep an open mind about my star witness.

Judge Stevens rapped his gavel sharply and warned that anyone who reacted verbally or visibly to any witness's testimony would be removed immediately and would be barred from attending further sessions.

When Jimmy was settled in the witness chair, Emily walked over to him slowly, her expression grave. Her strategy was to immediately elicit from him his prior criminal record, and the plea agreement he had made with her. She had addressed his background as a longtime felon in her opening statement and now she wanted to get the details out immediately. She hoped that facing these circumstances head-on would at least convey to the jury that she would be forthright with them and that this witness, despite his laundry list of crimes, should be believed.

I'm walking on thin ice, she thought, and maybe the ice will break. But as she asked question after question in a matter-of-fact tone, Jimmy Easton's response was everything she could hope for. His voice humble, his manner hesitant, he admitted to his many arrests and frequent prison terms. Then out of the blue he added gratuitously, "But never once did I hurt a hair on anyone's head, ma'am. That's why I couldn't go through with the deal to kill Aldrich's wife."

Richard Moore sprang to his feet. "Objection."

Way to go, Jimmy! Emily thought. So what if it was stricken from the record? The jury heard that loud and clear.

It was already late morning when Easton's testimony began. At twelve twenty, Judge Stevens, recognizing that Emily was about to transition her questioning to Easton's involvement with Gregg Aldrich, said, "Ms. Wallace, since we're close to the usual twelve thirty lunch break, I will recess until one thirty."

Superb timing, Emily thought. Now Jimmy's record will be at least somewhat separated from his testimony about Aldrich. Thank you, Judge.

Her face impassive, she waited at the prosecutor's table until Easton was escorted back to the holding cell by a sheriff's officer, and the jurors had left the courtroom. Then she hurried to Ted Wesley's office. He had sat in the courtroom all morning and she wanted to get his reaction to the way she had handled Easton.

In the two weeks since the announcement was made that he'd been nominated to be the attorney general of the United States, there had been a flurry of press about him and the coverage had been generally very favorable. Why wouldn't it be? Emily asked herself as she hurried down the corridor. Ted had been a prominent attorney and active in Republican circles before he was appointed prosecutor.

When she entered his office she could see a stack of clippings on his desk that she was sure were about his nomination. And it was obvious that he was in a very upbeat mood.

"Emily!" he greeted her. "Come on over here. Take a look at these."

"I'm sure I've seen most of them. You're really getting fabulous press. Congratulations."

"You're not doing so bad yourself. You've pretty much knocked me off the front page with the great job you're doing on this case."

He had sent for sandwiches and coffee. He pulled open the bag and started unpacking the food. "I ordered ham and swiss on rye for you. And black coffee. Right?"

"Perfect." She accepted the sandwich he held out to her.

"Then sit down and relax for a few minutes. I want to talk to you."

Emily had just started to unwrap her sandwich. Something's up, she thought and looked at him, a question in her eyes.

"Emily, I'm going to give you a piece of advice. You haven't wanted to publicize or even discuss the fact that you had a heart transplant two and a half years ago. Everyone in this office knows that you had heart surgery and, of course, you were out sick for several months. But because you were so quiet about the details, I think I'm the only one here who knows that your surgery actually involved a transplant."

"That's true," Emily said quietly as she opened the packet of mustard and squeezed it across the bread. "Ted, you know what Mark's death did to me. I was a basket case. People were so kind, but I was smothering in sympathy. Then, not even a year later, when out of the blue I had to have my aortic valve replaced, it was more of the same. Everyone expected me to be out for three months anyway. So, when the valve failed so quickly and I ended up needing a transplant, I was blessed to get one right away. I went back into the hospital quietly and only told a very few people, including you, what had happened."

Ted leaned forward in his chair, ignoring his own sandwich and looking at her with deep concern. "Emily, I absolutely understand and have always understood why you didn't want to talk about this. I saw your reaction when I asked you six months ago if you felt well enough to take this case. I know you don't want to be considered to be fragile in any way. But let's face it. You are trying a very high-profile case and are becoming very well known. The case is on *Courtside* every night and your name keeps coming up. They're talking about you. It's only a matter of days before they start really digging, and trust me, they'll find out about this. It's great human interest. Between the transplant and losing Mark in Iraq, you're going to be fodder for the tabloids, even though they'll probably be nice to you."

Emily took a sip of the coffee. "Your advice, Ted?"

"Be prepared. Expect the questions and don't let it upset you. Like it or not, you've become a public figure."

"Oh, Ted, I hate that thought," Emily protested. "I've never wanted to talk about it. You know that some of these guys make it tough enough to be a woman in the prosecutor's office."

Including and especially guys like your cousin, she thought.

"Emily, believe me, I've admired the fact that you absolutely have never allowed me to give you any slack because of the health problems you've had to deal with."

"There's something else," Emily said quietly. "Mark didn't expect to die. He was so sure he'd make it home. He had so many plans for what we would do the rest of our lives. We were even suggesting to each other the names we'd call our children. Now I am constantly and fully aware that I am alive because someone else died. Whoever that person was, he or she had to have plans and hopes for the future. That's never been easy for me to accept."

"I can understand that, too. But take my advice. Be prepared to be asked about it."

Emily took a bite out of the sandwich and forced a smile. "To change the subject, my guess is that you believe I'm doing okay so far with Jimmy Easton."

"Emily, I was watching Richard Moore squirming when Jimmy was laying out his prior record and the plea deal. You were taking the wind out of Moore's sails when you were dealing with it all up front. You managed to convey to the jury that you think Easton's a real lowlife, but that in this case he's not lying."

Emily took a few quick bites of her sandwich and wrapped the rest of it up. "Thanks, Ted. I was hoping you'd feel that way." She hesitated, trying to swallow over the lump in her throat. "And thanks for everything else . . . Your support when I lost Mark . . . When I got sick . . . And then giving me this case, I'll never forget it."

Ted Wesley stood up. "You've earned every bit of support I have ever given you," he said heartily. "And trust me, Em, if you convict this guy Aldrich, I can picture the new prosecutor offering you the first-assistant position. Believe me, that's not far-fetched. Go back in there and sell Easton to that jury! Make them think he got religion."

Emily laughed as she got up from her chair. "If I can do that, then as my grandfather used to say about me, I could sell a dead horse to a mounted policeman. See you, Ted."

19

Although he had no way of knowing, Jimmy Easton had exactly the same lunch as Emily, a ham and cheese on rye and black coffee. The only difference was that he complained to the guard at the holding cell that he would have liked more mustard.

"We'll remember that tomorrow if you're still here," the guard said, sarcastically. "We wouldn't want you to be unhappy with our cuisine."

"I'm sure you'll speak to the chef," Jimmy grumbled. "And tell him next time to throw in a slice of tomato."

The guard did not answer.

Apart from the lack of sufficient mustard, Jimmy was actually feeling pretty good about his performance so far. Reciting all of his past crimes had been sort of like going to confession. "Bless me, Father, for I have sinned. It's been thirty years, give or take, since my last confession, I've been arrested eighteen times, have been in prison three times for a total of twelve years. Then six months ago I ransacked four houses in one week and was dumb enough to get caught at the last one. But I always knew I had an ace in the hole."

Of course, he hadn't told that story to a priest. Instead, he had spilled the beans about Aldrich to that guy from the prosecutor's office, which is why he was sitting here all dolled up, instead of already serving a term of ten years.

Jimmy finished the last drop of coffee. Maybe he should tell the wise-guy cop who had brought him the sandwich that tomorrow, if he was still here, he'd like a bigger cup. And a pickle, he thought with a grin. He glanced at the clock on the wall. It was almost one. The judge would be back out there in half an hour. "All rise for the court." Why not "All rise for Jimmy Easton?" Later some of the guys from the jail would watch that *Courtside* program featuring him. He'd do his best to give them a good performance.

Jimmy got up and rattled the bars on the holding cell. "I want to go to the can," he shouted.

Promptly at one thirty he was back on the stand. As he sat down, Jimmy remembered Emily Wallace's instructions. "Sit up straight. Don't cross your knees. Look at me. Don't even *think* of playing to the jury."

But I bet she didn't mind that I tossed in that line about not ever hurting a hair on anyone's head, Jimmy thought. His expression now serious, he looked at Emily. Sometimes when she interviewed him in jail, she had worn her hair pinned up. Today it was loose on her shoulders, but not sloppy loose, just every strand even, kind of like a waterfall. She was wearing a pants suit in a kind of deep blue color, almost the same shade as her eyes. There was no doubt that she was a good-looking broad. He had heard from some of the guys that she could be one tough cookie if she was out to get you, but she wasn't out to get *him*, that was for sure.

"Mr. Easton, do you know the defendant, Gregg Aldrich?"

Jimmy closed his lips on the answer he would otherwise have given. "You bet I do." Instead, keeping his tone low but audible, he answered, "Yes, I do."

"When did you meet Mr. Aldrich?"

"Two and a half years ago, on March second."

"Under what circumstances did you meet Mr. Aldrich?"

"I was in Vinnie's-on-Broadway. That's a bar on West Forty-sixth Street, in Manhattan."

"What time were you there?"

"It was about six thirty or so. I was having a drink and the guy on the stool next to me asked me to pass the dish of nuts, so I did. But first I picked out a couple of the salted almonds and he said those were his favorites, too, and we got to talking."

"Did you exchange names?"

"Yeah. I told him I was Jimmy Easton and he said he was Gregg Aldrich."

"Is Mr. Aldrich in this courtroom?"

"Sure he is. I mean, yes."

"Will you please point to him and briefly describe what he is wearing?"

Jimmy pointed to the defendant's table. "He's the one

in the middle sitting between the other two guys. He's wearing a gray suit and blue tie."

"The record will reflect that Mr. Easton has identified Mr. Aldrich," Judge Stevens said.

Emily resumed her questioning. "Did you strike up a conversation with Gregg Aldrich, Mr. Easton?"

"I think I'd put it this way. Aldrich started talking to me. He had half a bag on—"

"Objection!" Moore shouted.

"Sustained," Judge Stevens said, then added, "Mr. Easton, please just answer the question that is posed."

Jimmy tried to look repentant. "Okay." He caught Emily's look and hastily added, "Your Honor."

"Mr. Easton, in your own words will you please describe the conversation you had with Mr. Aldrich?" This is it, Emily thought. My case begins and ends here.

"Well, you see," Jimmy began, "we had both had a couple of drinks and we both were kind of down in the dumps. I don't usually talk about being in jail, you know, it's kind of embarrassing, but I'd been looking for a job all day long and been turned down all over the place, so I told Aldrich it was hard for a guy like me to go straight even if I wanted to."

Jimmy shifted in the witness chair. "Which I do," he assured the courtroom.

"How did Gregg Aldrich react to your telling him that?"

"At first he didn't. He took out his cell phone and pushed a number. A woman answered. When she knew it was him, she got mad. I mean she was screaming so loud I could hear her. She yelled, 'Gregg, leave me *alone!*' Then she must have hung up, because he got flustered-looking and I could tell he was mad as hell. Then he looked at me and said, 'That was my wife. I could *kill* her!' "

"Will you repeat that, Mr. Easton?" Emily asked.

"He looked at me and said, 'That was my wife. I could *kill* her!' "

"Gregg Aldrich said, 'That was my wife. I could *kill* her!' " Emily repeated slowly, wanting the words to sink in with the jury.

"Yeah."

"And that conversation took place around six thirty on March second, two and a half years ago."

"Yeah."

Emily stole a look at Gregg Aldrich. He was shaking his head as though he could not believe what he had just heard. She could see the perspiration forming on his forehead. Moore was whispering something to him, obviously trying to calm him down. It won't work, she thought. I've barely scratched the surface.

"Mr. Easton, what was your reaction when Mr. Aldrich made that statement?"

"I knew he was really mad. I mean furious. I mean his face was all red and he slapped his phone down on the bar, but I still thought he was kidding. So just kidding around myself, I said, 'I'm broke. For twenty thousand bucks I'll do it for you.' "

"What happened then?"

"Some guy who just came into the bar spotted Aldrich and made a beeline for him."

"Did Mr. Aldrich introduce you to that man?"

"Naw. The guy stayed just long enough to say that he had seen Natalie in *Streetcar Named Desire* and she was superb. That's the word he used, 'superb.' "

"What was Mr. Aldrich's reaction?"

"He said in a kind of annoyed tone that Natalie was superb in any part she played, then turned his back on the guy. So the guy just shrugged and went into the dining room and I could see that he joined some people at a table."

"Were you aware that this man was talking about Natalie Raines?"

"I figured that out right away. I like to go to the movies and I saw her in the one where she was nominated for an Oscar. And I'd seen the ads for *Streetcar*."

Emily took a sip of water. "Mr. Easton, after that brief encounter, what did Mr. Aldrich say to you?"

"I said to him, just kidding, you know, 'Hey, your wife is Natalie Raines. My price to off her just went up.' "

"What was Mr. Aldrich's reaction to that statement?"

"He looked at me and didn't say anything for a minute, then he said, 'And what is your price, now, Jimmy?' "

"How did you respond to that question?"

"Still kind of kidding, I said, 'Five thousand down and twenty thousand when I deliver'."

"Then what did Mr. Aldrich say?"

"He said, 'Let me think about it. Give me your phone

number.' So I wrote it down for him, and then I started to leave, but I figured I'd stop at the can. I guess he thought I was gone because not five minutes later when I was washing my hands, my phone rang. It was Aldrich. He said that he was taking me up on my offer and that I should stop by his apartment the next day and pick up the five thousand in cash."

"Mr. Aldrich asked you to stop by the next day? That would be March third?"

"Yeah, about four o'clock. He said the housekeeper would be gone by then. He told me he'd be standing at the corner outside his building and he would walk me up himself so that the doorman wouldn't have to announce me. He said to wear dark glasses and a hat. So I did, and he met me at the corner. Then he waited till some other people got out of a cab and went into the building and we went up with them in the elevator."

"You went to his apartment and he gave you five thousand dollars to kill Natalie Raines?"

"Yeah, and he gave me the info on where she lived in New Jersey, and her schedule at the theatre."

"Can you describe Mr. Aldrich's apartment, Mr. Easton?"

"It's on the fifteenth floor. Real fancy. You know, only two apartments on the floor. Big foyer. The living room was painted a kind of white, and had a big marble fireplace with lots of carving on it in the center. The rug was one of those Orientals, mostly blue and red colors. I remember there was a blue couch facing the fireplace and chairs without arms on either side of it. There was another small couch under the window and lots of paintings on the walls."

"How long were you there?"

"Not long. He never even asked me to sit down. I could tell he was real nervous. Then he opened the drawer in a little table by the couch and took out money, and counted out five thousand bucks."

"What did you do next?"

"I asked him how I'd get the rest of the money after I did the job.

"He said that the cops would probably be questioning him after her body was found, being that they were in the middle of a divorce, so a week after the funeral he'd call me from a lobby phone somewhere and arrange to meet me at the movie house on Fifty-seventh Street and Third Avenue."

"That was the arrangement when you left Gregg Aldrich?"

"Yeah. But then I got to thinking. Being Natalie Raines is so famous, when something happened to her it'll be a big deal and the cops will be all over it. I could end up spending the rest of my life in prison. I mean, even when I was taking the five thousand bucks, I knew I probably wouldn't go through with it. I'm not a killer."

"How did you let Mr. Aldrich know that you wouldn't go through with it?"

"I wrote him a letter saying that I didn't think I was the right person for the job he had in mind and I was grateful to him for the nonrefundable advance he gave me."

The outright laughter in the courtroom caused an angry reaction from the judge, who once again warned against outbursts of any kind. Then the judge told Emily to continue.

"What did you do with the five thousand dollars, Mr. Easton?"

"The usual. I blew it all gambling."

"When did you mail the letter backing out of your deal to murder Natalie Raines?"

"The morning of March twelfth, I sent it to Gregg Aldrich at his apartment. I mailed it in the post office box near my rooming house in Greenwich Village."

"Why did you write to him?"

"'Cause he said not to phone him, that he had made a mistake calling me that one time. And I knew he'd get the letter. You know what they say, 'Neither rain, nor storm, nor dark of night will keep the postman from completing his appointed rounds.' And I've got to say he was always there with my bills." Jimmy couldn't help turning and smiling at the jury, hoping they appreciated that little joke. He knew they were eating up everything he said, and it felt good not to be the one on trial for a change.

"That letter backing out of your contract to murder Natalie Raines was mailed on March twelfth," Emily said slowly and turned to look at the jurors. She hoped they were doing their own calculations. Gregg Aldrich would have received that letter on Friday the 13th, or Saturday the 14th.

She hoped they were remembering what she had told them in her opening statement. On Friday evening the 13th, he went to see Natalie's final performance and the witnesses who saw him there stated that he sat stone-faced in the last row, and was the only one who did not participate in the standing ovation for her. On Saturday the 14th of March, he rented a car and followed his estranged wife to Cape Cod.

She waited a long moment then looked at Judge Stevens.

"No further questions, Your Honor," she said.

20

Richard Moore stood up slowly. For the next two hours, after reviewing Jimmy Easton's long criminal record with him, he began to attack his testimony. But the more Jimmy testified, the more he was actually strengthening our case, Emily thought with satisfaction.

Moore kept trying to put a different spin on the facts that Gregg had met Jimmy in Vinnie's-on-Broadway, that Gregg called Natalie in Jimmy's presence, that a chance acquaintance, Walter Robinson, commented to Gregg about Natalie's performance in *Streetcar*, and that shortly afterwards Gregg called Jimmy on his cell phone.

But skilled attorney that he was, Richard Moore could not rattle Jimmy or catch him contradicting himself. When he asked, "Isn't it a fact that Gregg Aldrich and you had only a casual conversation about sports?" Jimmy replied, "If you call asking me to kill his wife casual conversation, sure."

Moore's question: "Isn't it true that in a noisy bar it would be impossible for you to hear what Natalie Raines said to Gregg?"

Jimmy's answer was: "She was an actress. She knew how to project her voice. It's a wonder the whole bar didn't hear her screaming at him."

Jimmy's *loving* this, Emily thought. He's eating up being in the limelight. She worried about the fact that he was becoming too loquacious, and an increasingly irritated Judge Stevens kept reminding Jimmy to restrict his answers to the questions posed.

"As to the phone call from Gregg Aldrich's cell phone to yours, isn't it a fact that when you were at the bar you told Gregg you had mislaid your cell phone since you arrived there? Isn't it a fact that you asked him to dial your number so your phone would ring and you could find it? Isn't that what really happened?"

"Absolutely not. I never mislaid my cell phone," Jimmy answered. "I always kept it in a clip on my belt. I told you, he called me while I was washing my hands in the can."

Jimmy's account of his visit to the apartment was what worried Emily as being the weakest part of her case. The doorman had not seen him. The housekeeper had not seen him. It was his word against Gregg's that he had been there, that the money had been handed to him, and that he had backed out of the deal later.

There had been a number of magazine interviews with Natalie in the apartment when she lived there, and some of them had pictures of the living room. Emily was sure that Moore would make the most of those pictures to prove that the knowledge of the layout of the apartment and the way the living room was furnished was readily available.

That was exactly Moore's strategy. He presented to Easton one after another of the pages that showed the

living room, then asked him to tell the jury what he was
seeing.

Easton's answers were a word-for-word recital of what
he claimed to remember from being in the room.

"You met Gregg Aldrich in a chance encounter at the
bar," Moore snapped at him. "You knew who his wife
was. Then when she was murdered, you put together a
story for the next time you were caught stealing and had
it ready to trade?"

Scorn in his expression, derision in his voice, Moore
continued, "Now read for the jury the underlined sentences in this article about Gregg Aldrich and Natalie
Raines." He handed a page from *Vanity Fair* to Jimmy.

Completely unshaken by Moore's accusations,
Easton pulled reading glasses from his pocket. "The old
peepers aren't what they used to be," he explained. He
cleared his throat before reading aloud. "Neither Gregg
nor Natalie has ever wanted live-in help. Their housekeeper arrives at eight A.M. and leaves at three thirty. If
they are not going out for the evening, they have dinner
in the club in their building, or room service from it."

He put down the page and looked at Moore. "So
what?"

"Isn't it a fact that anyone reading that article would
know that the housekeeper would be gone at four
o'clock, the time you claim you were in the Aldrich
apartment?"

"You think I read *Vanity Fair*?" Jimmy asked
incredulously.

Once again the spectators laughed and once again

they were admonished by the judge. This time he was obviously very angry and said that if it happened again, he would point out to a sheriff's officer the people who had been laughing and they would be escorted out of the courtroom.

The final blow to Moore's attempts to portray Jimmy as a liar came when he asked him to study the pictures of the living room again and tell him if there was one single thing in the room that he would not have known about if he had seen those pictures before he testified.

Jimmy started to shake his head, then said, "Oh, wait a minute. You see that little table by the couch?" He pointed to it. "That's where Aldrich kept the money he gave me. I don't know if it still creaks but it sure was noisy then when he opened it. I remember thinking he oughta oil it or somethin'."

Emily glanced at Gregg Aldrich.

His complexion had gone so pale that she wondered if he was about to faint.

21

Because he had lied to Emily that his hours at work had been changed, Zach realized it was important she shouldn't see him or his car when she got home from the courthouse. And the problem was that now that the trial was under way, and court recessed at four P.M., she was getting home to her house early, between five thirty and six P.M. That meant he couldn't go home himself when he got off from work, but had to stay out until it was dark, then hope she didn't see him drive into his garage.

It was one more reason to dislike her.

Soon after he handed Emily back her key, she had installed a bolt on the door of her back porch. He had discovered that when he tried to sneak into her house, about a week after he stopped minding Bess. He had called in sick to work because he missed handling Emily's things. He tried to slip in her house one morning after she left, and was stopped by the new bolt. What she was too dumb to realize was that he had made a key that opened her front door, but he was afraid to try that. He knew it was very risky to be standing on her front porch. There was always the chance that a nosy neighbor might see him there.

The only real contact he had with her now was to listen to her in her kitchen in the morning when she was talking to Bess. He had considered planting a microphone or maybe even a camera in a few places in her house, but decided that was also too risky. If she had found one of them, she'd have had half the prosecutor's office swarming all over the place, and they'd have been on his doorstep in minutes. He was almost certain that she'd never notice the tiny microphone over her refrigerator. It was out of her line of sight.

Low profile, Zach reminded himself. Always keep a low profile. That means when the time comes I can do what I have to do, then disappear. It worked for me in Iowa and in North Dakota and in New Mexico. Charlotte, and Lou, and Wilma. Lou and Wilma didn't have families around when he got rid of them.

When Emily's time came, it would be necessary for him to disappear from New Jersey. He started to formulate a plan about where he might move.

One morning, toward the end of the third week of the trial, as he watched through the slats of the blinds, Zach saw Emily pour her first cup of coffee and get up suddenly. "Bess," he heard her say, "no time to waste. This is the big day. Gregg Aldrich is going on the stand and I'll get to cross-examine him. I'm going to make mincemeat of him."

Then as she passed the refrigerator on her way to the stairs, her steps slowing, she added: "Bess, it's absolutely crazy but in a way I feel sorry for him. I must be losing it."

22

Richard Moore had been confident that on the day he put Gregg Aldrich on the witness stand, Emily would get to her office early. That was why he was waiting for her at seven A.M. when she arrived at the courthouse. It was Friday, October 3rd.

The minute Emily saw him, she knew the reason he was there. She invited him into her office and offered to get him some coffee. "If you get a cup when it's just made, it's not that bad," she assured him. "But if you're craving Starbucks or Dunkin' Donuts, take a pass on it."

Moore smiled. "With an endorsement like that, I don't know how I can resist, but no thanks, Emily." The smile was gone as quickly as it came. "Emily, what I say now stays in these four walls, okay?"

"Okay, I think. It depends on what you say to me."

"My client absolutely insists that he is innocent. He doesn't know I'm talking to you now and would undoubtedly be furious if he found out about it. But here's the question: Is an aggravated manslaughter plea with a twenty-year sentence still on the table?"

The image of Gregg Aldrich, pale and shaken, rushed into Emily's mind but she shook her head. "No,

Richard," she said emphatically. "At this point, for any number of reasons, it's not. For openers, if Aldrich had taken the plea when it was offered months ago, I wouldn't have had to put Natalie's mother under all the stress and heartbreak of testifying." Moore nodded slowly, as if he'd expected this response.

Realizing how angry she sounded, Emily said, "Let me grab my own coffee. The pot is down the hall. Back in a second."

When she returned, she made sure to keep the emotion out of her voice. "Richard, you know the amount of preparation it takes to get ready for a trial. I've been working around the clock for months and now I have a lot of other cases piled up and waiting for some attention from me. At this point, I want the case to be decided by the jury."

Richard Moore stood up. "All right. I understand. And I repeat, Gregg Aldrich did *not* authorize this visit. He swears he is innocent and wants the jury to acquit him. Acquit? Actually, he wants to be exonerated."

Exonerated! He must be crazy, Emily thought. He'd better hope that at least one juror believes him and he gets a hung jury. At least that would buy him a few more months of freedom before a second trial. Without a hint of sarcasm in her voice, she said, "I sincerely doubt that Gregg Aldrich will be exonerated by this jury or any other."

"You may be right about that," Moore replied, glumly. At the door, he turned back. "I admit that Easton was better on the stand than I expected, Emily. And I don't mind telling you that you've done a good job."

Richard Moore was not known to give compliments. Sincerely pleased, Emily thanked him.

"And, Emily, one way or the other, I'm glad this will be over soon. It's really been a tough one."

He did not wait for her reply.

23

On the morning of October 3rd, Gregg Aldrich got out of bed at five A.M. Because he was going to be on the witness stand, he had gone to bed unreasonably early and it had been a mistake. He had slept for an hour until eleven P.M., then dozed fitfully for the next six hours.

I've got to clear my head, he thought. I'll take a run in the park. I can't testify feeling this groggy and stupid. He raised the shades and closed the window. The window looked across the street to the opposite building. Park Avenue never does give much of a view, he thought. On Fifth Avenue, you looked over Central Park. On East End Avenue, you could see the river. On Park you look at a building filled with people like yourself who can afford the fancy prices.

The view was better in Jersey City, he thought, wryly. I could get a glimpse of the Statue of Liberty from the old apartment. But after Mom died, I couldn't get away fast enough. Mom forced herself to stay alive until she'd seen me graduate from St. John's University. I'm glad she's not sitting in that courtroom now, he thought, turning from the window.

It was cool out, and he decided to wear a light running suit. As he dressed, Gregg realized how much he'd been thinking of his mother lately. He found himself remembering how, after she died, he'd invited a few of the close neighbors like Loretta Lewis to come into their five-story walk-up to help themselves to any furnishings they could use.

Why was he thinking that? Because Richard Moore is going to put Mrs. Lewis on the stand as a character witness to say what a "grand" son I was and how helpful to all the old people in the building. He seems to think that will create some sympathy for me. Father dead when I was nine, mother fighting cancer for years, working my way through college . . . Moore will have them in tears for me. But what has that got to do with Natalie's death? Moore says it could create doubt that I was capable of killing Natalie. Who knows?

At 5:20, after gulping a cup of instant coffee, Gregg opened the door to Katie's bedroom and looked in on her. She was fast asleep, hunched in a ball under the coverlet, only her long blond hair visible. Like him, she loved a cold room for sleeping.

But last night, after she had gone to bed, he heard her sobbing and went to her. "Daddy, why is that Jimmy Easton lying about you?" she wailed.

He sat on her bed and put a reassuring hand on her shoulder. "Katie, he's lying because he's going to spend a lot less time in prison by spinning that story."

"But, Daddy, the jury believes him. I can tell that they believe him."

"Do you believe him?"

"No, of course not." She quickly pulled herself up to sitting position. "How can you even *ask* me that?"

She had been shocked. And I was shocked that I asked her that question, Gregg thought, but if I'd seen any doubt in her eyes, it would have finished me. It had taken a long time before Katie fell asleep. Now he hoped she wouldn't wake up until at least seven o'clock. They had to leave for the courtroom at twenty of eight.

He let himself out of the apartment and began to jog the two blocks to Central Park, taking the path north when he reached it. Try as he would to organize his thoughts to prepare himself for the witness stand, his mind keep hurtling back to the past.

My first job in show business was taking tickets at the Barrymore, he reminisced, but I was smart enough to hang out in Sardi's and some of the other watering holes until Doc Yates offered me a job in his theatrical agency. By then I'd met Kathleen.

Kathleen had a small part in a revival of *The Sound of Music* at the Barrymore. It had been love at first sight for both of us. We got married the same week I took the job with Doc Yates. We were both twenty-four years old.

Deeply immersed in the past, Gregg jogged northward, aware of neither the chilling wind, nor of the other early-morning runners. We had eight years together, he thought. I went up the ladder fast at the agency. Doc groomed me for his job from day one. Kathleen worked pretty steadily but the minute she got pregnant, she said, happily, "Gregg, when our baby arrives, I'm staying home. You'll be the sole breadwinner in this family."

Gregg Aldrich did not realize that he was smiling.

Those years had been so tender, so satisfying. And then to have Kathleen diagnosed with the breast cancer that had killed his mother and to lose her so quickly, to come home from the funeral to a sobbing three-year-old Katie who was screaming for Mommy had been almost unbearable.

Work was the answer, and in those first years after Kathleen was gone, he had worked almost constantly. As much as possible, he handled things from home in the morning until Katie went to nursery school at noon. Then he arranged his hours to be with her in the late afternoon. He'd go to cocktail parties and first nights, and film openings with clients, only after they'd had a good amount of time together.

Then when Katie was seven, he had met Natalie at the Tony Awards. She was a nominee and was wearing an emerald green gown and jewelry that, she confided to him, was purely on loan from Cartier. "If I lose this necklace, promise to shoot me," she'd joked.

Promise to shoot me. Gregg felt his guts twist with pain.

She didn't win that night, and the guy who escorted her got drunk. I took Natalie back to her place in the Village, he remembered. I went upstairs for a nightcap and she showed me the play she'd been asked to read. I knew it and told her to forget it, that it had been bounced off half the major actresses in Hollywood and it was a lousy script. She told me her agent was really pushing her to sign for it and I told her in that case to drop her agent, then I finished my drink and gave her my card.

Two weeks later Natalie had called for an appointment, he recalled. And that was the beginning of a whirlwind romance that culminated in the Actors' Chapel of St. Malachy's Church. Three months after their first meeting, he and Natalie were married. By then he had taken over as her agent. In the four years we were together, I did everything I could to help her make her big breakthrough, Gregg thought. But didn't I always suspect that our marriage couldn't last?

He circled around the reservoir and began to run south. How much of trying to reconcile with her had to do with real love and how much did it have to do with obsession? he asked himself. I was obsessed with her. But I was also obsessed with the idea of recapturing what I had, a wife who loved me, a good mother for Katie. I didn't want to lose Natalie and begin all over again.

I didn't want Natalie to throw away her career and it was going to happen. Leo Kearns is a good agent but he would have tried to cash in on her, do what her first agent was doing all over again.

Why did I follow her to Cape Cod? What was I thinking? What was I thinking the morning that she died?

Without realizing it, Gregg had run all the way to Central Park South and started north again.

When he got back to the apartment, he found Katie, dressed and frantically worried. "Daddy, it's seven thirty. We've got to leave in ten minutes. Where *were* you?"

"Seven thirty! Katie, I'm sorry. I was thinking things through. I had no idea of the time."

Gregg rushed to shower. That's what happened the morning Natalie died, he thought. I had no idea of the time. And I didn't drive to New Jersey then any more than I drove there now.

For the first time he felt certain of it.

Almost certain! he corrected himself.

24

At nine o'clock Emily called the first of her two corroborating witnesses. Eddie Shea was a representative from Verizon, who testified that their records showed that a call had been made from Gregg Aldrich's cell phone at 6:38 P.M. to Natalie Raines on the evening of March 2nd two and a half years ago and a call to Jimmy Easton was made that same evening at 7:10 P.M.

The second witness was Walter Robinson, the Broadway investor who had spoken to Gregg at Vinnie's-on-Broadway and remembered seeing Easton sitting next to him at the bar.

When Robinson left the witness stand, Emily turned to the judge. "Your Honor, the state rests."

The courthouse is packed, she thought, as she took her seat at the prosecutor's table. She recognized some familiar faces in the audience, people whose names popped up on Page Six of the *New York Post*. As usual the proceedings were being videotaped. Yesterday she had been stopped in the corridor by Michael Gordon, the host of *Courtside*, complimenting her on the job she was doing and asking her to be a guest on his program after the trial was over.

"I'm not sure," she had answered, but later, Ted

Wesley had told her that it would be a great boost for her reputation to make a guest appearance on a national program. "Emily, if there's any advice I hope you take from me, it's to get any good publicity that comes your way."

We'll see, she thought, as she turned her head to look at the defense table. Today Gregg Aldrich was wearing a well-tailored pinstripe dark blue suit, a white shirt, and a blue and white tie. He had more color in his face than yesterday and she wondered if he had been jogging earlier. He seemed more confident, too, than he had appeared to be yesterday. I don't know what you have to be confident about, she thought, with just a tinge of fear.

Today, his daughter, Katie, was sitting in the first row directly behind her father. Emily knew she was only fourteen but she seemed oddly mature as she sat there, her carriage erect, her expression grave, her blond hair soft on her shoulders. She was a very pretty girl, Emily thought, not for the first time. I wonder if she looks like her mother.

"Mr. Moore, call your first witness," Judge Stevens directed.

For the next three hours, Moore called both character and fact witnesses. The first one, Loretta Lewis, had lived next door to Gregg when he was growing up. "You couldn't meet a nicer young man," she said earnestly, her voice hoarse with emotion. "He did everything for his mother. She was never well. He was so responsible always. I remember one winter when our building lost electricity, he went from one apartment to another, there were twenty in the building, knocking on doors and carrying candles so that people could see. He even made sure that everyone was warm. The next day his mother told me that he took the blankets from his own bed and brought them down to Mrs. Shellhorn because the ones she had were so thin."

One of Katie's retired nannies told the jury that she'd never known a more devoted father. "Most two-parent families don't give the time and the love Mr. Gregg gave to Katie," she testified.

She had been there four of the five years that Natalie and Gregg had been married. "Natalie was more of a pal than a mother to Katie. When she was around, she'd let her stay up later than her usual bedtime, or if she helped her with her homework, she'd just give her the answers instead of making her work out a problem. Gregg would tell her not to do that, but he didn't get angry about it."

The new agent Natalie had hired prior to her death, Leo Kearns, was a surprising witness for the defense. He was on the witness list but Emily had not expected that Richard would call him. Kearns explained that he and Gregg differed fundamentally about the course Natalie's career should take. "Natalie was thirty-seven years old," he said. "She had received an Academy Award nomination for Best Actress but that was three years earlier. Not enough people go to Tennessee Williams plays for Natalie to stay in the limelight. She needed a few well-publicized action movies. I was sure they would create a buzz for her. She was a great actress but it's pretty common knowledge that turning forty in show business can be the beginning of the end unless you're hot by then."

"Notwithstanding that you were becoming Natalie Raines's agent, therefore replacing him, did Gregg Aldrich ever exhibit any animosity to you?" Moore asked.

"No. Never. The only difference Gregg and I had was in our opinions of how Natalie's career should progress."

"Had you ever competed for a client with Gregg Aldrich before?"

"In the past, two of my clients switched to him. Then one of his switched to me. We both understood the game. Gregg is a consummate professional."

Aldrich's secretary, Louise Powell, testified that no matter how frantic events in the office could get, Gregg never lost his temper. "I've never heard him even raise his voice," she swore. She testified about his relationship with Natalie. "He was crazy about her. I know he phoned her a lot after they broke up but he did that when they were married, too. She told me once that she loved having him so attentive. I think those calls were his way of showing her that he was still attentive to her. Natalie craved attention and Gregg knew it."

At 12:10, after Powell left the stand, Judge Stevens asked Moore if he had any further witnesses.

"My next and final witness will be Mr. Gregg Aldrich, Your Honor."

"In that case, we will recess now and resume at 1:30," the judge decreed.

* * *

The witnesses were pretty good, Emily admitted to herself. During the lunch break she brought a sandwich and coffee to her office and closed her door. She realized that she was suddenly experiencing a drop in her emotional level. I'm going in for the kill and right now I feel sorry for him, she thought. The loving son, the single father, the guy who has a second chance at happiness and then it blows up in his face.

Planning his activities around his daughter's schedule certainly doesn't match with my image of the playboy agent, she thought.

If Mark and I had ever been blessed enough to have a child, would she look at me the way Katie Aldrich looks at her father? She certainly knows him better than anyone else in the world.

Her sandwich tasted like cardboard. Is this what prison food was like? Yesterday after Jimmy was escorted back to prison, the guard had told her that Jimmy had said if he was around today he wanted a second cup of coffee and a pickle.

He'd been a fantastic witness, Emily thought now— but what a piece of work he is!

Gregg Aldrich looked as though he was going to faint when Jimmy talked about the drawer that squeaked. That piece of evidence clinched Easton's testimony. It was the first nail in the coffin, deciding the way Gregg would spend the rest of his life.

The crazy question that kept coming through Emily's mind was, why did Gregg Aldrich go so pale when Jimmy talked about the drawer? Was it because he knew he was finished, or was it because it was so incredible to him that Jimmy Easton would have remembered that detail?

Would I have remembered it? Emily asked herself, as she visualized Easton standing in the Park Avenue living room, contracting to commit a murder, and greedily waiting for the five thousand dollars that was about to be placed in his hands.

Impatiently shrugging off her own questions, Emily picked up the notes she would use when she cross-examined Gregg Aldrich.

25

Step by step, Richard Moore led Gregg Aldrich through the story of his life, growing up in Jersey City, moving to Manhattan after his mother's death, success as a theatrical agent, his first marriage and the death of his first wife, then his marriage to Natalie.

"You were married four years?" Moore asked.

"Actually, for almost five years. We were separated, but not yet divorced, when Natalie died a year after she moved out of our apartment."

"How would you describe your relationship with your wife?"

"Very happy."

"Then why did you separate?"

"That was Natalie's choice, not mine," Gregg explained, his voice even, his manner quiet, but seemingly confident. "She decided that our marriage wasn't working."

"Why did she decide that?"

"On three occasions during our marriage, she had accepted roles in a movie or play that required her to be on location or on tour. I will certainly admit that I was sad about those separations, but I flew out frequently to see her. Katie went with me on a couple of those occasions, if they occurred during a school break or summer vacation."

He looked directly at the jury as he continued, "I'm a theatrical agent. I certainly knew that a successful actress has to be away from home for extended periods of time. When I objected to Natalie insisting on going into a play that would take her on the road, it was because I thought the play was wrong for her, not because I wanted her home to cook dinner for me. That was her interpretation, not mine."

Oh, sure, Emily thought as she scribbled a question that she would ask Aldrich when it was her turn to cross-examine him: "Weren't her career decisions smart enough that she was already a star when she met you?"

"Did that cause tension in your home?" Moore asked.

"Yes, it did. But not for the reason Natalie believed. I will say it again. When I objected to the quality of a script, she thought I was using that as an excuse to keep her home. Would I have missed her? Of course. I was her husband and her agent and her biggest fan, but I knew I had married a successful actress. The fact that I would miss her was not why I objected to some of the contracts she insisted on signing."

"Couldn't you make her understand that?"

"That was the problem. She understood how much Katie and I missed her when she was away, and came to believe that it would be less painful if we separated and remained friends."

"In the beginning, isn't it true that after the separation, she planned to retain you as her agent?"

"Initially, yes. I truly believe Natalie loved me almost as much as I loved her, and that she wanted to remain close to Katie and me. I really think she was quite sad after we had separated but while I was still her agent, when we would meet for business, then leave at the end of the meeting to go our separate ways. It became painful for both of us."

How about the pain in your wallet when you lost her as a client? Emily scribbled on her pad.

"A number of Natalie's friends have testified that she was upset by your frequent phone calls to her after your separation," Moore stated. "Would you please tell us about that?"

"It's exactly what you heard from my secretary, Louise Powell, this morning," Aldrich replied. "Natalie may have acted as if she didn't want me pursuing her, but I really believe she had very mixed emotions about whether to go through with the divorce. While we were together, she loved the fact that I called her frequently."

Moore asked about the noisy drawer where Jimmy Easton had claimed Gregg kept the money that was a down payment on his contract to kill Natalie.

"That piece of furniture has been in my home since Kathleen and I bought it at an estate sale seventeen years ago. The squeak in it is something of a family joke. We called it a message from the departed spirits. How Jimmy Easton heard of it, I'll never know. He was never in my living room when I was there and as far as I know he was never there under any circumstances."

Moore asked Gregg about meeting Easton at the bar.

"I was sitting at the bar by myself having a couple of drinks. I completely acknowledge that I was pretty down in the dumps. Easton was sitting on the stool next to me and he just started talking to me."

"What did you talk about?" Moore inquired.

"We talked about the Yankees and the Mets. The baseball season was close to starting."

"Did you tell him that you were married to Natalie Raines?"

"No, I did not. It was none of his business."

"While you were there, did he find out that you were married to Natalie Raines?"

"Yes, he did. Walter Robinson, a Broadway investor, saw me and came over. He said that he just wanted to tell me how wonderful he thought Natalie was in *Streetcar*. Easton heard him and picked right up on the fact that I was Natalie's husband. He told me that he had read in *People* magazine that we were getting a divorce. I politely told him that I did not want to discuss it."

Moore asked about the calls from Gregg's cell phone to Natalie and then to Easton the night they were in the bar. "I called Natalie to say hello. She was resting in her dressing room. She had a headache and was very tired. She was annoyed at the interruption and *did* raise her voice, as Mr. Easton testified. But as I said, she had mixed emotions. The day before she had stayed on the phone for twenty minutes while she told me how tough the separation was for her."

Moore then asked about the call to Easton's phone. Emily's stomach tightened because she didn't know how Aldrich would try to explain it away. His lawyer had supplied one alternate theory during cross-examination, but Gregg had given no further statements after Easton had come forward. She knew that this piece of testimony could make or break the case.

"A little while after he asked about Natalie, Easton said he was going to the men's room. I certainly didn't care what he did, particularly after he asked about Natalie. At that point, I felt hungry and decided to order a hamburger and eat right at the bar. About five minutes later, Easton came back and told me that he couldn't find his cell phone and thought he might have left it somewhere in the bar. He asked me to dial his number so that the phone would ring and hopefully he would find it."

Gregg paused and looked toward the jury. "He gave me his number and I dialed it. I could hear it ring on my phone but there was no ringing sound in the bar area. I let it ring about fifteen times so that he could walk around and see if he could locate it. I remember that no voice mail message came on, it just kept ringing. About thirty seconds later, as it was still ringing, he answered it and thanked me. He said he had found it in the men's room. That was the last I saw or heard of him until he got arrested for the house burglary and then gave the police that ridiculous story."

"As far as you know, did anyone else hear him ask you to dial the phone?"

"I really don't think so. The bar was very noisy. I didn't know anybody else who was there. Easton came up with this outrageous lie two years later. I wouldn't even know who to call to ask if they remembered anything."

"By the way, did Mr. Easton ever tell you that he was a career-criminal and that he was having a hard time finding a job?"

"Absolutely not!" Gregg replied.

"On Friday, March 13th, two and a half years ago," Moore continued, "you went to see Natalie in her final performance of A *Streetcar Named Desire*. Witnesses have stated that you sat in the last row, stone-faced, and did not join in the standing ovation. How do you explain that?"

"I had not intended to see the play, but I heard so much about her performance that I could not resist going there. I deliberately bought a ticket in the last row. I didn't want Natalie to see me because I was afraid it would upset her. I didn't jump up to applaud because I was emotionally spent. I think at that moment I realized once again what a magnificent actress she was."

"Did you receive a phone call from her the next morning?"

"I received a message from her on my cell phone, saying she had gone up to Cape Cod, that she would be at our scheduled meeting on Monday, and asking me not to call her over the weekend."

"How did you react to that call?"

"I certainly admit that I was upset. Natalie had previously hinted to me that she had met someone else. It was very important to me to know if that was true. So, I made the decision to drive to Cape Cod. I made up my mind that if I saw her with someone else, I would have to accept that our marriage was over."

Ask him why he didn't hire a private investigator to check this out, Emily wrote on her pad.

"Why did you rent a car, a green Toyota, to drive to the Cape when your own vehicle, a Mercedes-Benz, was in the garage of your apartment building?"

"Well, of course, Natalie would recognize my car. The license plates on it had both our initials on them. I didn't want her or anyone else to know that I was checking on her."

"What did you do when you got to the Cape, Gregg?"

"I checked into a little motel in Hyannis. We know a lot of people who live on the Cape and I didn't want to bump into any of them. I just wanted to see if Natalie was alone."

"You drove past her house several times?"

"Yes. Years ago, the garage was converted into a recreation room and no one ever got around to building a new one. There was no garage that another car could have been in. When I drove past the house, I saw only her car in the driveway, and I knew she was alone."

Suppose she had picked someone up along the way? Emily wrote on her pad. How could you assume she was alone just because there wasn't another car there?

"What did you do then, Gregg?" Moore asked.

"I drove past her house Saturday afternoon and late

Saturday evening, and three times on Sunday. Her car was always the only one in the driveway. It was overcast both days and there were lights on inside the house, so I assumed she was there. Then around eight o'clock Sunday evening I started back to Manhattan. There was a nasty storm predicted and I wanted to get home."

"At that point, had you made any decision about continuing your efforts to reconcile with Natalie Raines?"

"On the drive home, I remember that I thought about something I had read. I'm not sure if it was written about Thomas Jefferson, but I think it was. Anyhow, the quote was 'Never less alone than when alone.' "

" 'Never less alone than when alone.' Did you decide that was true of Natalie?" asked Moore.

"Yes. I believe that on the drive home that Sunday evening, I resigned myself to that reality."

"What time did you arrive home?"

"About one A.M. I was exhausted and I went right to bed."

"Monday morning, what did you do?"

"I went for a jog in Central Park. Then I returned the rental car."

"What time did you go out to jog?"

"About 7:15 A.M. or so."

"And you returned the rental car at 10:05 A.M."

"Yes."

"Was that an unusually long amount of time for you to jog?"

"Usually, I jog for about an hour and sometimes after

that I just keep walking. Sometimes, especially when I'm thinking things through, I lose track of the time."

Sure you do! Emily thought.

"How often does it happen, Mr. Aldrich, that you may lose track of time when you're jogging or walking?" Richard Moore asked, his voice sympathetic.

"There's no pattern. But when I have a lot on my mind, it can happen." Gregg remembered that it had happened just this morning. I left the apartment before five thirty and got back at seven thirty. I had to rush to shower and change to be here on time. I won't tell the jury that, he thought to himself. They'll think I'm nuts.

There's no pattern. But it happened the morning Natalie died, Emily thought. How convenient.

Richard Moore's next questions were about Gregg Aldrich's reaction when he received the call saying that Natalie was dead.

"I couldn't believe it. It seemed impossible. I was devastated."

"What did you do when you got that news?"

"I left my office immediately and went to see Natalie's mother." Gregg looked directly at Alice Mills who was seated in the third row. Although the witnesses were sequestered, she had been permitted, once her testimony was finished, to watch the rest of the trial. "We were bewildered and shocked. We cried together. Alice's first thought was of Katie." His voice grew strained. She knew how much Katie and Natalie loved each other.

She insisted that I go right away to break the news to Katie before she heard about it from someone else."

It was getting close to four o'clock. Moore's going to drag this out so that he can leave the jurors feeling sorry for Gregg over the weekend, Emily thought.

Intensely disappointed that she would not be able to start cross-examination until Monday, she was careful to maintain her impassive demeanor.

26

That evening, Michael Gordon's *Courtside* panel was in agreement that Gregg Aldrich had fared well during direct examination and that, if he could stand up to the prosecutor's cross-examination, he had a reasonable chance of a hung jury, and a fighting chance at an acquittal.

"The verdict in this case hinges on the testimony of a crook," retired judge Bernard Reilly reminded the panel. "Find some reasonable explanation as to how Jimmy Easton could have learned about that squeaky drawer and this jury will have reasonable doubt. All of the other evidence involving Easton comes down to his word against Aldrich's."

Judge Reilly smiled. "I've batted the breeze with a guy in a bar any number of times, and if one of them showed up saying that I told him I wanted to kill my wife, it would be his word against mine. And I have to tell all of you, I found Aldrich's explanation of the phone call to Easton quite possible and plausible."

Michael Gordon suddenly felt a welling of emotion, and he realized that a part of him still expected his friend to be vindicated.

"I'm putting something on the table," Gordon heard

himself saying. "When Jimmy Easton came out of the woodwork, I honestly believed that he was probably telling the truth, that Gregg Aldrich had committed this crime. I was an eyewitness on many occasions to how crazy Gregg was about Natalie and how upset he was at their breakup. I really thought that he had just snapped and killed her."

Gordon looked around at the questioning faces of his panel. "I know this is a first for me. It's been my policy to be neutral during a trial, and, if anything, I've overdone it in this case. As I disclosed on day one, Gregg and Natalie were my close friends. I have intentionally stayed away from Gregg since he was indicted and, hearing him on the witness stand and looking at all of the rest of the evidence, I now intensely regret that I doubted him. I believe that Gregg is telling the truth. I believe he is innocent and that this accusation against him is a great tragedy."

"Then who do you think shot Natalie Raines?" Reilly asked.

"She could have walked in on a burglary," Gordon suggested. "Even though nothing was taken, the intruder could have panicked and fled after killing her. Or it could have been a crazed fan. Any number of people have those fake rocks with hide-a-keys in their backyards. An experienced crook would know to look for one of them."

"Maybe they should ask Jimmy Easton if he ever looked for one," Brett Long, the criminal psychologist, suggested.

As they all laughed, Michael Gordon reminded the viewers that on Monday, Emily Wallace, the beautiful young prosecutor, would begin the cross-examination of Gregg Aldrich. "He is going to be the final defense witness. Then, after the attorneys present their summations and the judge instructs the jury on the law, the case will go to the jury. When they start deliberating, we will conduct another poll on our Web site. Be sure to weigh the evidence and cast your vote. Many thanks for watching *Courtside*. Good night."

It was ten o'clock. After a few words with the departing panelists, Michael went to his office and dialed the number that he had not dialed for seven months. When Gregg answered, he said, "By any chance were you watching?"

Gregg Aldrich's voice was husky. "Yes, I was. Thanks, Mike."

"Have you had dinner yet?"

"I wasn't hungry."

"Where's Katie?"

"At a movie with one of her girlfriends."

"Jimmy Neary doesn't close the kitchen until late. No one will bother you there. How about it?"

"Sounds good, Mike."

As Michael Gordon replaced the receiver, he realized his eyes were moist.

I should have been there for him all along, he thought. *He sounds so alone.*

27

As Emily watched *Courtside* in her living room, she sipped a glass of wine. I agree, she thought, as she listened to the comments of the retired judge. My case depends on the testimony of a witness who is as glib as any human being I've ever encountered.

She realized how deflated and down she felt. I know why, she explained to herself. I was so psyched to get at Aldrich. Then Richard managed to drag out the testimony of the neighbor from Jersey City, the secretary, the nanny, who all thought Gregg Aldrich walked on water. I was right to just about give them a pass. If I'd tried to make them look bad, I'd have made a huge mistake.

Leo Kearns, the other agent? Should I have dug into him more? Maybe. Nobody's all that altruistic when he loses a client. Being a theatrical agent has to be a tough business. Kearns made it sound like a tennis match—Love all.

Gregg Aldrich. The pain on his face when he talked about his first wife . . . I'm getting mushy, Emily thought. I was feeling with him the kind of pain I felt when I learned that Mark was dead.

"Way up on the mountain, there's a new chalet . . . and Jean so brave and true . . . has built it all anew." A folk song from her childhood ran through Emily's mind. Gregg Aldrich tried to rebuild his life, she thought. He remarried. He obviously was very much in love with Natalie. Then, when she was murdered, he was not only grieving, but had to defend himself against the cops who thought he killed her.

She gulped the rest of the wine. God, what's the matter with me? she asked herself, angrily. My job is to prosecute this guy.

Then, toward the end of *Courtside*, Michael Gordon came out in support of Aldrich. Knowing that Gordon was considered to be a fair analyst, Emily was shocked.

But then she felt her resolve harden. If he's typical of the people watching this show, and if he's typical of the way the jury may be thinking, I've got my work cut out for me, she thought.

28

Well, isn't that a surprise?" Isabella Garcia asked her husband, Sal, as they sat in their small living room on East Twelfth Street in Manhattan. She had been engrossed in watching *Courtside* and could hardly believe her ears when Michael Gordon told the rest of the panel that he now believed that Gregg Aldrich was innocent of the murder of Natalie Raines. But although she was absolutely shocked, she remarked to Sal that when you really thought about it, what Gordon was saying made a lot of sense.

Sal was sipping a beer and reading the sports page. Except for the news, and baseball or football games, he couldn't care less about watching television and had the gift of tuning both the picture and the sound out when he was reading.

He hadn't really paid attention yesterday when Belle told him to take a look at the clips that they were showing of the crook, Jimmy, on the witness stand. But from his one quick glance, Sal felt as if the guy seemed vaguely familiar for some reason. But he couldn't remember where he might have met him, and anyhow he didn't care.

Knowing that now, with the program over, Belle

wanted to talk, Sal dutifully lowered his newspaper. After watching *Courtside*, she liked to air her opinion of the day's events at the trial. Unfortunately, her elderly mother was on a cruise in the Caribbean with several of her friends who were also widows, and so was not available for their customary lengthy telephone chat.

"I have to say that Gregg came off beautifully," Belle began. "You know, he has a nice way about him. Why Natalie would have left him in the first place is hard to fathom. If she were *our* daughter I would have sat her down and told her that a very wise man wrote, 'At the end of his life, no one ever said I wish I'd spent more time in the office.' "

"She was on the stage, not in an office," Sal pointed out. You'd think this case depended on Belle's opinion, he thought, half amused, half irritated, as he looked across the room at his wife of thirty-five years. She'd been dyeing her hair for decades, so it was, at age sixty, the same coal black shade it had been when he first met her. Her body was thicker, but not very. The corners of her mouth turned up because she smiled so easily. He always tried to remember to thank God that Belle had such a good disposition. His brother was married to a battle-axe.

"Stage, office, you know what I mean." Belle dismissed Sal's comment. "And Katie is such a pretty girl. I like to see the clips of her that Michael shows on the program."

Belle had a way of referring to people as if they were, or had been, close friends, Sal thought. Sometimes when she was telling him a story, it was several minutes before he realized that she wasn't talking about someone they knew intimately. Michael Gordon, the host of *Courtside*, was always just "Michael." Natalie Raines was always "Natalie." And, of course, the accused murderer was affectionately referred to as "Gregg."

At twenty of ten, Belle was still going strong. She was talking about how it had been a good thing that Suzie, the housekeeper who worked next door to where Natalie lived, had been so nosy that she had gone in to check on Natalie and found her dying on the kitchen floor. "I don't know whether or not I would have the nerve to go into that kitchen myself," Belle said.

Oh, please, Sal thought. To Belle, a closed door was an invitation to see what was going on. He stood up. "Well, I'm sure you would have helped if you had had the chance," he said wearily. "That's it for me. We've got an early-morning pickup in Staten Island. People moving to Pearl River."

As he got into bed fifteen minutes later, the name Jimmy Easton popped back into Sal's head. No wonder that guy looked familiar, he thought. He worked for us on and off a couple of years ago.

Not too reliable.

He didn't last.

29

On Saturday morning, as he did every day, Zach watched through the blinds as Emily ate breakfast. It was already eight thirty. She gave herself a couple of extra hours to sleep, he thought. Yesterday she had left the house at six thirty A.M. Today, she took the time to have a second cup of coffee while she was reading the newspaper. Her dog, Bess, sat on her lap. He hated that dog. He envied her closeness to Emily.

When Emily went upstairs to dress, he felt the familiar disappointment that he could not then see or hear her. He stayed at the window for about twenty minutes, until he saw her getting into her car. It was a warm early-October day and she was wearing jeans and a sweater. She didn't get dressed up when she went to the office on the weekend. He was sure she was going in to work on her case.

He had his day planned until she got home again— the first of the leaves had begun to fall, and he spent the morning raking and gathering them, then putting them into large plastic bags for the town pickup.

Zach was sure that Emily wouldn't be back until late afternoon at the earliest. After he had lunch, he drove to the local nursery and picked up some autumn plantings. He especially liked the yellow mums, and decided to line the walk from the driveway to the porch with them, even though he wouldn't be around long enough to enjoy them.

As he piled the flowers into a shopping cart, he found himself wishing that he could buy some for Emily. They would look nice on her walk, too. With the way she works, she hardly has any time for herself, let alone for her yard, he thought. But he knew if he tried to be nice to her like that, she would take it the wrong way. And then . . .

It really doesn't matter anyway, he decided, as he paid the cashier. *She* won't be around much longer to enjoy them, either! He still was angry with himself that he'd been stupid enough to be sitting in her enclosed porch when she came home that night a few weeks ago. It had ruined their growing friendship, and now she totally avoided him.

He was glad at least he'd taken that fancy nightgown from her bottom drawer the last day he went through her house. He was sure she wouldn't miss it. She had at least eight of them in that drawer, and from what he had seen in her hamper she usually slept in a long T-shirt.

He drove the short distance home, reflecting that in the couple of weeks since it had been clear that Emily had rejected him, he had begun his preparations to leave New Jersey.

As soon as he had killed her.

His house was a month-to-month rental. He had informed the owners he would be moving out on November 1st. He had also given notice at work that he would be leaving at the end of October. His story to all of them was that his elderly mother who lived in Florida had serious health problems, and he needed to be with her.

Zach knew he had to disappear right after Emily died but before her body was found. He was sure that the cops would investigate all of her neighbors, and that he had undoubtedly been seen walking her dog. And it was always possible that Emily had commented to her family or friends that she thought the guy living next door to her was strange and made her feel uncomfortable. You can bet that they would tell *that* to the police, he thought.

He thought about how Charlotte, his third wife, had thrown him out of his own house. Afterwards she had told her new boyfriend that he was weird and that she was afraid of him. You were right to be afraid of me, sweetheart, he told himself with a chuckle. I'm only sorry I didn't take care of my former good buddy, who became your boyfriend, at the same time.

In total he bought twenty-six flats of mums. He really enjoyed spending the rest of the afternoon planting them. Just as he expected, Emily came home around five o'clock. She waved to him as she got out of her car, but quickly hurried into her house.

He could see she looked tired and stressed. He was pretty sure that she'd be in for the night and fix her own dinner. He hoped so. But at twenty after six he heard the sound of her car engine starting through the open side window. He got to the window in time to see her backing out of the driveway and caught a glimpse of the silk blouse, pearls, and big earrings that she was wearing.

All dolled up, he thought bitterly. She was probably meeting friends for dinner. At least no one picked her up, so she probably didn't have a date. He could feel his anger growing. I don't want her to have anyone else in her life. Not *anyone!*

He felt himself getting very upset. He knew it wouldn't take him a minute to cut out a windowpane and be waiting in her house when she got home. Her alarm would be no problem. It was a cheap basic system. He could easily disarm it from the outside.

Not yet, he warned himself. You're not ready yet. You need to get a different car, and rent a little place in North Carolina. A lot of people were relocating there all the time and with a new identity, he was sure he could blend in easily.

Determined to take his mind off what Emily was doing, he went into his kitchen, took out the packet of hamburger he had bought for tonight's supper, and turned on the television. He liked several Saturday-night programs, particularly *Fugitive Hunt*, which came on at nine P.M.

Twice in the last couple of years they'd presented a segment on *him*. He enjoyed watching them and mocking the computer images that they said might look like him today.

Not even close, he had snickered.

30

Ted Wesley had invited Emily to have dinner at his home on Saturday evening. "We're just having a few friends in," he explained. "We want a chance to be with people we really *care* about before we move."

He would be starting his new job in Washington on November 5th. Emily knew that the house in Saddle River was already on the market.

It was the first time she had received a dinner invitation from Ted and Nancy Wesley. She knew it was a reaction to the favorable publicity she'd generated in the media during the trial. Ted liked to be associated with people in the limelight. *Successful* people!

Win or lose, the newspapers with my pictures plastered all over them will be lining next week's garbage pails, she thought, as she drove through Saddle River and turned onto Foxwood Road. If I lose, it'll be an awfully long time before I'm invited back, she warned herself wryly.

Ted's house was one of the largest of the mini-mansions on the winding street. He certainly didn't buy this on a prosecutor's salary, Emily thought. Of course before he became prosecutor, he was a partner in his father-in-law's prestigious law firm, but the real money, she knew, came through his wife, Nancy. Nancy's maternal grandfather had founded a chain of upscale department stores.

Emily parked the car near the house's rotunda at the end of the driveway. The evening had turned cool and as she got out of the car, she inhaled several deep breaths of fresh air. It felt good. I've barely been outdoors often enough to clear my lungs, she thought. Then she quickened her step. She had not bothered to bring a jacket and could have used one.

But she was glad that she had decided to wear the silk blouse with the splashy print. She knew the fatigue, caused by the long hours she was putting in, showed on her face. Carefully applied makeup helped to somewhat conceal it. So did the vivid colors in the blouse. After this trial is over, no matter how much is piled up on my desk, I'm taking a few days off, she decided, as she rang the bell of the house.

Ted answered the door himself, let her in, then said admiringly, "You're looking very glamorous tonight, Counselor."

"I agree," Nancy Wesley said. She had followed her husband to the door. A slender blond in her late forties, she had the unmistakable stamp of someone who was born to privilege and wealth. But her smile was genuine, and she took Emily's hands in hers as she placed a fleeting kiss on her cheek. "We've invited just three others to be with us. I know you'll enjoy them. Come in and meet them."

Emily managed a quick glance around the foyer as

she followed the Wesleys. Very impressive, she thought. Marble double staircase. Balcony. Antique chandelier. And I *did* dress properly. Like her, Nancy Wesley was wearing black silk pants and a silk blouse. The only difference was that her blouse was a pastel shade of blue.

Three other people, Emily thought. She was afraid that the Wesleys might have invited a single man as a sort of dinner companion for her. In the past year, that had occurred several times in other circumstances. Since she still missed Mark so much, it had not only been annoying, but painful. I hope I'll be ready again someday, she mused, but not yet. She tried to stifle a grin. Even if I *had* been ready, she told herself, the jokers they've trotted out for me so far have been pretty bad!

She was relieved to see that the three people in the living room were a man and woman, who both appeared to be in their early fifties, sitting on a couch by the fireplace, and another woman who appeared to be in her late sixties, seated in a wing chair. She recognized the man, Timothy Moynihan, as an actor in a long-running evening television show. He played the chief surgeon in a hospital drama.

Ted introduced him and his wife, Barbara, to Emily.

After greeting his wife, Emily, smiling, asked Moynihan, "Should I call you 'Doctor'?"

"I'm off duty, so Tim will do."

"The same with me. Please don't call me 'prosecutor.'"

Ted then turned toward the older woman, "Emily, this is another dear friend, Marion Rhodes—and she's a real-life doctor, a psychologist."

Emily acknowledged the introduction and in a moment was seated with the group and sipping a glass of wine. She felt herself beginning to unwind. This is so civilized, she thought. There really *is* life outside the Aldrich case, even if only for an evening.

When they went into the dining room and Emily saw the beautifully set table, she thought briefly about the soup or sandwich at her desk for lunch, or the take-out food for dinner that had pretty much constituted her haute cuisine for the past few months.

The dinner was delicious and the conversation was both pleasant and amusing. Tim Moynihan was an accomplished raconteur and shared stories of what went on behind the scenes of his show. As she listened and laughed, Emily commented that this was even better than reading the gossip columns. She asked how he and Ted had first met.

"We were college roommates at Carnegie Mellon," Wesley explained. "Tim majored in drama, and believe it or not I was in a few plays myself. My parents wouldn't let me become an actor because they thought I would end up starving to death. I was planning on law school, but I do think the little bit of acting I did helped me in the courtroom as a trial lawyer and also as the prosecutor."

"Emily, we were warned by Nancy and Ted that this is your night off from talking about your case," Moynihan said. "But I have to tell you, Barbara and I have been following it closely on *Courtside*. The clips I've seen of you in the courtroom tell me you could have been a very successful actress. You have tremendous presence and poise and there's also something else—the way you ask the questions and your reactions to the answers you get convey so much to the spectators. I'll give you one example: The withering look you gave Gregg Aldrich several times during Easton's testimony spoke volumes."

"I don't know if Ted will bite my head off if I bring this up," Barbara Moynihan said, somewhat hesitantly. "But, Emily, you couldn't have been happy about Michael Gordon announcing that he thinks Gregg Aldrich is innocent."

Emily could sense that Marion Rhodes, the psychologist, was awaiting her answer with intense interest. And she was acutely aware that while this was a social setting, her boss, the county prosecutor, was also sitting at the table.

She chose her words carefully. "I would not, and could not, be prosecuting this case if I didn't believe strongly that Gregg Aldrich killed his wife. The tragedy for him and his daughter and Natalie Raines's mother is that he probably *did* love Natalie very much. But I am sure Dr. Rhodes has seen many times over the years that people who are otherwise very decent can do terrible things when they're very jealous or sad."

Marion Rhodes nodded in agreement. "You're absolutely right, Emily. From everything I have heard and read, Natalie Raines probably still loved her husband. If they had gone to counseling, and had really talked out the problems caused by the frequent separations when she was on the road, things really might have turned out differently."

Ted Wesley looked at his wife and, with surprising candor, said, "Thanks to Marion, that's the way it worked out for us. We got the help we needed from her when Nancy and I hit a rough patch many years ago. If we had broken up then, look at everything we would have thrown away. Our boys never would have been born. We wouldn't be about to move to Washington. And after the counseling, Marion became our cherished friend."

"Sometimes, when people experience emotional trauma or conflict in an important relationship, it can be very helpful to work with a good therapist," Rhodes said quietly. "Of course not all problems can be solved and not all relationships can be, or should be, salvaged. But there are happy endings."

Emily had the uncomfortable feeling that Marion Rhodes was directing those comments at her. Could it be that Ted was setting her up to meet not a man, but a therapist? Surprisingly, she did not feel resentment. She was sure that Ted and Nancy had told the others about Mark's death and her surgery. She recalled that Ted had once asked her if she had ever seen a therapist to talk about all she had been through. She had responded by saying she was very close to her family and had plenty of good friends. She told him that the best therapy for her, like so many who experienced loss, was work. Hard work.

Maybe Ted has also told Marion that both my father and my brother and his family have moved away, Emily thought. And Ted also knows that with the work schedule I've had, there's been very little time to spend with friends. I know that he has been sympathetic about everything that has happened. But, as I was thinking when I arrived here tonight, if I lose this case there will be plenty of Monday-morning quarterbacking about him assigning it to me. Let's see how much he cares about me if *that* happens.

The evening broke up at ten o'clock. By then Emily was more than ready to go home. The brief escape she had enjoyed for the last few hours was over. She wanted to get a decent night's sleep and be in her office early Sunday morning. After the favorable impression Gregg Aldrich had made so far on the stand, she was again feeling deep anxiety about the cross-examination.

Or was it more than that? she asked herself as she drove home. Am I really worried about the cross-examination and the verdict?

Or is it that I am terrified that we have made a terrible mistake and that someone else killed Natalie?

31

At nine P.M. Saturday night, Zach, settled in the small living room of his rented house, and sitting where he could see Emily's driveway, switched the channel so that he could now watch *Fugitive Hunt.* A couple of beers had helped to quiet his nerves, and he was physically tired from all the yard work and planting the mums. He wondered if Emily had noticed when she came home from work or when she went out again a little bit later how nice the yellow mums looked along his walkway.

The background music for *Fugitive Hunt* came on. "Tonight we will have three segments on old cases," the host, Bob Warner, began. "Our first segment is an update on the two-year-old search for the man last known as Charley Muir. You may recall our prior two segments on him — one right after the multiple murders in Des Moines, Iowa, two years ago, and another follow-up segment last year.

"The police allege that Muir was very bitter about the divorce, and was incensed when the judge awarded their home to his wife. They say that was the motive for the murder of his wife, her children, and her mother. By the time the bodies were found, he was gone and has not been seen since.

"The continuing investigation has uncovered startling new evidence that he is responsible for the murders of two other women, whom we now know were his first and second wives. The first one, Lou Gunther, died in Minnesota ten years ago. The second one, Wilma Kraft, died in Massachusetts seven years ago. During each of his three known marriages, he used a different identity and continuously changed his appearance. In Minnesota he was known as Gus Olsen, and in Massachusetts he was known as Chad Rudd. We don't even know what his real name is."

Warner paused, the tone of his voice changing. "Stay with us for the rest of this incredible story. We'll be right back after these messages."

They're still at it, Zach thought, scornfully. But give them credit—they've now connected me to the other two. They didn't have that last time. But let's see how I'm supposed to look at this point.

As the commercials were playing, Zach got up to get another beer. He was all set to get a laugh at the upcoming pictures, but he couldn't help feeling uneasy. The fact that they had linked him to both Minnesota and Massachusetts worried him.

Beer in hand, he sat down again in front of the television. The program was coming back on. Warner began by showing pictures of Zach's third wife, Charlotte, with her children and her mother, followed by pictures of Lou and Wilma. He described the brutal nature of their deaths. Charlotte and her family had been shot. Lou and Wilma had both been strangled.

To Zach's growing dismay, Warner displayed pictures of him that had been provided by family members of his victims. The pictures over the ten-year span, between Minnesota, Massachusetts, and Iowa, demonstrated that at various times he had been bearded or clean-shaven, and had worn his hair long or in a crew cut. He was pictured wearing thick glasses, granny glasses, or no glasses at all. The pictures also revealed that his weight would fluctuate from very thin to chubby, then back again to very thin.

Warner continued by exhibiting computer age-enhanced images of Zach, which interchanged the various potential differences in his head and facial hair, weight, and glasses. To Zach's horror, one of them substantially resembled the way he looked now. But anyone watching the show is looking at all of those pictures at once, he tried to reassure himself—they'd never recognize him.

"FBI profilers believe that, based upon his known prior employment, he could be working in a warehouse or a factory," Warner continued. "He also worked briefly as an electrician's helper. His only known hobby is that he enjoyed working in his yard and took pride in maintaining a garden. We have been provided pictures of his homes and will show them to you now. All three pictures were taken in autumn and as you can see, he was very partial to bright yellow mums. He always lined his driveway or walkway with lots of them."

Like a shot out of a cannon, Zach leaped from his chair. Frantic, he raced outside, grabbed a shovel, and began digging up the plants. Realizing that the porch light substantially illuminated the walkway area, he hurried to turn it off. Working in near darkness, his breath coming in short gasps, he clawed at the plants, tossing them into heavy plastic bags. He realized that Emily could be turning into her driveway at any moment and he didn't want her to see him doing this.

He also realized that she must have noticed the plantings this afternoon and would wonder why they were gone. The first thing tomorrow morning he would buy different beds of flowers to replace them.

What would be going through Emily's head? Would she hear anybody in her office talking about this program? Would they talk about the mums? Would anybody at his job, or on this block, notice that one lousy picture and think about the fact that he had lived and worked here for two years—exactly the right time frame for leaving Des Moines?

Zach had just finished pulling up the last of the flowers when Emily's car came up her driveway. He crouched down in the dark shadow of the house and watched as she got out of the car, hurried to her front door, and went inside. Is there any chance, wherever she had been, that she had seen this program? Even if she had only glanced at it, at some point her professional instincts would be bound to kick in. If not right away, then soon.

Zach knew that he had to step up his preparations and be ready to leave much sooner than he had planned.

32

Michael Gordon ended up spending most of his waking hours during the weekend with Gregg and Katie. At dinner at Neary's on Friday night, the usually reticent Gregg had been surprisingly open. Waving away Michael's repeated apologies for doubting his innocence, Gregg said: "Mike, I've been thinking a lot about something that happened to me when I was sixteen. I was in a horrible car crash and was in intensive care for six weeks. I don't remember a single moment of it. Afterwards, my mother told me that for the last three weeks, I was talking a blue streak, and begging them to take the tubes out of me. She told me that I thought the nurse was my grandmother, who died when I was six."

"You never talked about that," Mike said.

"Who wants to talk about being in a near-death experience?" Gregg had smiled—a wry smile—as he added, "For that matter, who wants to hear about it? There's enough doom and gloom in the world to go around without someone filling your ear with his hard-luck tale from twenty-six years ago. Anyway, let's change the subject."

"As long as you keep eating," Mike replied. "Gregg, how much weight have you lost?"

"Just enough to make my clothes fit better."

Early Saturday morning, Mike had picked up Gregg and Katie and they had driven to his ski lodge in Vermont. It was almost two months too early for skiing but in the afternoon, Gregg and Katie had gone for a long walk together, while Mike worked on his book about major crimes of the twentieth century.

For dinner, they drove into Manchester. As usual, Vermont was significantly cooler than New York and the fire blazing in the dining room of the cozy inn was warming, both emotionally and physically, for each of them.

Late that evening, after Katie, with a book under her arm, had gone to bed, Gregg went into Mike's study where he had resumed working after dinner. "I think I remember you telling me that you're doing a chapter on Harry Thaw, the millionaire who shot Stanford White, the architect, at Madison Square Garden in New York?"

"That's right."

"He shot him in front of a crowd of people and then got off on an insanity plea, didn't he?"

Michael wondered what Gregg was driving at. "Yes, but Thaw *did* have to spend some time in an asylum," he said.

"Then, when he got out of the asylum not very long afterward, he moved into a nice big house on Lake George, as I remember?"

"Gregg, come on. What are you getting at?"

Gregg shoved his hands in his pockets. To Mike he looked curiously vulnerable. "Mike, after that accident when I was a kid, I had long stretches where I couldn't remember things that had happened. That all passed, but what hasn't passed is my concept of time. I can get so engrossed that I don't realize if a couple of hours have gone by."

"That's called the ability to concentrate," Mike said.

"Thanks. But it happened the morning Natalie died. That was a March day. The weather was lousy. It's one thing to be sitting at your desk and be unaware of time. It's another when you're outside in crummy weather. The point is, I know I couldn't have killed Natalie. God, how much I loved her! But I wish I could remember those two hours. I do remember turning in that rented car. If I'd been running for two hours, was I in that deep a funk that I didn't feel cold or out of breath?"

Heartsick at the doubt and confusion he saw on his friend's face, Michael got up and grasped Gregg's shoulders. "Gregg, listen to me. You came off great on the stand yesterday. I believed you about that Jimmy Easton character and about the reason you called Natalie frequently. I remember being with you when in the middle of a conversation, you'd push the button on your cell phone and have a ten-second conversation with her."

"Natalie, I love you," Gregg said, his voice emotionless. "End of message."

33

Emily allowed herself to sleep until seven thirty on Sunday morning. She planned to get to the office by eight thirty and spend the day there. "Bess, you've been very patient with me. I know I've been neglecting you," she apologized as she plucked Bess from the other pillow. She was longing for a cup of coffee but seeing the plaintive look in the eyes of her little dog, she threw on jeans and a jacket and announced, "Bess, you're not just going out in the backyard this morning. I'm taking you for a walk."

Bess's tail was wagging furiously as they went downstairs, and Emily grabbed the leash and fastened it to her collar. She slipped a key in her jacket pocket and headed for the front door. Since she had put the bolt on the porch door, it was easier to go out that way.

With Bess excitedly pulling at the leash, they started down the walk to the driveway. Then Emily stopped abruptly and stared in amazement. "What in God's name is going on?" she asked aloud as she saw the freshly dug dirt where only late yesterday she had admired the newly planted mums.

Were they loaded with bugs? she wondered. Is that possible? I mean, that is really strange. He lined his whole walkway with them just yesterday. And when did he pull them up? They were there when I left to go to the Wesleys' last evening. I didn't notice one way or the other if they were gone when I got home. That was sometime after ten o'clock.

She felt a tug on the leash and looked down. "Sorry, Bess. Okay, we'll start moving."

Bess elected to turn left at the sidewalk which took Emily past Zach's house. He has to be home, she thought, because his car is parked in the driveway. If that guy wasn't so creepy, I'd ring his doorbell later and ask him what happened. But I don't want to give him an excuse to latch onto me again.

The image of Zach rocking in the chair in her enclosed porch once again permeated her thoughts. It was more than a feeling of discomfort, she concluded. *He scared me.*

And he still does, she acknowledged, as she passed his house again on the way back fifteen minutes later. I've been so wrapped up in this case that I don't think it hit me right away.

34

This is the day the Lord has made," Gregg Aldrich thought grimly as he looked out his bedroom window at six o'clock on Monday morning. It was pouring outside, but even if it had not been, he would not have gone for a run. I would hope I wouldn't be stupid enough to lose track of time on this of all days, he thought, but I'm not taking any chances.

He swallowed against the dryness in his mouth. Last night he'd taken a low-dose sleeping pill and had slept for seven hours without waking up. But he didn't feel rested, and if anything was even a little groggy. Strong coffee will take care of that, he promised himself.

He reached into the closet for a robe and, as he was putting it on, stuffed his feet into slippers, then walked down the carpeted hallway to the kitchen. As he approached it, the fragrance of the brewing coffee lifted his spirits.

The weekend with Mike in Vermont was a life preserver, he thought, as he took his favorite mug from the cabinet over the coffeemaker. Talking to Mike about the morning Natalie died, when I hadn't even been aware of the cold after jogging for two hours, had been reassuring. And then Mike had reminded him he had to do as well today on the witness stand as he had on Friday.

On the drive home from Vermont yesterday afternoon, Mike had talked about that again. "Gregg, show the same resolve that you showed on Friday. Your answers came across as completely credible. You heard Judge Reilly on my show say that if he was at a bar and had a conversation with some stranger, it would be his word against the other guy that he didn't make a deal with him to kill his wife. A nationwide audience heard Reilly say that, and I really believe that plenty of people out there thought the same thing."

Mike had paused and then continued. "These were the kind of circumstances where anybody can accuse anybody else of anything. And don't forget, Jimmy Easton is getting a big reward for testifying against you. He doesn't have to sweat about growing old in prison."

I pointed out to Mike the one little factor he was forgetting, Gregg thought. The judge's wife didn't end up shot to death.

Confidence, he thought bitterly. I don't have any. He poured coffee into the mug and carried it into the living room. Kathleen and he had bought the apartment when they were expecting Katie. I really was taking a leap to sign up for the maintenance, Gregg thought. But in those days I was sure I was going to make it big as an agent. Well, I did, and where has it gotten me?

Kathleen had been like a little kid choosing paint colors and furniture and carpets. She had instinctive good taste and a genuine talent for hunting down bargains.

She'd always joked that like him, she'd grown up with the silver spoon in someone else's mouth. He stood in the living room, remembering.

If she had lived, Gregg thought, I never would have become involved with Natalie. And I wouldn't be on my way to court to try to persuade a jury that I'm not a murderer. A tidal wave of nostalgia washed over him. In that instant he longed for her physically and emotionally. "Kathleen," he whispered, "watch over me today. I'm frightened. And if I'm convicted, who will take care of our Katie?"

For a long moment, he swallowed against the lump in his throat, then bit his lip. Stop it, he told himself. Stop it! Go back in there and start fixing some breakfast for Katie. If she sees you feeling like this, she'll be a wreck.

On the way to the kitchen he passed the table with the drawer where Jimmy Easton had claimed he'd kept the five-thousand-dollar advance for killing Natalie. He stopped, reached for the handle of the drawer, and yanked it open. As he did so, the raucous squeak that Jimmy Easton had accurately described assailed his senses. With bitter anger, Gregg slammed the drawer shut.

35

Loaded for bear, I hope."

Emily looked up. It was seven thirty A.M. on Monday morning and she was in her office. Detective Billy Tryon was standing in the doorway. One of my least favorite people in the world, she thought, irritated at what she perceived to be his condescending tone.

"Is there anything I can do for you this morning, Emily? I know it's a real big day for you in court."

"I think I'm pretty well set, Billy. But thank you."

"As Elvis would say, 'It's now or never.' Good luck with Aldrich today. I hope you destroy him on the stand."

Emily wondered whether Tryon really wished her well, or hoped that she would fall on her face. At the moment she didn't care. I'll think about that later, she decided.

Tryon was not about to leave. "Don't forget you're fighting it for Jake and me, too," he said. "We put a lot of legwork into this one. And that guy Aldrich is a killer, and we all know it."

Realizing that he was fishing for a compliment, Emily reluctantly replied, "I know you and Jake really worked hard and I certainly hope the jury thinks the way you do."

You finally got a haircut, she thought. If you knew how much better you looked, you'd visit your barber more often. She had to admit that when he didn't look sloppy, Tryon had a sort of a tough-guy, swaggering manner that some women probably considered attractive. Word in the office was that he had a new girlfriend who was a nightclub singer. Why was she not surprised?

It became immediately apparent that he was looking her over, too.

"You sure got all dolled up for the camera today, Emily. You look great."

In a superstitious moment earlier that morning, Emily had rejected the jacket and skirt she had been planning to wear. She had reached in her closet for the charcoal gray pants suit and bright red turtleneck that she remembered having on when Ted Wesley assigned her the case. "I'm not dolled up," she said sharply. "This suit is two years old and I've worn it any number of times to court."

"Well, I'm trying to pay you a compliment. You look great."

"Billy, I guess I should thank you, but as you can obviously see, I'm going over my notes and in a little more than an hour, I'm going to go into court to try to get a murderer convicted. Would you mind?"

"Sure, sure." With a smile and a wave, he turned and left, closing the door behind him.

Emily felt rattled. I didn't dress for the camera, did I? she asked herself. No, I didn't. Is the red turtleneck too bright? No, it isn't. Forget it. You're getting wacky, like Zach. She thought again about the missing mums. He must have spent most of Saturday planting them. They looked beautiful. Then when I walked Bess yesterday morning they were gone. Nothing but dirt where they had been. But when I got home at five o'clock his walkway was lined with asters and pansies. I liked the mums better, she thought. But that guy is really strange. Looking back, it's probably a blessing that I found him lounging inside my house at ten o'clock at night. What a wake-up call!

Dismissing any further thought about her wardrobe or her oddball neighbor, Emily looked down and once again perused the notes she would use when she cross-examined Gregg Aldrich.

The trial resumed promptly at nine A.M. Judge Stevens indicated to Gregg Aldrich that he should return to the witness stand.

Aldrich was wearing a charcoal gray suit, white shirt, and black and gray tie. You'd swear he was going to a funeral, Emily thought. I'll bet Richard Moore put him up to wearing that outfit. He's trying to convey the image of the bereaved husband to the jury. But if I have anything to say about it, it won't do him any good.

She glanced quickly over her shoulder. A sheriff's officer had told her that the corridor had been packed with would-be spectators long before the doors to the courtroom opened. It was clear that every seat was taken. Katie Aldrich was sitting in the front row directly behind her father. On the other side of the aisle, Alice Mills, accompanied by her two sisters, sat just behind Emily.

Emily had already greeted Alice before she took her place at counsel table.

Judge Stevens noted for the record that the witness had been previously sworn, then said, "Prosecutor, you can now begin your cross-examination."

Emily stood up and said, "Thank you, Your Honor." She walked over to the ledge at the far end of the jury box. "Mr. Aldrich," she began, "you have testified that you loved your wife, Natalie Raines, very much. Isn't that correct?"

"That is correct," Gregg Aldrich said quietly.

"And you have testified that you were her agent. Is that correct?"

"That is correct."

"And as her agent, you were entitled to fifteen percent of her income. Isn't that correct?"

"That is correct."

"And would it be fair to say that Natalie Raines was an acclaimed actress and achieved major celebrity status, both before and during your marriage?"

"That is correct."

"And isn't it a fact that if Natalie had lived, there is every indication that she would have continued to be very successful?"

"I am sure she would have been."

"And isn't it a fact that if you weren't her agent anymore, you wouldn't be getting a portion of her income?"

"That is true, but I was a successful agent for years before I married Natalie, and I continue to be a successful agent."

"Mr. Aldrich, I am only going to ask you one more question in this area. Did your income substantially increase when you married Natalie and became her agent? Yes or no?"

"Yes, but not substantially."

"Well, are any of your present clients as successful as Natalie Raines was?"

"I have a number of clients, particularly recording artists, who make a great deal more money than Natalie did." Gregg Aldrich hesitated. "We are talking about a different kind of success. Natalie was well on her way to assuming the mantle once held by the late Helen Hayes: 'First Lady of the American Theatre.' "

"You wanted very much to have her viewed in that light?"

"She was a magnificent actress. She deserved that accolade."

"On the other hand, you were saddened when, to further her career, she went on the road for extended periods of time, weren't you, Mr. Aldrich? Isn't it a fact that you constantly badgered her by wanting it both ways?" As her tone began to rise, Emily stepped closer to the witness stand.

"As I have testified here and will now tell you again, my concern was that Natalie insisted on accepting roles that I felt could hurt her career. Of course I missed her when she was away. We were very much in love."

"Of course you were. But isn't it a fact that you were so angry and frustrated at the frequent separations that Natalie became tormented, so much so that she finally gave up on the marriage?"

"That was absolutely not the reason she decided to separate."

"Then if you were so accepting of Natalie's schedule, aside from your professional opinion about the roles she was taking, why did she hire another agent? Why did she beg you to stop calling her? Why did she end up *demanding* that you stop calling her?"

As Emily pounded away at Gregg Aldrich, she could sense that there was an awareness in the courtroom that his composure was beginning to break down. His answers were becoming hesitant. He kept looking away from her.

"Natalie phoned you for the last time on Saturday morning, March 14th, two and a half years ago. Let me quote to you exactly what you said under oath about the call." She looked down at the paper she was holding and then read: "'I received a message from her on my cell phone, saying she had gone up to Cape Cod, that she would be at our scheduled meeting on Monday, and asking me not to call her over the weekend.'"

Emily stared at Gregg. "She wanted to be left alone, didn't she, Mr. Aldrich?"

"Yes." A thin bead of perspiration was forming on Gregg Aldrich's forehead.

"But instead of respecting her wishes, you immediately rented a car and followed her to Cape Cod, didn't you?"

"I respected her wishes. I did not phone her."

"Mr. Aldrich, that's not what I asked. You followed her to Cape Cod, didn't you?"

"I didn't plan to talk to her. It was necessary for me to see if she was alone."

"And it was necessary to drive a rented car that nobody would recognize?"

"As I explained last week," Gregg answered, "I wanted to go there quietly and I didn't want to upset her or confront her. I just wanted to see if she was alone."

"If you wanted to find out if she was seeing anyone else, why didn't you hire a private investigator?"

"That never occurred to me. I made a spontaneous decision to drive up to Cape Cod. I would never have hired anyone to spy on my wife. The thought is revolting to me," Gregg said, his voice quivering.

"You testified that, by Sunday evening, you were satisfied that she was alone because you didn't see any other cars in the driveway. How do you know that she didn't pick up someone before you got there? How could you be so sure that there was no one else inside?"

"I was sure." Gregg Aldrich's voice was rising.

"How could you be so sure? This was the most important issue in your life. How could you be so sure?"

"I looked in the window. I saw her sitting alone. That's how I knew."

Emily, stunned at this new revelation, recognized

instantly that Gregg Aldrich had just made a big mistake. Richard Moore knows it, too, she thought.

"Did you get out of your car and walk up her lawn and look in her window?"

"Yes, I did," Gregg Aldrich said, defiantly.

"What window did you look in?"

"The window on the side of the house that looks into the den."

"And what time of the day or night was it when you did this?"

"It was just before midnight on Saturday night."

"And so you were hiding in the bushes outside her home in the middle of the night?"

"I didn't think of it that way," Gregg answered, the defiance gone, his voice now hesitant. He leaned forward in the witness chair. "Can't you understand that I was worried about her? Can't you understand that if she had found someone else, I knew I had to go away?"

"Then what did you think when you saw her alone?"

"She looked so vulnerable. She was curled up like a child on the couch."

"And how do you think she would have reacted if she had seen a figure in the window at midnight?"

"I was very careful not to let her see me. I did not want to frighten her."

"Were you then satisfied that she was alone?"

"Yes, I was."

"Then why did you drive past her house again several times on Sunday?" Emily demanded. "You admitted it in your direct examination."

"I was worried about her."

"So let me get this straight," Emily said. "First, you tell us that you went there in your rented car just to find out if she was alone. Then you tell us that you were satisfied that she was alone after you peered in her window while you hid in the bushes at midnight. Now you tell us that on Sunday, even though you *believe* she's alone, you're driving around her neighborhood a good part of the day and into the evening. Is that what you're telling us?"

"I'm telling you that I was worried about her and that's why I was there on Sunday."

"And what were you so worried about?"

"I was worried about Natalie's emotional state. The way she had been curled up like that said to me that she was very upset."

"Did it occur to you that the reason she appeared to be upset might be your fault, Mr. Aldrich?"

"Yes, it did. That was why, as I testified on Friday, on the drive home from the Cape, I think I made my peace with the fact that it was over between us. It's hard to explain but that was my thinking. If I was the cause of whatever was upsetting her, then I had to leave her alone."

"Mr. Aldrich, you did not find your wife with another man. Then on the way home, to quote you, you decided that Natalie was one of those people who are 'never less alone than when alone?' Aren't you telling this court-room that either way you had lost her?"

"No, I am not."

"Mr. Aldrich, isn't it fair to say that she simply didn't

want to be with you anymore? And if something else was troubling her, she didn't turn to you for help. Isn't it true that she wanted you out of her life?"

"I remember feeling on that drive down from the Cape that there was no point in hoping that Natalie and I would get back together."

"That upset you, didn't it?"

Gregg Aldrich looked into Emily's eyes. "Of course I was upset. But something else was happening, a feeling of relief that at least I knew it was over. At least I wouldn't be consumed by her any longer."

"You wouldn't be consumed by her anymore. Was that your resolution?"

"I guess that's one way of putting it."

"And you didn't drive out to her home the next morning and shoot her?"

"Absolutely not. Absolutely not."

"Mr. Aldrich, immediately after your wife's body was found, you were questioned by the police. Didn't they ask you if you could give them the name of even one person who might have seen you jogging in Central Park between, and I quote you, '7:15 or so and 10:05 when I returned the rental'?"

"I wasn't looking at anyone that day. It was cold and windy. On days like that everyone who is jogging or running is bundled up. Some people have headphones on. The point is it's not a social get-together. People are into themselves."

"Would you say that you were into yourself for two and a half hours on a cold, windy March day?"

"I used to run the November marathon. And I have clients who were professional football players. They tell me that no matter how frigid the weather, the adrenaline would start pumping when they were on the field and they simply didn't feel the cold. I didn't either on that morning."

"Mr. Aldrich, let me ask you if this scenario is true. I suggest that your adrenaline was pumping that Monday morning when, by your own admission, you had decided that your wife, Natalie Raines, was lost to you. I suggest that knowing she would be home at sometime that morning, you got in that rental car, made the thirty-minute drive to Closter, picked up the hide-a-key you knew was there, and waited inside her kitchen. Isn't that what happened?"

"No. No. Never."

Emily, her eyes blazing, pointed her finger at the witness stand. Her tone loud and sarcastic, she said, "You killed your wife that morning, didn't you? You shot her and then you left her, thinking that she was already dead. You drove back to New York and then maybe jogged around Central Park, hoping you'd be seen. Isn't that right?"

"No, it is not!"

"And then a little while later, you returned the rental car that you had used to spy on your wife. Isn't that right, Mr. Aldrich?"

Gregg Aldrich was now standing up and shouting. "I never hurt Natalie. I could never hurt Natalie."

"But you did hurt Natalie. You did more than hurt her. You killed her," Emily shouted back at him.

Moore was on his feet. "Objection, Your Honor, objection. Counsel is badgering the witness."

"Sustained. Prosecutor, lower your voice and rephrase the question." Judge Stevens's tone left no doubt that he was irritated.

"Did you kill your wife, Mr. Aldrich?" Emily asked, her voice now gentle.

"No . . . no . . . ," Gregg Aldrich protested, his voice breaking. "I loved Natalie, but . . ."

"*But*, you had admitted to yourself . . ." Emily began.

"Objection, Your Honor," Moore thundered. "She won't let him complete his answers."

"Sustained," Judge Stevens said. "Ms. Wallace, you are directed to allow the witness to complete his answers. I don't want to have to admonish you again."

Emily nodded in acknowledgment of the judge's instructions. She turned back to Aldrich. Her voice lowered, she said, "Mr. Aldrich, didn't you go to Cape Cod because Jimmy Easton had backed out of the deal to kill your wife for you?"

Gregg shook his head hopelessly. "I met Jimmy Easton in a bar, had a few minutes' conversation with him, and I never saw him again."

"But you had paid him to stalk and kill her. Isn't that the way it happened?"

"I didn't hire Jimmy Easton and I could never hurt Natalie!" Gregg protested, his shoulders shaking, his eyes filled with tears. "Can't you understand that? Can't *anyone* understand that?" His voice cracked and he broke into dry, racking sobs.

"Your Honor, may I request a recess?" Moore urged.

"We will take a fifteen-minute break," Judge Stevens ordered, "to give the witness a chance to compose himself."

A short time later, court resumed. Gregg had calmed down and returned to the witness stand. He appeared pale and seemingly resigned to enduring more of Emily's scathing cross-examination.

"I just have a few more questions, Your Honor," Emily said as she walked past the bench toward the witness stand. She stopped directly in front of it and, for a long moment, looked at him intensely.

"Mr. Aldrich, you acknowledged on direct examination that in the living room of your apartment in New York, you do have a side table with a drawer that, when it is opened, emits a loud and distinctive squeak."

"Yes, that is true," he answered faintly.

"And would it be fair to say that Jimmy Easton accurately described that table and that sound?"

"Yes, he did, but he was never in my home."

"Mr. Aldrich, you told us that this drawer is somewhat of a joke in your family, and that you all referred to it as 'a message from the departed spirits.' "

"Yes, that is true."

"Sir, as far as you know, did Mr. Easton know any members of your family?"

"As far as I know, he did not."

"Did you have any mutual friends with Mr. Easton who might have joked about this drawer in his presence?"

"As far as I know, we have no mutual friends."

"Mr. Aldrich, do you have any explanation whatsoever as to how Jimmy Easton could have so accurately described this piece of furniture and the sound it gave off if he has never been in your living room?"

"I have racked my brain as to how he could have known. I have no idea." Gregg's voice was beginning to break again.

"One more thing, Mr. Aldrich. In the articles that appeared in various magazines about Natalie, was this drawer ever mentioned?"

"No, it was not," he said, despairingly. Clutching the arms of the witness chair, he turned to the jury. "I did not kill my wife," he shouted. "I did not kill her. Please believe me. I . . . I . . . ." Unable to continue, Gregg buried his face in his hands and wept.

Ignoring the devastated figure on the witness stand, Emily said crisply, "Your Honor, I have no further questions," then walked back toward her chair at counsel table.

Moore and his son whispered quickly and decided against posing any further questions themselves. Richard Moore stood up. "Your Honor, the defense rests."

Judge Stevens looked at Gregg Aldrich. "Sir, you may step down."

Wearily, Gregg arose, murmured, "Thank you, Your Honor," and slowly, as if every step were painful, went back to his chair.

Judge Stevens then addressed Emily. "Is there any rebuttal from the prosecutor?"

"No, Your Honor," Emily said.

The judge then turned toward the jury. "Ladies and gentlemen, the testimony in this case is completed. I will take a forty-five-minute break to allow the attorneys to gather their thoughts for their summations. Under our rules of court, the defense attorney goes first, and then the prosecutor. Depending upon how long the summations take, I will give you my final legal instructions either late this afternoon or tomorrow morning. After my instructions are finished, we will randomly select the alternates and the final twelve jurors will begin their deliberations."

36

When court recessed on Monday afternoon, Emily had just finished her powerful summation. Moore did his best, she thought, but he couldn't get around that drawer. She had left the courtroom cautiously optimistic that soon Gregg Aldrich would be in a prison cell. The case would be given to the jury tomorrow. How long will it take them to decide? she wondered. And hopefully there *will* be a decision. She shuddered at the thought of a hung jury and having to do this all over again.

On the way home she stopped in the supermarket, intending only to pick up some basics like milk, soup, and bread. But when she passed the meat counter, she stopped. The thought of a steak and baked potato for dinner, particularly after all of the take-out food the last few months, was suddenly very appealing.

Exhaustion was seeping into her bones as she took the items to the checkout counter. By the time she was pulling into her driveway fifteen minutes later, she wondered if she would have the energy to grill the steak.

There was no sign of Zach's car and she remembered that he had told her that his hours at work had changed. The new flower beds had been soaked in the driving rain that had lasted most of the day. She found it unsettling to look at them.

As she unpacked the grocery bag, she let Bess run in the backyard for a few minutes, then went upstairs to her bedroom. She changed into an old pair of cotton jogging pants and a long-sleeved T-shirt and stretched out on the bed. Bess snuggled up to her and she pulled the coverlet over both of them. "Bess, I have fought the good fight. Now let's see what happens," she said as she closed her eyes.

For two hours she slept and was awakened by her own voice whimpering "Please don't . . . please don't . . ."

She bolted upright from the pillow. Am I crazy? she asked herself. What was I dreaming?

Then she remembered. I was frightened and I was trying to stop someone from hurting me.

She realized that she was trembling.

She could see that Bess was aware that she was upset. She pulled her dog close to her and said, "Bess, I'm glad you're here. That dream was so real. And pretty scary. The only person I know who would really want to get me is Gregg Aldrich, but I'm certainly not afraid of him."

A thought suddenly struck her. And neither was Natalie. She, too, believed he would never hurt her.

My God, what's the matter with me? she asked herself, impatiently. She looked at the clock. It was ten of eight. Time to cook a decent dinner, catch up on the paper, and then watch *Courtside*.

After everything that went on today, she thought, let's see if Michael Gordon is still so sure his buddy is innocent.

37

"It was not a good day in court for Gregg Aldrich," Michael Gordon said somberly as the opening credits for *Courtside* appeared on-screen. "A confident and seemingly credible Gregg Aldrich on direct examination last Friday came across very differently today. The courtroom was stunned when for the first time, he admitted that he had hidden in the bushes at midnight outside his wife's Cape Cod home and watched her as she sat alone. This occurred just about thirty-two hours before Natalie Raines was shot in the kitchen of her New Jersey residence, after returning from Cape Cod."

The *Courtside* panel all nodded their heads in agreement. Judge Bernard Reilly, who on Friday evening had expressed understanding of how a chance encounter in a bar could lead to bizarre and unfair accusations, now acknowledged that he was deeply troubled by Gregg Aldrich's performance under blistering cross-examination. "I felt for Richard Moore when Aldrich admitted he had his nose pressed against the windowpane at midnight. I'll bet anything that he had never told Moore he did that."

Georgette Cassotta, a criminal psychologist, said, "Let me tell you. That image sent shivers through the women on the jury. And you can bet that the men on the jury also reacted strongly. He went from the concerned husband on direct examination to a Peeping Tom on cross-examination. And going back past her house again on Sunday, after he admitted that he was satisfied by Saturday night that she was alone, could have sealed his fate."

"And there's something else that really helped the prosecution's case today," Judge Reilly added. "I think Emily Wallace was very effective in the way she approached the issue of the squeaky drawer. She gave Aldrich every opportunity to suggest an explanation for Easton's knowledge of that table and that drawer. He couldn't come up with anything. He and Moore had to know that she was going to pound on that. The problem is that he didn't come across as someone who honestly just didn't have an explanation. He came across like someone who had been cornered."

"But if he really didn't do it," Gordon said, "and if he really doesn't know, couldn't that have been the reaction of a man who feels entrapped and in despair?"

"I think at this point that Gregg Aldrich's best shot is that one or two jurors react that way and he gets a hung jury," Judge Reilly responded. "I just don't see twelve jurors voting not guilty, frankly."

Just before the program ended, Michael Gordon reminded his viewers that as soon as Judge Stevens finishes his instructions on the law, the jurors would begin to deliberate. "Probably around eleven o'clock," he said. "And at that time you will be able to vote on our

Web site as to whether you believe Gregg Aldrich will be found guilty or not guilty of the murder of his wife. Or, whether there will be no unanimous decision either way, which would result in a hung jury and another trial.

"I seriously doubt that we will have a verdict by broadcast time tomorrow evening," Michael continued. "You can cast your vote right up until the jury informs Judge Stevens that they have reached a verdict. If there is no verdict by tomorrow night, we'll talk about the results of the voting so far. And now good night from all of us."

38

It got really bad today," Belle Garcia glumly told her husband, Sal, as Michael Gordon said good night to his viewing audience. "I mean, only last Friday, Michael came out and said that he thought Gregg was innocent. But tonight, he admits that Gregg's performance didn't help him one bit."

Sal looked up over his glasses. "Performance? I thought actors performed."

"You know what I mean. I mean he didn't come across like he didn't do it. He got confused and tripped up on what he was saying. He started crying when Emily got after him about Jimmy Easton and that loud drawer. I bet he wishes now he had had it oiled. And, to make matters worse, he really started blubbering and they had to take a break. I felt sorry for him but, being totally neutral, I have to say this: I think today he was coming across as sorry that he had killed his wife."

Fully aware that Belle was geared to have a serious discussion about the trial right now, Sal knew that it was time to put down his newspaper. He asked Belle a question that he was sure would evoke a lengthy response and require only minimal reaction from him. "Belle, if you were on the jury, as of right now how would you vote?"

Looking pensive and troubled, Belle shook her head. "Well . . . It's so hard . . . It's all so sad. I mean, what's going to happen to Katie? But, oh, Sal, if I were a member of that jury, I'm forced to say, with my heart breaking, I'd vote guilty. On Friday I really thought that Gregg was starting to make sense out of what had looked, even to a real dope, to be so suspicious. That squeaky drawer worried me, but anyone can tell Jimmy Easton is a born liar. But just now, when I saw those clips of Gregg on *Courtside*, I felt as if I was looking at a man who was going to confession. You know what I mean, not quite confessing as in admitting you did something you're not proud of, but kind of confessing by explaining how it happened, if you know what I mean."

Jimmy Easton, Sal thought.

Belle was looking straight at him and he hoped he didn't show the worry that the sound of Jimmy's name evoked in him. He had not told Belle that Rudy Sling had phoned him this afternoon. Nearly three years ago, his crew had moved his old friends Rudy and Reeney from their apartment on East Tenth Street up to Yonkers.

"Hey, Sal, by any chance have you been watching that *Courtside* show about the big-shot agent who shot his wife in the Garden State?" Rudy had asked.

"I'm not really paying attention to it, but Belle wouldn't miss a moment of it. And then I have to hear all about it."

"That guy Jimmy Easton was one of your crew when you moved us to Yonkers three years ago."

"I don't remember. He was an occasional backup when we were busy," Sal answered cautiously.

"The reason I'm telling you is because of something Reeney talked about this morning. She reminded me that when you moved us, you said we could tape the dresser drawers closed so we didn't have to unload everything."

"That's right. I told you that."

"My point is that when your guy Easton was pulling the tape off the drawers of the bedroom furniture, Reeney caught him going through them. She couldn't find anything missing, but she's always believed he was looking for something that was worth stealing. That's why we both remembered his name. You weren't on the job that day. Remember I called and told you to watch out for him?"

"Rudy, I never hired him again. So all I can say now is, so what?"

"So nothing. I mean, it just makes it kind of interesting that a guy who worked for you is making the headlines testifying he was hired by Aldrich to kill his wife. Reeney wondered if he maybe delivered something to that Aldrich guy's apartment for you and maybe opened that drawer, and *that's* how he knew it squeaked."

Easton is also one of the many guys I've paid off the books, Sal thought, nervously. "Rudy," he said, "I gave you a pretty nice break on that move, didn't I?"

"Sal, you were a prince. You moved us without a nickel down and waited two months till we paid you."

"And I've never delivered anything to Park Avenue where that Aldrich guy lived," Sal snapped angrily. "And you'll do me a real favor if you don't talk to anyone about Easton. I'll be honest. I paid him off the books. I could get in trouble."

"Sure, sure," Rudy replied. "You're my pal. Anyway, I guess there's nothing to it. I thought you'd get a chance to be a hero and maybe get a reward if you could honestly tell them that Easton had made a delivery to Aldrich's apartment. And you know how much Belle would love it if you guys got your picture in the newspaper."

My picture in the newspaper! Sal thought with dread. That's all I need!

His conversation with Rudy rushed through Sal's mind as Belle finished explaining how Emily, the prosecutor, had just about destroyed Gregg on the stand. "She was like one of those avenging angels," Belle said.

At that point in the narration, she sighed, reached down, and pulled over the hassock. She put her feet on it and continued. "Sometimes the cameras were on Alice Mills, Natalie's mother. Oh, I should tell you, Sal. Natalie's real name was Mills but she didn't think it was a good show business name so she changed it to Raines in a tribute to Luise Rainer, an actress who won the first two back-to-back Academy Awards that were ever presented. That was in *People* magazine today. She didn't want to take exactly the same name, but she wanted it close."

39

On Monday afternoon, after the disastrous day in court, Cole Moore walked with his father to their cars in the courthouse parking lot. "Why don't you and Robin come over around six thirty and have dinner with your mother and me?" Richard suggested quietly. "And we'll have a couple of drinks. We can both use them."

"Good idea," Cole replied. As he opened the car door for his father, he said, "Dad, you did everything you could. And don't give up yet. I still think we've got a decent shot at a hung jury."

"We had a decent shot until he admitted to being a Peeping Tom," Richard said, angrily. "I can't believe he never told me about that. At least we could have gone over it so that he could have explained it somewhat better. And if we'd had a chance to prepare him, he wouldn't have gotten so flustered over it. It makes me wonder what *else* he didn't tell me."

"Me, too," Cole said. "See you later, Dad."

* * *

At seven P.M. Richard and his wife, Ellen, and Cole and his wife, Robin, were at the dinner table, somberly discussing the trial.

Throughout their forty years of marriage, Ellen had always been an invaluable sounding board for Richard about his cases. A sixty-one-year-old woman with silver hair and the trim body of a disciplined athlete, her hazel eyes were filled with concern. She knew the toll this case was taking on her husband.

It's a blessing that Cole has been working with him, she thought.

Robin Moore, a twenty-eight-year-old real estate lawyer with auburn hair, had been married to Cole for two years. Now she shook her head in frustration. "Dad," she said, "I absolutely believe that somewhere along the line Easton had access to that apartment. In my mind that's the difference between a conviction and an acquittal. It's that miserable drawer that is going to be the sticking point during the deliberations."

"I completely agree," Richard replied. "As you know, we had our investigator, Ben Smith, go through Easton's background with a fine-tooth comb. When he wasn't in prison, he never had a regular job. So when he wasn't stealing enough to keep him going, he has to have been working off the books."

"Robin, we have a list of every store that regularly delivered to that apartment," Cole said, his tone frustrated. "You know, the laundry, the dry cleaner, the supermarket, the drugstore, you name it. No one admits ever having hired him, either on or off the books."

He picked up his glass of pinot noir and took another sip. "I really don't think Easton ever worked for one of those local stores. If he ever set foot in that apartment, I think he might have been making an isolated delivery for a vendor who paid him off the books. And remember, we couldn't even show Easton's picture to the Aldrich housekeeper after he was arrested seven months ago and came up with this whole scenario. She had already retired and then passed away about a year after Natalie died."

"Is there any chance he ever committed a burglary there?" Robin asked.

Richard Moore shook his head. "The security's too good. But if Jimmy Easton had ever managed to break in, he certainly would have stolen something, and the theft would have been noticed. Trust me, he wouldn't have left empty-handed."

"Naturally, everyone at the club is talking about this," Ellen said. "Richard, you certainly know that I don't talk about anything confidential, but sometimes it's helpful to hear how other people are reacting."

"How *are* they reacting?" Richard asked. The expression on his face indicated that he knew what she would say.

"Tara Wolfson and her sister, Abby, were in our golf foursome yesterday. Tara said that the thought of Gregg Aldrich reaching into that drawer and counting out five thousand dollars as a down payment on Natalie's life sickens her. She hopes he gets life."

"What does Abby think?" Robin asked.

"Abby was just as strongly convinced that Aldrich is innocent. They talked about it so much yesterday they barely focused on the game. But Abby called me a little while ago, just before you got home. After hearing the news reports on what happened in court today, she's changed her mind. Now she thinks he's guilty, too."

For a moment there was complete silence at the table, then Robin asked, "If Gregg Aldrich is convicted, will the judge let him go home to settle his affairs before he's sentenced?"

"I have no doubt that Judge Stevens will revoke his bail immediately," Cole replied. "Dad has tried a number of times to make Gregg face that possibility and at least make tentative arrangements for Katie."

"On that subject, to this day, he always cuts me off," Richard explained, his tone resigned. "He has his head in the sand, and refuses to face the consequences of being found guilty. If they have a verdict tomorrow—and I don't think it will happen that fast—I don't even know if he's made arrangements to have Katie driven home from the courthouse. Worse than that, I doubt that he's appointed a guardian to take care of that poor kid. Gregg was an only child and so was Katie's mother. And except for a few cousins in California that he almost never sees, there is no other family."

"God help that child," Ellen Moore said sadly. "God help both of them."

40

After *Courtside* ended, Michael Gordon walked from Rockefeller Center to Gregg's apartment on Park and Sixty-sixth Street. It was a little over a mile but he was a fast walker and now that the rain had ended, it felt good to have the cool, damp air on his face and hair.

That afternoon, as he was leaving the courthouse, Gregg had said, "I'm having dinner with Katie in the apartment tonight, just the two of us. It may be the last time that we can ever do that. But would you mind coming over after your program? I need to talk to you."

"Sure, Gregg." It had been on the tip of Mike's tongue to say something reassuring to Gregg, but looking at the drawn, sad face of his friend, he had stopped himself. It would have been insulting. Gregg's expression told him that he was painfully aware that he had damaged himself badly in his testimony.

Natalie.

Her face was in Michael's mind as he crossed Park Avenue and started walking north. When she was happy, she was funny and warm and great to be around. But if she was in the dumps because a rehearsal was going badly, or if she was fighting with a director on how a role should be interpreted, then she was impossible. Gregg had the patience of a saint with her. He was her confidant and protector.

And wasn't that what he was really trying to convey when he testified about looking in the window of the house at Cape Cod? Wasn't that what he was trying to explain when Emily Wallace pounded on him about driving around that house the next day? What were the words he had used in his response to her? He said, "I was worried about her emotional state."

Knowing Natalie, that made sense, Mike thought.

The prosecutor, Emily Wallace, had rattled Gregg. He'd admitted that much over the weekend in Vermont. It wasn't so much that Wallace looked like Natalie. Oh sure, in a general way, maybe there was something of a resemblance, Mike reflected, that struck me, too.

They were both lovely-looking women. They both had beautiful eyes and chiseled features. But Natalie's eyes had been green, and Emily Wallace's were midnight blue. They were both slender, but Emily Wallace is at least three inches taller than Natalie had been.

On the other hand, Natalie carried herself so gracefully and held her head so high that she always appeared to be taller than she actually was.

Wallace's perfect posture also gave her a commanding presence. And there was something about the way she used her eyes that was compelling. Those side glances at the jury, as though she knew they were sharing her scorn for Gregg's hesitant answers, were downright theatrical.

But no one had used side glances to better advantage than Natalie . . .

It was starting to drizzle again and Michael quickened his pace. So much for the weatherman on our station, he thought. At least the one we had before him used to make better predictions. Or better guesses, he added wryly.

It occurred to him that another resemblance of sorts between Natalie and Emily Wallace was the way Wallace walked. She moved between the jury box and the witness stand like an actress on a stage.

A half block before he reached Gregg's apartment building, the rain turned into a near cloudburst. Michael began to run.

The longtime doorman saw him coming and held the door open for him. "Good evening, Mr. Gordon."

"Hello, Alberto."

"Mr. Gordon, I don't think I'll see Mr. Aldrich tonight. And I won't be on duty tomorrow morning when he leaves for court. Please give him my very best wishes. He's a fine gentleman. I've been working here twenty years. That's even before he moved in. In my job you get to know what people are really like. It's a damn shame if that rotten liar Jimmy Easton can make a jury think that Mr. Aldrich ever brought him into this building."

"I agree, Alberto. We'll keep our fingers crossed."

As Michael walked through the tastefully appointed lobby and stepped into the elevator, he found himself praying that at least one person on the jury would feel the way Alberto did.

Gregg was waiting at the door when the elevator stopped on the fifteenth floor. He looked at Mike's dripping raincoat. "Don't they give you cab money at that cable station?" he asked with an attempt at a smile.

"I trusted our weatherman's forecast and decided to walk. A serious mistake." Michael unbuttoned his coat and slipped it off. "I'll hang it over the tub," he suggested. "I don't want it dripping on the floor."

"Good idea. Katie and I are in the den. I was about to pour my second scotch."

"While you're at it, pour me my first."

"Consider it done."

When Mike came into the den a few moments later, Gregg was sitting in his club chair. Katie, her eyes swollen with tears, was sitting on the hassock at his feet. She got up and ran to Mike. "Mike, Daddy said he thinks he's going to get convicted."

"Hold on, hold on," Gregg said, as he stood up. "Mike, your drink's over there." He pointed to a table next to the couch. "Come back here, Katie."

She obeyed, this time settling next to him in his chair.

"Mike, I'm pretty sure that you've been going over in your mind how to find something cheerful to say to me. I'll save you the trouble," Gregg said quietly. "I know how bad it is. And I know I've been wrong not to face the fact that I could be convicted."

Mike nodded. "I didn't want to bring that subject up to you, Gregg, but, yes, I've been worried."

"Don't worry about not bringing it up to me. Richard Moore has been doing that for months and I've been blowing him off. So let's get to it now. Would you consider being Katie's legal guardian?"

"Absolutely. It would be an honor."

"Of course, I don't mean to say that Katie should live with you. That wouldn't be appropriate, even though she'll be at Choate for most of the next three years. I have friends who have offered, but when you're trying to figure out what is the best situation for Katie, it's pretty damn tough."

Katie was crying silently, and Gregg's eyes were moist but his voice was composed. "On the business side, I made some calls tonight when I got home from court. I spoke to two of my top guys in the agency. They would be willing to buy me out for a fair price. That means I'll have enough money to finance an appeal. And there will be an appeal. Richard and Cole have done a good job but I had the feeling when we left court today that they looked at me differently. I may have to hire different lawyers for the next round."

He tightened his arm around his daughter. "Katie has a trust fund that will see her through to a graduate degree at an Ivy League college if that's what she wants."

Michael felt as though he were watching a terminally ill man making a living will. He also knew that Gregg had not finished revealing his plans.

"I have enough behind me to maintain this apartment for at least a couple of years. By then I hope I may be back here."

"Gregg, I agree that it is inappropriate for me to live with Katie, but she certainly can't live here by herself when she's not at school," Michael protested. "And I'm still not conceding that this worst-case scenario will happen," he added hastily.

"She's not going to be alone," Gregg responded. "There is a wonderful lady who loves her and wants to be with her."

As Michael looked at him, Gregg Aldrich seemed to be gathering strength. "Mike, I know that today, in the eyes of most of the people in the courthouse and most of the people in your audience, I came across horribly. But one person, a very important person, believed me."

Gregg tugged his daughter's hair. "Come on, Katie, cheer up. We've got the vote of someone who, unfortunately, is not on the jury but whose opinion means everything to us. She has sat in that courtroom every day from the very beginning. Of all people, she was the one most emotionally invested in seeking justice for Natalie."

Momentarily stunned, Michael waited.

"Mike, Alice Mills called while Katie and I were having dinner. Alice told me that when I was on the stand today, she understood what I was saying. She absolutely believes that I was looking out for Natalie, not spying on her. She was crying and said how much she has missed Katie and me, and that she bitterly regrets ever thinking that I could have hurt Natalie."

Mike saw that there was a difference in Gregg; a sort of calm had come over him.

"Alice told me that she has always considered Katie as her granddaughter. If I am convicted, she wants to be with Katie. She wants to take care of her. I told Alice that she was like a gift from heaven. We talked for a few minutes. Alice agreed that she would move here if things don't go well in court."

"Gregg, I guess that I should be stunned, but I'm really not," Michael said, his voice hoarse with emotion. "I could tell when Alice testified, and as I have watched her every day in court, that her guts were being torn out. I could almost sense her wanting to help you when Emily Wallace was beating on you."

"I know it sounds insane, Mike," Gregg said quietly, "but what so upset me today was I felt as if I were trying to explain to Natalie why I followed her to Cape Cod."

41

Zach had concocted a story to tell Emily and any of the other neighbors who might nosily inquire about the change of plants in his walkway. He planned to say it was the first time he had ever planted mums, that they had brought on a severe asthma attack, and that one of his friends had dug them up for him. He was almost sure that since it had been dark when he removed them, no one could have seen him.

It's a pretty believable excuse, he decided nervously—anyway, it was the best he could do.

On Tuesday morning he watched Emily having breakfast just before seven A.M. As usual, she was talking to Bess. The recording device he had planted over the refrigerator was acting up, but he could still hear most of what she was saying.

"Bess, after the judge instructs the jury this morning, then they start to deliberate. I'm fairly certain that they're going to convict him, but I wish I could feel good about it. For some reason I keep thinking about the other side of the picture. I hate knowing how much depends on Jimmy Easton's testimony. I wish I had one speck of DNA to prove that Gregg Aldrich is guilty."

If I ever come to trial, the prosecutor won't have *that* problem, Zach thought, as he remembered the *Fugitive Hunt* episode. The host had talked about the DNA that connected him to the murders of his three wives.

As Emily's voice began to crackle and fade, he fiddled with the volume on his receiver. I'm losing her, he thought, frustrated. I'm going to have to get back in there somehow and adjust the microphone.

He waited until seven forty, when Emily left for court, before he got into his own car to drive to work. Madeline Kirk, the elderly woman who lived directly across the street from him, was sweeping her walk. He gave her a friendly wave as he backed out of his driveway.

She did not return it. Instead she turned her head and looked away.

Another woman rejecting him. They're all alike, Zach thought bitterly. That old bag wouldn't even give me the time of day. The couple of other times he had seen her outside, he thought she had at least nodded in his direction.

He pressed his foot on the accelerator, and the car roared past her. Then a chilling possibility occurred to him. Maybe she saw that show? She's certainly got nothing else to do. She lives alone and never seems to have any visitors. Maybe she noticed the mums when I planted them, and wondered why they were gone.

Would she call in a tip to the show? Or would she think about it before she did it? Does she talk to anybody on the phone? Would she bring it up?

He was driving too fast. All I need is to be stopped by a cop, he thought nervously. As he slowed to the twenty-five-mile-an-hour speed limit, he was going over and over the way Madeline Kirk had rebuffed him.

And deciding what to do about it.

42

On Tuesday morning at nine A.M. Judge Stevens began his legal instructions to the jury. He explained, as he had done when the jury was initially being selected, that Gregg Aldrich was charged with the burglary of Natalie Raines's home, the murder of Natalie Raines, and possession of a firearm for an unlawful purpose. He instructed them that in order to convict Gregg Aldrich, they must be unanimously convinced that the prosecutor had proven his guilt beyond a reasonable doubt.

"I will define for you what we mean by the phrase 'beyond a reasonable doubt,'" the judge continued. "It means that in order to convict, you must be firmly convinced that the defendant is guilty. If you are not firmly convinced of guilt, then you must find him not guilty."

Emily listened as the judge explained this burden of proof.

You must be firmly convinced that Gregg Aldrich is guilty, Emily thought. *Am* I firmly convinced? Do I have a reasonable doubt? I have never felt this way trying a case. I have never argued to a jury to convict someone when I wasn't completely sure myself. But the truth here, she thought, is that sometimes I have a reasonable doubt about Aldrich, and sometimes I don't.

She looked over at him. For a man who had been so distraught yesterday, and who was facing the possibility of being in a jail cell tonight if there was a quick verdict, he seemed remarkably composed. He was wearing a jacket and slacks, with a blue shirt and a striped blue and red tie, a somewhat more casual outfit than he had been wearing during the trial. It becomes him, she thought reluctantly.

Judge Stevens continued to address the jurors: "You must carefully weigh and evaluate the credibility of each of the witnesses. You should consider the manner in which they testified and whether they had any interest in the outcome of this case."

He paused, his tone becoming even more serious. "You have heard the testimony of Jimmy Easton. You have heard about his prior criminal record. You have learned that he has cooperated with the prosecutor and that he will receive a benefit as a result of his cooperation. He will receive a substantial reduction in his own sentence."

Emily was studying the seven men and seven women in the jury box. She wondered which two would be randomly selected to become the alternates after Judge Stevens was finished. She hoped that jurors number four and eight would end up as the alternates. Both women seemed to cringe when the judge referred to the reduction in Easton's sentence. She knew that they could picture him ransacking their own homes. She doubted very much that they would believe a word that he said.

She looked back up at Judge Stevens. She was grateful for his businesslike tone when he spoke about Jimmy Easton. If the jurors detected even a hint of disapproval of his testimony, it could be very damaging.

"You will consider that substantial reduction," the judge was saying, "as well as all of the surrounding circumstances, when evaluating his testimony. This testimony must be scrutinized carefully. As with any other witness, you may believe all of it or you may believe none of it. Or, you may believe some of it and reject the remainder. Again, ladies and gentlemen, the ultimate determination of the credibility of his testimony is completely up to this jury."

This morning the courtroom was less than half full. There is no excitement for spectators in hearing the legal instructions to the jury, Emily thought. The real drama is in the testimony during the trial—and in that moment when the jury files back in with the verdict.

Judge Stevens smiled at the jury. "Ladies and gentlemen, I have completed my legal instructions to you. We now have reached the point where I know that it's going to be very disappointing for two of you. We are now going to select the alternates. Your juror cards have been placed in this box, and the court clerk will now randomly select two cards. If your name is called, please have a seat in the front row and I will then give you further instructions."

Emily crossed her fingers under the table and prayed that the numbers four and eight would come up. The court clerk, a slight woman of about fifty, her expression emotionless and professional, rotated the box and, when it had stopped, opened the top, looked away so that the jurors could be assured this was random, and took out the first card. "Juror number fourteen," she read, "Donald Stern."

"Mr. Stern, please sit in the front row of the courtroom," Judge Stevens directed. "The clerk may now indicate the second alternate."

Once again looking away, the clerk reached in the box and retrieved a second card. "Juror number twelve, Dorothy Winters," she read.

"Ms. Winters, please sit in the front row of the courtroom," Judge Stevens said.

An obviously reluctant and visibly frustrated Dorothy Winters rose from her juror chair and, shaking her head, walked to the front row and sat down next to Donald Stern.

Turns out I really dodged a bullet getting rid of that lady, Emily thought. From the way she's been looking sympathetically at Aldrich and Katie, she probably would have led the charge to acquit.

Emily only half listened as Judge Stevens addressed the alternates, telling them that they would remain with the case. He explained that if any of the deliberating jurors became ill or had a family emergency that prevented them from continuing, it was important that alternates still be available to deliberate.

"You are instructed not to discuss the case between yourselves or with anyone else until all of the proceedings are finished. You can remain in the central jury room on the fourth floor while the deliberations are ongoing."

God forbid that any juror has a problem and Winters ends up deliberating, Emily thought. Unless I'm totally misreading her, she would have ended up causing a hung jury, at the very least. And I think both of the Moores know that. They look as if they've just lost their best friend.

Judge Stevens then addressed juror number one, a heavyset, balding man in his early forties. "Mr. Harvey, our rules of court provide that juror number one serves as the foreperson of the jury. You will be responsible for overseeing the deliberations and for delivering the verdict when the jury has reached its decision. When the jury has reached its verdict, you will send me a note by handing it to the sheriff's officer who will be stationed just outside the jury deliberation room. Do not indicate in this note what the verdict is, but only that you have reached a verdict. The verdict will be announced by you in open court."

The judge glanced at his watch. "It is now eleven fifteen. Lunch will be delivered to you around twelve thirty. Today you may deliberate until four thirty. If you have not reached a verdict by that time, and I stress that you should take all the time that you reasonably need to be fair to both sides, I will release you overnight and you will resume your deliberations at nine o'clock tomorrow morning."

He turned to Emily. "Ms. Wallace, is all of the evidence ready to go into the jury room?"

"Yes, Your Honor, it's all here."

"Ladies and gentlemen, you may now go into the jury room. The officer will immediately bring the evidence in to you. As soon as he leaves the room, you may begin your deliberations."

Almost in unison, the jurors stood up and slowly filed into the immediate adjacent jury room. Emily watched intently to see if there were backward glances, either sympathetic or hostile, directed at Gregg Aldrich by any of them. But they all looked straight ahead and gave no clues at that moment as to how they might be thinking.

Judge Stevens then quickly reminded the attorneys and Gregg Aldrich that they must all be on a ten-minute call for any jury request, or for a verdict. "Court is adjourned," he concluded, lightly tapping his gavel on the bench.

The remaining spectators began to file out. Emily waited until the Moores, Gregg Aldrich, and Katie had left the courtroom. Then she got up to go. Outside in the corridor, she felt a tug on her sleeve and turned. It was Natalie's mother, Alice Mills. She was alone.

"Ms. Wallace, may I speak to you?"

"Of course." Compassion filled Emily as she looked at the red-rimmed eyes of the older woman. She's been doing a lot of crying, she thought. It's got to have been agony for her to sit here day after day and listen to all of this. "Why don't we go down to my office and have a cup of tea?" she suggested.

The elevator was crowded. Emily caught the interested looks of the other people in it as they recognized Natalie's mother.

As they walked into her office, Emily said, "Mrs. Mills, I know this has been torture for you. I'm so glad that we're near the end."

"Ms. Wallace . . . ," Alice Mills began.

"Please call me Emily, Mrs. Mills." Emily smiled. "I thought we had agreed on that."

"All right," Alice Mills replied. "It's Emily. And remember I had asked you to call me Alice." Alice's lips were quivering.

"Why don't I get us that tea?" Emily asked. "How do you take it?"

When she returned a couple of minutes later, Alice Mills seemed composed. With a murmured thank-you, she accepted the cup and took a sip.

Emily waited. Obviously Natalie's mother was nervous about whatever she was going to say.

"Emily, I don't know quite how to put this. And I know you've worked so hard and I know you want justice for Natalie. Heaven knows, so do I. But yesterday when you were questioning Gregg, I know that to a lot of people he came off terribly. But I was seeing something different."

Emily could feel her throat closing. She had thought Alice Mills was coming to tell her how much she had appreciated Emily's efforts to convict Gregg. That obviously wasn't going to happen.

"I was remembering all the times when Natalie was

in rehearsal and was upset or anxious about how it was going. Gregg would quietly slip into the theatre and watch her. Sometimes she didn't even know it because he didn't want to interrupt her or distract her. Other times, when she was on the road, he would drop everything and fly out to see her because he knew she needed reassurance. Yesterday, when he was on the witness stand, explaining what he did in Cape Cod, I realized it was Gregg doing what he had always done. He was protecting Natalie."

"But, Alice, didn't all that happen under very different circumstances? Wasn't that before Natalie separated from him and then filed for divorce?"

"Gregg never stopped loving Natalie and never stopped trying to protect her. The Gregg that I saw on the witness stand yesterday is the Gregg that I have always known. Emily, I have thought this whole thing through until I almost can't think anymore. There is absolutely no way that Gregg could have ever hurt Natalie and then left her to die. I will go to my grave believing that."

"Alice," Emily said, gently, "I'm going to say this with the deepest respect for you. When a tragedy like this happens, and a family member is accused, it is often almost impossible to accept that the family member could be responsible. In a terrible and sad sort of way, in a crime like this, it is more merciful if it had been committed by a stranger. At least then the victim's family endures it together."

"Emily, I don't care about other cases. I beg you, if Gregg is found guilty, to investigate this further. Can't you see for yourself what I can so plainly see? Jimmy Easton is a liar."

Alice stood up defiantly and glared at her.

"And why do I think that you know that, too, Emily?" she asked.

43

On Tuesday night, Michael Gordon opened the discussion on *Courtside* by indicating that the jury had completed its first day of deliberations without reaching a verdict. "We're now going to reveal the results of the voting on our Web site and where our viewers stand on whether Gregg Aldrich is guilty or not guilty."

He looked around at the other members of the panel. "And quite frankly, I think we are all surprised. Last night after Aldrich was cross-examined, and we believed that he had stumbled badly, we fully expected that the poll numbers would weigh heavily for a guilty verdict."

Clearly buoyed by what he was saying, Gordon announced that forty-seven percent of the four hundred thousand respondents had actually voted not guilty. "Only fifty-three percent are ready to convict," he said dramatically.

"After all these years in the business, you think you have a pretty good feel for how people are reacting and then you get a result like this," Judge Bernard Reilly said, shaking his head. "But there's another thing being in the business a long time also teaches you: You just never know."

"If the prosecutor, Emily Wallace, happens to be

watching, she can't be too thrilled. A bare majority doesn't cut it in the criminal courts," Michael Gordon said. "Any verdict, guilty or not guilty, must be unanimous, twelve to zero either way.

"If the jurors are thinking like our viewers, we are headed for a hung jury and a retrial."

44

The jurors resumed their deliberations at nine o'clock on Wednesday morning. Emily tried to concentrate on some of her other files but could not. Her exchange with Alice Mills yesterday had caused her a troubled night's sleep.

At noon, she went to the courthouse cafeteria to pick up a sandwich and bring it back to her desk. But when she got there she was sorry she had not asked someone else in the office to go for her. Gregg Aldrich, his daughter, Katie, Richard and Cole Moore, and Alice Mills were seated at a table she had to pass to get to the lunch counter.

"Good afternoon," she murmured quietly as she went by. She tried to avoid making direct eye contact with them but could not help but see the tearful anguish on young Katie's face.

She doesn't deserve this, Emily thought. No fourteen-year-old does. She's smart enough to understand that at any moment we could be summoned back to the courtroom and hear a verdict that may send her father to prison for the rest of his life.

Emily ordered a turkey sandwich and a diet soda. Back in her office, she nibbled at the sandwich, then put it down. Though she had felt hungry a few minutes ago, seeing Katie Aldrich had taken away any semblance of an appetite.

Alice Mills. Emily's thoughts turned back to her. If she had been convinced of his innocence back in April when I first met her here, would I have done anything different? she asked herself.

It was a possibility that frightened her. Billy and Jake did most of the investigation on the case, including interviewing Jimmy Easton and checking out the details of his story. There was no question that Gregg Aldrich had placed a phone call to him and there was no question that he had accurately described Aldrich's living room.

But so much of the rest of his story could not be corroborated. Gregg Aldrich completely denied ever getting a letter from Easton backing out of the deal to kill Natalie.

Easton just doesn't seem like the type to write a letter, Emily thought. It would be so much more like him to leave a cryptic message on Aldrich's cell phone saying he was leaving town and was no longer available to provide services.

But maybe Easton didn't want to get involved in any conversation if Gregg had answered the call, Emily rationalized. He couldn't count on just getting Gregg's voice mail. So he wrote a letter.

I'm finished trying this case, she reminded herself. Let it go. There is a ton of evidence against Gregg Aldrich. Whatever the jury does, I can live with.

*   *   *

At four thirty that afternoon, Judge Stevens sent the jury home, reminding them again not to discuss the deliberations, either among themselves or with anyone else.

They've been deliberating for about twelve hours now, Emily thought as she watched the somber-faced jury file out. That doesn't surprise me. I just hope we get a verdict by Friday afternoon. She smiled ruefully. After watching *Courtside* last night and hearing the poll results, she didn't want the jurors exposed over the weekend to family and friends dying to offer helpful comments.

Richard Moore lingered in the courtroom after Cole escorted Gregg and Katie out, with Alice Mills a few steps behind them. He came over to Emily. "The jurors are making both of us sweat, Emily," he remarked cordially.

"I guess they are, Richard," Emily agreed. "But I always thought this would take a few days."

"I understand that Alice Mills came to see you yesterday."

"She certainly did," Emily replied. "She's a lovely lady and she's been through hell, but I'm sure glad she's not on the jury."

Richard Moore chuckled. "I guess you are." The momentary hint of humor then disappeared. "Emily, I swear to you. You've got the wrong guy. You may get a conviction, but if you do we're going to keep looking for how Easton got his information, especially about that damn squeaky drawer. There's got to be another explanation."

"Richard, you've done a great job for him. I have prosecuted him in good conscience. If any legitimate new evidence ever came up, I would be the first to want to see it."

They walked out of the courtroom together. "See you in the morning," Richard said.

"Take care," Emily replied.

When she got to her office, there was a note on her desk. "Em," it read, "come to Solari's at 6:30 for dinner. It's Billy Tryon's birthday and we're taking him out. Ted Wesley is going to stop by." The note was signed "Trish," an investigator in the office.

Trish had added a good-natured P.S. "You'll be home in time to watch your favorite show—*Courtside*!!!!"

The thought of sharing in a birthday celebration for Billy Tryon was singularly unappealing, but there was no way she could decline, particularly since Ted Wesley, Tryon's cousin, was going to be there.

It's almost five o'clock, she realized. Since I'm stuck with this, I'd better get going so that I can feed Bess and let her out. And I'll get out of this suit and these heels and put on something more comfortable.

An hour later, after having treated Bess to a twenty-minute walk, Emily put out her food, changed her water dish, and went upstairs. Bess had been so frantic to go out that she hadn't taken the time to change when she first got home.

45

Detective Billy Tryon was clearly enjoying his fifty-third birthday dinner at Solari's, the popular restaurant located around the corner from the Bergen County Courthouse. His arm around the chair of his latest young girlfriend, Donna Woods, he commented how good it was to get away from the tension of waiting for the Aldrich verdict.

"Jake and I put in a load of hours on this one," he said, a hint of boasting in his tone. "Too bad he couldn't make it tonight. His kid is in some game."

"Billy, I didn't think you liked Jake," Donna protested earnestly. "Why would you want him here?"

Thoroughly enjoying Tryon's obvious embarrassment as he shot an angry glance at his girlfriend, Emily felt an immediate kinship with Jake. Too bad I don't have a kid in a game tonight, she thought. I'd really rather be almost anywhere else.

The others at the table were two assistant prosecutors, two veteran detectives, and Investigator Trish Foley, the one who had left the note inviting Emily to the dinner.

Trish is such a good friend, Emily thought, but she doesn't realize how I feel about Billy Tryon. I'm sure that she invited me here because she knows I'm worried about the Aldrich jury. She thinks that getting out tonight will be good for me. I'd much rather be home with Bess, she sighed.

She had not seen Ted Wesley today but she knew he had been in his office. It surprised her somewhat that he hadn't stopped by to say hello. That wasn't like him when a jury was out on a major case.

Billy Tryon, still squirming from Donna's indiscreet comment about his opinion of Jake, tried to change the subject. "Come on, Em, stop worrying. When you've got such a model citizen as your star witness, getting a conviction is a piece of cake," he joked. "Didn't you love Easton's story about the letter he sent Aldrich backing out of the deal and keeping the 'nonrefundable advance'? That was my line and he used it. It got a big laugh in court."

"That was *your* line!" Emily exclaimed in shock.

"Well, you know what I mean. When I first interviewed him, he told me that in his letter to Aldrich, he wrote that he wasn't going to return the money. I joked to him that it was like a sort of nonrefundable advance. And that's the way it came out when he testified."

"Hello, everybody." Ted Wesley pulled out a chair and sat down. They had not noticed him approaching but it was clear that he had overheard Billy's remark. "Let's get off that subject," he said brusquely. "We don't need to create problems."

And happy birthday, Billy, Emily thought sarcastically. She studied the prosecutor's face. Something is bothering Ted, she thought. I wonder if he saw *Courtside* last night. I bet he did. And he can't be happy when nearly half the viewers think that his office is prosecuting an innocent man. That's not exactly the best image for the incoming United States Attorney General, the chief law enforcement officer in the whole country.

She was aware that Ted's greeting had been directed to the whole table and that she had not received her usual warm recognition. Of course, that should have been what I expected, she reminded herself. I know Ted is a fair-weather friend, not just to me, but to pretty much everybody. If Aldrich is convicted, I predict plenty of fair weather—nothing but balmy breezes and plenty of sunshine.

Trish tried to reinstate the festive mood that Donna's revelation had obliterated. "So, Billy, what do you really want for your birthday?" she asked cheerfully.

"What do I want? Let me see." Tryon was also obviously trying to shift the conversation away from any reference to Easton. "To keep doing whatever it takes to get the bad guys. To win the lottery so I can have a fancy pad in a Park Avenue building. And to visit my cousin the new attorney general in Washington." He looked at Ted and smiled. "I want to see how it feels to put my feet up on your desk."

Ted Wesley was clearly in no mood for humor. "As I told you earlier, I could only stop by for a few minutes. Enjoy the rest of the evening."

He got up abruptly.

He never did get around to wishing his cousin a happy birthday, Emily observed. The waiter was handing out menus. They ordered, and the tension began to dissipate for everyone, except the birthday boy, who, Emily could see, was still rattled by both his girlfriend's stupid comment and his cousin's chilliness. Fortunately for Donna, she was oblivious and having a good time.

The food was delicious. As the evening went on, Billy seemed to get over his anger. He joked that Donna, who was drinking only soda, was his designated driver, and helped himself to four generous glasses of wine.

Dessert consisted of Billy's birthday cake, served with coffee. As they finished and got ready to leave, Trish told them the prosecutor had called her this afternoon and told her to put it on his tab.

Billy smiled and said, "That's my cousin, my best buddy since we were little kids."

And you're an embarrassment to him, Emily thought. I just hope you don't end up being an albatross around his neck. She realized how deeply upset she was about what she had learned at this dinner. First, he was obviously at odds with his partner, Jake Rosen, a fine and ethical investigator. Second, he had given Easton a quotable quote for the jurors about not giving the money back to Aldrich.

And finally, a birthday wish had been to keep doing "whatever it takes to get the bad guys."

"Whatever it takes," she thought.

And what does that mean?

46

At 11:15 on Thursday morning Emily received a call from Judge Stevens's secretary that the jury had sent a note to the judge. "Is it a verdict?" Emily asked, anxiously.

"No, it's not a verdict," the secretary replied. "Judge Stevens wants to see you and the Moores in his chambers in five minutes."

"Okay, I'll be right up."

Emily made a quick call to Ted Wesley's office to let him know that something was happening.

Ted got on the phone. "Verdict?"

"No," Emily said. "It could be a request for readback or it could be a hung jury. If they're saying they're hung, I'm sure that Moore will move for a mistrial."

Before she could finish what she was going to say, Wesley said angrily, "You *object* to that. They've only been out a couple of days, after weeks of trial."

Emily tried not to sound irritated. "That's exactly what I plan to do. Of course, I will argue that they should be instructed to continue to deliberate. Anyhow, I don't think Judge Stevens would do it this soon."

"All right. Good. It's much too early to let them throw in the towel. I'll see you up there."

A few minutes later, Emily and the Moores were in Judge Stevens's chambers. The judge had the note in his hand and read it to them: "Your Honor, we would like to hear the testimony of Jimmy Easton and Gregg Aldrich again. Thank you." The note was signed by juror number one.

"I've notified the court reporter and she'll be ready to go in about fifteen minutes," Judge Stevens told them. "Both witnesses gave lengthy testimony, and I anticipate that the readback will take the rest of the day."

Emily and both of the Moores agreed. They thanked the judge and went out to the courtroom. Ted Wesley was standing by the prosecutor's table. "We're going to have readback of both Easton and Aldrich's testimony," Emily informed him. "It will take the rest of the day."

He looked relieved. "Well, that's a lot better than a hung jury. If it's going to take all day, and the judge then sends them home, you're obviously not going to get a verdict today. All right. I'm out of here," he said briskly.

With the jury seated in the box and intensely attentive, Easton's testimony came first. Emily cringed as the court reporter read back his flippant answers about the nonrefundable deposit. This is supposed to be Easton's testimony, but I wonder how much of it is really from Billy Tryon, she asked herself.

The court reporter finished Easton's readback at 1:15. Judge Stevens indicated that there would be a forty-five-minute lunch recess and that they would resume at two o'clock for the readback of Gregg Aldrich's testimony.

Rather than having to walk through the cafeteria and encounter Gregg and Katie Aldrich and Alice Mills again, Emily asked a young intern in the office to get her some soup. In her office, with the door closed, she took comfort in the fact that the readback had been delivered in a low-key and professional tone by the court reporter.

This had been in marked contrast to Easton's flippant and smirking demeanor when *he* had testified. Hopefully, any jurors who had been, understandably, disgusted by him would realize that there was a lot of substance to what he had said and a lot of corroboration . . . She touched the wood of her desk.

At ten minutes of two, she stepped back into the elevator to go up to the courtroom. She knew it would not be easy to sit through Gregg Aldrich's tortured testimony. She also reflected that while she had hopefully benefited from the crisp readback of Easton's testimony, so might Aldrich benefit from an equally crisp readback of *his* testimony, which would not reflect the quivering hesitancy that had been in his voice and his demeanor.

With everyone again in place, the readback began promptly at two o'clock. With total focus and intensity, the jurors seemed to absorb every word. Occasionally some of them would look over at Gregg Aldrich, then at Alice Mills, who in the last several days had sat next to Katie, frequently putting her arm around her.

She's letting the jury know that she's changed her mind, Emily recognized. And the jurors have probably seen her these past few days, when they are leaving to go home, standing with Gregg and the Moores out in the hall. I wonder how that's going to affect the jurors who still haven't made up their minds?

We'll probably get a verdict or a hung jury by sometime tomorrow, Emily thought. She knew from past experience that a jury that has already been out for a few days, and has just heard a lengthy readback of the most important witnesses, will usually either reach a verdict or decide that they cannot agree pretty quickly.

The court reporter finished at 4:05. "All right, ladies and gentlemen, we will recess until tomorrow morning at nine o'clock," Judge Stevens told the jury. As Emily turned to leave, she saw that Alice Mills was staring at her.

She had the distinct feeling that Alice had been studying her for a long time.

As Emily stood there, Natalie's mother reached over the railing and tenderly put her hands on Gregg's shoulders, a gesture that seemed oddly familiar to Emily.

Blinking back the tears that began to sting her eyes, Emily hurried from the courtroom, trying to escape the overwhelming and inexplicable nostalgia she suddenly felt when she looked at those three devastated figures, Alice, Gregg, and Katie.

47

W̲hat's your best guess?" Gregg Aldrich asked Richard Moore at ten minutes of nine on Friday morning, as they returned to their all-too-familiar places at the defense table.

"Sometime today," Moore answered.

Cole Moore nodded in agreement.

Promptly at nine o'clock, Judge Stevens took the bench. He called for the jurors to be brought into the box and directed that a roll call be taken. He then ordered the jurors to resume their deliberations.

As they filed back into the jury room, Gregg commented, "Richard, last night the poll on Mike's *Courtside* Web site had forty-seven percent of the viewers in my corner. By any chance were you watching it?"

"No, I wasn't, Gregg."

"I doubt that you'll ever find yourself in my predicament, but if you do, and if Mike covers it on his show, I suggest that you tune in. You'll find out that it's like being two people at once. You're the guy who's being thrown to the lions, yet at the same time you're a spectator in the arena who's betting on whether or not the guy in the pit can outrun them. Actually, it's a very interesting place to be."

I'm not making much sense, Gregg thought. I guess I'm worn out. It's crazy that I slept so well last night, but then woke up this morning with this terrible feeling that I'm going to get convicted. I thought all along that I wanted to get this over with, but now I'm begging God for at least a hung jury. If I'm found guilty, the appeal process could take years, and I can tell that Richard thinks I wouldn't have much chance on appeal.

A convicted murderer.

They assign you a number, don't they?

I want my life back. I want to get up in the morning and go to work. I want to drive up to Katie's school and watch her play soccer. I want to get out on the golf course. I hardly played all summer and when I did, I couldn't concentrate.

The judge was leaving the bench. Gregg looked over at the prosecutor's table. Emily Wallace was still seated. Today she was wearing a dark green jacket over a black turtleneck sweater, with a black skirt. Her legs were crossed under the table and he could see that as usual she was wearing high heels. The clicking of those heels when she had first entered the courtroom this morning reminded him of the sound of Natalie's heels, which he used to hear when the apartment was quiet and she came home around eleven o'clock after a performance . . .

Unless I was going to meet her at the theatre, I always waited up for her, Gregg thought. Her steps on the hardwood floor in the foyer would wake me up if I was dozing.

And then I'd get both of us a drink and fix a snack for

her if she was hungry. I enjoyed doing it, even though she'd be worrying that she was keeping me up and it wasn't fair.

Natalie, why did you stress so much over things that were never a problem? Why were you so damn insecure that you just couldn't accept the fact that I loved you and loved doing things for you?

As Gregg glanced again at the prosecutor's table, he saw one of the detectives who had interviewed him right after Natalie died, and again seven months ago right after Easton was arrested, walk over to Emily Wallace.

Tryon, Gregg thought. What's his first name again? Oh, yes, it's Billy. It was obvious watching him testify at the trial that he thinks he's James Bond. As Gregg watched, Tryon put his hand on Emily Wallace's shoulder in a familiar manner that she clearly did not appreciate as she looked up and frowned.

He's probably wishing her luck, Gregg thought. Let's face it. If I'm convicted, it's a victory for both of them. Another notch in their belts. I'm sure they'll all go out and celebrate together.

It's going to be today, he thought.

I know it's going to be today.

Richard and Cole Moore picked up their briefcases. Now we're off to our home away from home, Gregg thought.

The cafeteria.

*   *   *

At eleven thirty, as they were sitting at a table near the busy coffee section, Richard Moore's cell phone began to ring. Gregg and Katie had been playing Hearts. Alice Mills had been attempting to read a magazine. Cole and Richard had been reviewing other cases.

Richard answered the phone, listened, and looked around the table. "We have a verdict," he said. "Let's go."

Emily got the call as she was attempting to concentrate once again on a different file. She pushed it aside and called Ted Wesley, then, her footsteps clicking on the marble floor, she rushed out to the hall and decided to take the stairs rather than wait for the elevator.

When she reached the third floor, she could see that word was already spreading that the verdict was in. People were scrambling to get a seat in the courtroom before they were all gone. She arrived at the door at the exact moment Gregg Aldrich came from the other direction. They almost collided, then both stepped back. For an instant they stared at each other, then Aldrich motioned her to precede him.

Ted Wesley surprised Emily by sitting down next to her at the prosecutor's table. Now that he knows we've got a verdict, not a hung jury, he's pretty certain that we've got a conviction, she thought. So now *he's* front and center. She noticed that Ted had taken the time to change his tie and jacket. All spruced up for the cameras, she thought, with a trace of resentment.

Judge Stevens came out and formally announced what everybody already knew. "Counsel, fifteen minutes ago I received a note from the jury indicating they have reached a verdict." He turned to the sheriff's officer and said, "Bring in the jury."

As the jurors filed back in, everyone in the courtroom looked at them, seeking some hint of what their decision was.

Judge Stevens addressed juror number one, Stuart Harvey. "Mr. Harvey, would you please rise? Has the jury reached verdicts in this case?"

"Yes, we have, Your Honor."

"And are the verdicts unanimous?"

"Yes, they are, Your Honor."

The courtroom was absolutely silent.

Judge Stevens looked at Gregg. "The defendant will rise."

His face impassive, Gregg Aldrich and the Moores stood up.

Judge Stevens asked, "On count one, which charged burglary, is your verdict guilty or not guilty?"

"Guilty, Your Honor."

There was a collective gasp in the courtroom. If he's guilty of going into her home, then we've got him on everything, Emily thought. This is all or nothing.

"On count two, murder, is your verdict guilty or not guilty?"

"Guilty, Your Honor."

"No . . . no . . ." Katie Aldrich jumped up from her seat next to Alice Mills and before anyone could stop her, ran around the railing and threw her arms around her father.

Judge Stevens looked at her, motioned gently for her

to return to her seat, waited as she obeyed, then turned back to the foreman. "On count three, possession of a firearm for an unlawful purpose, is your verdict guilty or not guilty?"

"Guilty, Your Honor."

As Emily watched, Gregg Aldrich turned and tried to comfort his sobbing daughter. Over the buzz in the courtroom she could hear him say, "Katie, it's all right. It's only the first round. I promise you that."

Judge Stevens, in a firm but sympathetic tone, looked at Katie and said, "Ms. Aldrich, I must ask that you compose yourself as we finish these proceedings."

Katie cupped her hands over her mouth and buried her face in Alice's shoulder.

"Mr. Moore, do you wish to have the jury polled?" Judge Stevens asked.

"Yes, Your Honor."

"Ladies and gentlemen, your foreman has announced that you have found the defendant guilty on all counts," the judge said. "As your name is called, please indicate how you voted, guilty or not guilty."

"Guilty."

"Guilty."

"Guilty." . . . "Guilty." . . . "Guilty." . . .

Two of the women jurors had tears running down their cheeks as they responded.

Gregg Aldrich, his face deathly pale, shook his head in denial as the final juror echoed the word that had condemned him.

His tone now brisk, Judge Stevens formally confirmed that the verdict was unanimous. He ordered that the sheriff's officer go into the jury room with the foreman, bring out the evidence, and return it to the attorneys.

When they emerged a minute later from the jury room, Emily quickly reviewed the state's exhibits and Richard Moore the defense exhibits. Both indicated that they had everything back.

For the last time, the judge addressed the jury. "Ladies and gentlemen, with the return of your verdicts, your service in this case is complete. On behalf of the judiciary and everyone connected with this case, I want to thank you very much. You have been most attentive. I instruct you that under our rules of court, no one connected with this case may engage in any conversation with you about your deliberations in this case or your role in the outcome. I also caution you about speaking to other people about your deliberations. Do not say anything that you would not be willing to repeat in the presence of the other jurors. Again, thank you. You are dismissed."

As the jurors stood up to leave, Alice Mills sprang to her feet and shouted, "I don't thank you. You have it wrong, all of you. My daughter was shot and left on the floor to die, but her murderer is not in this courtroom. Gregg, my son-in-law, is innocent. He didn't do it."

Enraged, Alice pointed her finger at Emily. "Your witness is a liar and you know it. I saw that in your face yesterday. And don't you deny it. You know that this is a travesty and in your heart you're ashamed to be part of it. Emily, for God's sake!"

The judge banged the gavel. "Mrs. Mills, I fully understand how sad and upset you are, and I am very sorry for you. But I must insist that you remain quiet as the jurors leave the courtroom."

Clearly shaken by what they had witnessed, the jurors departed.

There was one more motion left to make. Emily stood up. "Your Honor, Mr. Aldrich has been convicted of three offenses, burglary, possession of a firearm, and murder. He is now facing life in prison and the state submits that he is a serious risk of flight. He certainly has the financial means to flee. The state moves to revoke his bail."

Richard Moore, his own complexion gray, responded. Knowing that his argument would be futile, he pleaded that Gregg Aldrich be allowed to go home until sentencing so that he could put his affairs in order and make arrangements for his motherless child.

"I must agree with the prosecutor that there is considerable risk of flight," Judge Stevens said. "Mr. Aldrich had to know that this verdict was possible and he should have made any necessary arrangements before today. The sentence will be imposed on December fifth at nine A.M. Bail is revoked. Mr. Aldrich will be taken into custody."

His face deadly pale, Gregg Aldrich quietly obeyed the officer's instructions to place his hands behind his back. He did not change his expression as the handcuffs were placed around his wrists and snapped shut.

As he was led from the courtroom into the holding cell, the two impressions that were burned into his mind were the intensely troubled face of Emily Wallace, and the openly satisfied smile of Prosecutor Ted Wesley.

48

Emily did not join the victory celebration Friday night at Solari's. Pleading exhaustion, she told Ted Wesley that before he left for Washington, she wanted to take him and Nancy out to dinner. Though her fatigue was certainly real, she could not bear the thought of celebrating a verdict that had devastated not only Gregg Aldrich, but also his young daughter and Natalie's mother.

"You know that this is a travesty and in your heart you're ashamed to be part of it." The agonized accusation Alice Mills had screamed in court repeated itself over and over in Emily's mind. Her sympathy for Alice was mixed with anger. I've given seven months of my life to this case, she thought as she left the courthouse. Mercifully, all of the media had left and no one approached her on her way to the car.

I wanted justice for an extraordinarily gifted human being who gave so much pleasure to so many people and who walked into her own home and was shot by an intruder, she thought.

"I know in my heart. . . ."

What does Alice Mills know about my heart? For that matter, what do *I* know about my heart? It isn't even my own. My own heart was put in a dish on a surgical table, then discarded.

The tears she had fought since Alice Mills's attack began to fall as she got into her car. She remembered what one of the reporters had said during the media barrage after the verdict. "You're going to be famous, Emily. Everybody is going to write about you. I didn't know until this morning that you'd had a heart transplant. A couple of people were talking about it. And another thing. I didn't know that your husband died in Iraq. I'm really sorry."

All of this is going to be splattered all over the media, Emily thought. Oh, God, I wouldn't even care that much about the heart transplant stuff, but I'd give anything to be going home to Mark right now. I could handle *anything* if he was with me . . .

When she arrived home and opened the front door, the frenzied barking she could hear from the back porch was a welcome greeting that instantly lifted her spirits. As she hurried to Bess, she thought with gratitude of the unconditional love that her little dog always gave to her.

49

On Friday evening, nine hours after the verdict had been delivered, *Courtside* went on the air. Michael Gordon began with the dramatic clips of the guilty verdict and the outbursts of Katie Aldrich and Alice Mills. "We have a terrific show for you tonight," he exclaimed. "Not only will you hear from our distinguished panelists, you will also hear from members of the deliberating jury, the alternates who didn't get to participate, and the witness who was with Natalie Raines when she died."

The panelists—retired judge Bernard Reilly, former prosecutor Peter Knowles, and criminal psychologist Georgette Cassotta—all expressed surprise that the jury had been able to reach a unanimous verdict. Cassotta acknowledged that she had not thought that unanimity was possible, given all of the problems with Jimmy Easton.

Dorothy Winters, the disappointed alternate, did not wait for an invitation to speak. "I am furious," she said. "This would never have happened if I had been in there. There's nothing that anybody could have said that would have changed my mind. I think the judge let the prosecutor badger Mr. Aldrich when that poor man was trying to explain why he went to Cape Cod. If you ask me, he was too good to Natalie. I didn't think she treated him very well. It was always all about her career, but he was still devoted to her and always trying to take care of her."

Juror number three, Norman Klinger, a civil engineer in his midforties, shook his head. "We examined this case from every angle," he said flatly. "Whether or not Mr. Aldrich was too good to Natalie is not the bottom line. Jimmy Easton is what he is, but everything he said was corroborated."

Suzie Walsh had been thrilled to receive the phone call asking her to be on the program. She had rushed out to get her hair done and even paid to have her makeup put on at the beauty parlor. She had learned only when she arrived that there was a hair and makeup person in the studio. I could have saved the money, she thought, wistfully, especially since the lady here rebrushed my hair and toned down the makeup.

Michael Gordon then asked her a question. "Ms. Walsh, you were the last person to see Natalie Raines alive. What are your thoughts about this verdict?"

"At first I thought he was definitely guilty," she said earnestly. "But then I realized that something has been bothering me all along. You see, she was still alive when I found her. She didn't open her eyes but she was moaning. I think she understood that I was calling to get help for her. If she knew who had shot her, and by that I mean her husband, why didn't she whisper that to me? In my opinion she knew she was dying. Wouldn't she want the person who did this to her to get caught?"

"Exactly," Dorothy Winters chimed in.

"Ms. Walsh, you must understand that all of this was thoroughly discussed in the jury room," Klinger told her. "You say yourself that Natalie Raines was dying. You said she never opened her eyes. The fact that she was moaning does not mean that she had any ability to communicate with you."

"She was aware of me. I'm sure of it," Suzie insisted. "And anyhow, I didn't think people could moan when they were unconscious."

"I am not saying she was necessarily completely unconscious. But she was gravely injured, and again, we did not think that she had any ability to communicate."

"They were separated for over a year. Maybe there was another boyfriend in the picture nobody knew about," Dorothy Winters said stubbornly. "Don't forget she had hinted to Gregg Aldrich there was someone else. That's why he went to Cape Cod to check it out. Or maybe it was some crazy fun? She may have had an unlisted telephone number, but anybody could have gotten her address and a map to her house off the Internet. Just look it up. It's the easiest thing in the world to do."

"The defense attorney didn't talk much at all about the possibility of another boyfriend," Donald Stern, the other alternate juror, pointed out. "If there was such a guy, even if he wasn't at Cape Cod, it still doesn't mean that he didn't know his way around the house in New Jersey. Frankly, I was still leaning to a guilty vote, but if I'd been in the deliberations with Mrs. Winters, I might have been persuaded to change my mind. And listening here, I'm very sure she wouldn't have changed hers."

Hearing this exchange, Michael Gordon wondered aloud at the monumental twist of fate that had occurred when the court clerk pulled out Dorothy Winters's card, making her an alternate. "Gregg Aldrich is in a jail cell tonight," he said, "facing a life sentence. If Dorothy Winters had been in that jury room, he would have had a hung jury and he'd be having dinner at home with his daughter tonight."

"Life is full of twists and turns that end up having enormous consequences," Judge Reilly agreed. "The cards that a court clerk randomly pulls out, keeping two jurors like Mrs. Winters and Mr. Stern out of the deliberations, have undoubtedly changed the outcome of some criminal trials, as we're seeing here."

When the program ended and Mike was back in his office, he found a note propped up on his phone. It read: "Mike, some woman phoned. Wouldn't give her name. Had no caller I.D. Wants to know if there's a reward for information about who Jimmy Easton was working for when he was in the Aldrich apartment. Would you find out and mention it on your show next week?"

50

With an ever increasing sense of urgency, Zach spent most of Saturday searching for a car. He had no intention of going to a dealership where there would be a trail of documents for the Motor Vehicle Department. Instead he responded to the classified ads listing used cars and the owners' telephone numbers.

He had seen the television news last night and the newspaper this morning, all filled with pictures and stories about the Aldrich verdict. He worried that there was so much publicity about Emily. He knew what could happen. Some reporter could do a follow-up story on her standing in front of her house and catch me on camera when I'm outside and didn't notice them coming. I could end up in the national news. Somebody, somewhere, could recognize me.

I have to be ready to leave.

The last ad he had responded to turned out to be exactly what he wanted. The dark brown van was eight years old but in pretty decent shape. It was the kind of vehicle that wouldn't attract attention. No one would even look at it twice. Just like me, he thought bitterly.

The owner, Henry Link, lived in Rochelle Park, a nearby town. He was an elderly man who liked to chat.

"This was my wife, Edith's, car," he explained. "She's been in a nursing home for six months. I always hoped she would be able to come home, but that's never going to happen. We had a lot of good times in it."

He was smoking a pipe. The air in the small kitchen was heavy with the odor of stale smoke. "Not that we went very far," he emphasized. "That's why the mileage is so low. We just drove up the Hudson a little way in good weather, then found a place to have a picnic lunch. She made the best fried chicken and potato salad in the world! And . . ."

Zach had been sitting across from him at the kitchen table for fifteen minutes, listening to the seemingly endless details of Henry's life with Edith. Unable to waste any more time, he stood up abruptly. "Mr. Link, your ad said four thousand dollars for the van, as is. I'll give you three thousand in cash right now. I'll take care of turning in the license plates and registering the other paperwork. You won't have to be bothered with any of it."

"All right," Henry said, sensing that, as usual, he had lost his audience. "That's fair, seeing that you have the cash. Thanks for doing the paperwork. I hate standing in those long lines at the Motor Vehicle place. When do you want to pick it up? I mean, you can't drive two cars at once. You gonna come back with a friend?"

I don't have any, Zach thought, and if I did, they wouldn't know about this. "Leave it in the driveway and give me the keys. I'll get a ride back later tonight and pick it up. I won't even have to ring the doorbell."

"That'll work fine," Henry Link answered, heartily.

"That will give me time to take Edith's things out of the car. You know, like her St. Christopher medal that's hanging from the visor. Unless you'd like to have it yourself. It kept her safe."

But then, frowning, he hesitated. "No, I'm sorry. You know what, she'd kill me if I gave it away."

51

Emily watched *Courtside* in her nightshirt, propped up in bed. As she listened to the comments of everyone, her emotions ranged between concern and dismay—concern that there was this much doubt about the verdict, and dismay that she found herself wishing that Dorothy Winters had been in the jury room.

If she had been, I'd be preparing this case for trial all over again. Is that what I really wanted to happen? she asked herself.

She turned off the light as soon as the show ended, but sleep was a long time coming. A heavy feeling of deep sadness had settled like a blanket upon her. She thought about the dozens of psychiatric reports she had read as a prosecutor, in which a doctor would write about a defendant's depression. Many of the symptoms that they discussed were the ones she had been feeling today. Weariness, tears, and pervasive sadness.

And resentment, she added. I've tried so hard to be sensitive to what Natalie's mother had been going through. How could she have turned on me like that today?

At midnight, she opened the drawer of the night table and reached for the mild sedative that she occasionally took when sleep eluded her. Within twenty minutes she had drifted off, but not before she envisioned Gregg Aldrich in a tiny cell, probably shared with another inmate who had also been convicted of a serious crime.

At seven A.M. she woke long enough to let Bess out for a few minutes, then brought her back upstairs and fell asleep again. The ringing of the phone at ten A.M. woke her. It was Investigator Jake Rosen.

"Emily, we missed you last night, but I can sure understand how you just wanted to get home. I was sorry the victim's mother lambasted you the way she did. Don't let it get you down. You did a great job."

"Thanks, Jake. How was it last night?"

"In a way you were better off not being there. I know that Billy isn't your favorite person."

Now fully awake, Emily interrupted, "That's putting it mildly."

Jake chuckled. "I know. Anyhow, he was at his loud-mouth best last night, and finally Ted Wesley told him to quit drinking and shut up."

Instantly reacting, Emily asked, "What was Billy talking about?"

"He was bragging at what a great coaching job he did with Jimmy Easton. He said that he basically handed the case to you on a silver platter. Emily, I wouldn't normally talk like this but that guy's ego is really out of control."

Emily sat up and slid her feet over the side of the bed. "He was talking the same way at his birthday dinner the other night. Jake, did you ever hear him feed Easton any information, or do you know if he did?"

"When Easton was arrested, I got to the police station just a couple of minutes after Billy," Jake replied. "Billy was talking to the local police and as far as I know he hadn't seen Easton yet. I was with him when he spoke to him a little while later. I didn't see him do anything wrong. As far as I know, I've been there whenever Billy has spoken to Easton since then."

"Jake, we both know that over the years Billy has been accused of putting words into other people's mouths when it helped his case. Are you positive that he's never been alone with Easton?"

"I think so. And Emily, don't forget, Billy is a blowhard and a bragger, but he also has been investigating homicides for a long time. He's got great instincts and he knows where to look."

"All right, Jake, let's leave it at that. Maybe I'm getting paranoid. Or maybe I've been watching too much *Courtside*."

Jake laughed. "Right. Switch to *Fugitive Hunt*. It's on tonight. It's pretty good. They should call it *Wacko Hunt*. I can't believe all the creeps that are on the loose. Good talking to you, Em."

"You, too, Jake."

After she hung up, Emily went straight into the shower. As she dried her hair, she planned out her day. I'll see if I can get an appointment for a trim and a manicure, she thought. I've been so busy that my hair is practically in my eyes. Then I want to get over to

Nordstrom's to get some stockings and makeup. I'll take a look at their suits. I could use a couple of new ones.

Before she made coffee, she walked out to the driveway to pick up the morning paper. Knowing what awaited her, she took it back into the kitchen and spread it open. A picture of Gregg Aldrich showing him slumped in his chair after the verdict had been delivered covered the top half of the front page. She cringed as she looked at the lower picture which showed a distraught Alice Mills pointing a finger at her.

She skimmed the article then threw the paper down. As she had expected, it had dramatically exploited the irony of Alice Mills's reference to her heart with the reality of Emily's medical history.

Disgusted, she vowed to put it out of her mind, and while she had coffee and toast, she made an appointment at the salon. There had been a noon cancellation and they were able to fit her in. "Something's going right, Bess," she said. "At least I can get a haircut. It's so long, I'm starting to look like you."

Four hours later, Emily pulled into the Garden State Plaza parking lot and headed into Nordstrom's. My luck's holding out, she thought forty-five minutes later as she handed her credit card to the saleslady.

"They're you!" the saleslady beamed cheerfully as she neatly folded the three new suits and placed them in a large shopping bag.

"Thanks very much for your help," Emily answered pleasantly. "I'm going to enjoy them."

She had already picked up stockings. Her final stop

would be the makeup counter. While she was heading toward that area of the main floor, Emily felt a tap on her shoulder and turned around.

"Emily, it's so good to see you. We met at the Wesleys last week. Marion Rhodes."

It was the psychologist who had been at the dinner party. Emily thought of her mother, who had always told her never to assume that people she had only met casually would be able to remember either her name or where they had met. Marion's mother must have told her the same thing.

Today Marion was dressed casually in a cardigan and slacks, but she still had that same indefinable air of elegance that Emily had admired. Her smile was as warm as the tone in her voice. Emily was genuinely pleased to run into her.

"You've had quite a week, Emily. I've been reading about your case in the papers. Ted told me how proud he is of the job you did. Congratulations on getting a guilty verdict. You must be very pleased."

Emily realized that her eyes were suddenly moist. "By any chance did you see this morning's paper with the picture of Natalie Raines's mother pointing at me and basically accusing me of knowing in my heart that Gregg Aldrich is innocent?"

She knew that Marion, as a close friend of the Wesleys, had to have been told by them about her heart transplant.

"I know, Emily. I read the paper. It can't be easy when something like that happens."

Afraid to answer for fear her voice would break, Emily nodded. She was aware that Marion was studying her intensely.

Marion opened her bag, reached into it, and took out her card. "Emily, I wish you would call me. Maybe if we talked a few times, I could be of some help to you."

As Emily willingly accepted the card, she managed a half smile. "I remember Ted saying at dinner that you had helped him and Nancy through a rough patch, as he called it, a long time ago.

"I'm not embarrassed to admit that I feel kind of over-whelmed now. I'll call you next week."

52

Years of evading capture had taught Zach to be cautious. He returned home from Henry Link's smoky kitchen, had an early dinner, and was now thinking about how he would get back there to pick up the car. He would not call for a cab at his house because there would be a record of it.

Instead, he walked a mile to Fair Lawn and got on a bus to the Garden State Plaza in Paramus. From there he walked the half mile to Link's home in Rochelle Park. He hoped that Henry Link wouldn't see him and then come out and start talking his ear off again.

But there was no sign of Henry as he unlocked the door and started the van. At Route 17 he turned south and headed for the Turnpike, which would take him to Newark Airport, where he would leave the van in the long-term parking lot. His plan was to take a cab back to Fair Lawn and walk the rest of the way home.

It was 8:45 P.M. when he got back to his neighborhood. He looked over at Madeline Kirk's home. He could tell that the nosy old lady's house had the same layout as his, which meant that the light that was on was coming from her den next to the kitchen. She's probably watching television, he thought, maybe waiting for *Fugitive Hunt* to come on at nine o'clock.

I wonder if they'll do an update to last week's segment about me? I wonder if they'll talk about tips that have come in?

Zach's feet were turning up his own driveway. But then he stopped. If Kirk *did* watch the show last week, she couldn't have called in a tip yet because the cops would have been all over me. But if she did watch and she wasn't sure about whether to call, seeing an update tonight might push her to do it. You never know . . .

He had to be sure. But first he had to get gloves from his house so that there would be no fingerprints. He hurried inside, took tight-fitting leather gloves from his hall closet, and put them on.

It was fairly dark on the street, making it easier to slink along the overgrown hedges that separated Kirk's property from her neighbor without being seen. He crouched as he reached the side window that looked into the den, then cautiously raised his head above the level of the sill.

Wearing a bathrobe and nightgown, the slight figure of Madeline Kirk was settled in a threadbare armchair with an afghan over her lap. He saw a phone, a pencil, and a small writing pad on the wooden end table next to her.

He had a good view of the television and the volume was so high that he could catch most of what was being said. It was a couple of minutes before nine and he heard the promo telling viewers to stay tuned for *Fugitive Hunt.*

He was certain that his instincts were correct. He couldn't wait any longer to see if she would write down the tip telephone number. If he stayed outside and she did begin to dial the number, he might not be able to stop her in time.

There could be an unlocked window or door somewhere, he thought. As he slithered around the outside of the house, he saw no evidence of wiring on the windows that would indicate an alarm. On the other side of the house, he found what he was looking for, a ground-floor window that was slightly raised. When he looked inside, he could see that it led into a small bathroom. A lucky break, he thought. And the door is closed so she won't be able to see me climbing in. Or hear me. With the television on so loud, she's probably almost deaf.

He used his pocketknife to cut away the netting of the screen. The old window's peeling frame shed paint particles that fell to the ground as he placed his gloved fingers in the small opening at the bottom and pushed upward. When he had it raised as far as it would go, he leaned his body forward, stood on his toes, grasped the sill with his hands, and hoisted himself through the opening.

With noiseless steps he made his way down the short hall to the den. Madeline Kirk's chair was positioned so that he was behind her.

Fugitive Hunt was in progress and the host, Bob

Warner, was presenting an update on Zach. "We've received dozens of tips since last week's segment, and so far none of them has panned out. But we're still on his trail."

The computer-enhanced pictures of him, including the one that looked frighteningly similar to him now, were flashed across the screen. "Take a close look at them again," Bob Warner urged. "And remember, this guy likes to plant yellow mums around his home. And here again is our tip number."

As the telephone number appeared on the screen, Zach heard Madeline Kirk say aloud, "I was right. I was right."

As she reached to grab the pencil and pad, Zach tapped her on the shoulder. "You know what, old girl? You *were* right. Too bad for you."

As Madeline Kirk let out a horrified gasp, Zach's gloved hands closed around her throat.

53

Michael Gordon had intended to go to Vermont for the weekend and try to concentrate on his book, but he decided to stay in Manhattan for Katie's sake. Besides that, he knew it would be impossible to concentrate on famous crimes of the twentieth century when only one crime, Natalie's murder, was absorbing all of his attention.

The phone call to his office.

The question about a reward.

Was all that on the level? *Was* there someone out there who might be able to provide proof that Jimmy Easton had been in Gregg's apartment while he was working at some kind of job?

He knew it could be a crank call. But on the other hand, Gregg and the Moores had always believed that if Easton was ever in the apartment, he would have been making some kind of service call or delivery.

What about the reward? Mike asked himself as he went through the motions of exercising at the gym in the Athletic Club on Central Park South. The minute I mention the word "reward" on air, we'll get hundreds of phony tips. And if it is a crank call, talking about it would raise false hope for Gregg and Katie and Alice . . .

He jogged on the treadmill, thinking. He'd been

astonished to read in the morning papers that Emily Wallace had had a heart transplant. His people had done a pretty thorough bio of her, with the thought that she might be a *Courtside* guest, and that fact had not come out. Of course they'd learned that her husband, an army captain, had been the victim of a roadside bomb in Iraq three years ago.

He knew that after the verdict Richard Moore drove to New York to talk further with Katie and Alice. He could have written the script of what he would say. Promising that there would be an appeal. Pointing out that almost half the people who responded to the *Courtside* voting poll voted *for* Gregg, not against him. The problem was that, as of now, Moore really didn't have any strong arguments for an appeal—the judge hadn't made any controversial rulings.

But if that call about the reward was on the level, if someone had evidence that Jimmy Easton had been in the apartment at any time before Natalie's death, Richard would certainly file a motion for a new trial . . .

How much of a reward should I offer? Five thousand? Ten thousand? Twenty-five thousand? These thoughts kept churning in his mind as he headed for the locker room.

After Mike left the gym, he had lunch in the club grill. He sat at a table by the window and looked out at Central Park. The leaves were at their peak, scarlet and golden and orange. The horse-drawn carriages were doing a brisk business, he observed. It was the kind of autumn day, sunny but with a cool breeze, that drew people to the park to walk or skate or jog.

If there's no new trial or successful appeal, Gregg will never again walk down this block and meet me at this club, Mike thought. As it is, he'll undoubtedly be expelled from it at the next board meeting. The least of his problems, of course.

As he ordered a hamburger and a glass of wine, the enormity of what had happened to his friend began to seep into his being. I knew the verdict could be guilty, but when I saw the handcuffs go on Gregg, it hit me like a ton of bricks, he mused. Now, watching these people enjoying Central Park, I'm beginning to have some concept of what it must be like to experience the total loss of freedom.

I'm going to put up the reward myself, he decided. I'll post it on the Web site. It will be big enough so that if the person who called feels badly about whoever employed Easton off the books getting in trouble, the money will overcome their qualms.

Twenty-five thousand dollars. *That* will get everybody's attention. With a gut feeling of having made a good decision, Mike started to eat the hamburger that the waiter had placed in front of him.

On Saturday evening, just before Mike went out to have dinner with friends, he called Gregg's apartment. Alice Mills answered. "After we got back here yesterday, Katie was so upset that Richard Moore called a doctor he knows who lives in the next building. He sent over a sedative for her. She slept until noon today, woke up, and started crying. But later on some of her girlfriends came over and that helped. They all went to a movie."

"I'll take both of you out to lunch tomorrow," Mike said. "Do you know what the visiting hours are at the jail?"

"Richard will let us know when we can see Gregg. Katie is adamant that she must see her father again before she goes back up to school in a couple of days. Getting back into some kind of routine is bound to be good for her."

"How are *you* doing, Alice?"

"Physically, not bad for someone pushing seventy-one. Emotionally, I don't have to tell you. I guess you saw the morning papers?"

"Yes." Mike thought he knew what was coming.

"Mike, I'm not proud of the scene I made in court. I absolutely couldn't help myself. And I certainly would never have referred to Emily Wallace's heart."

"I wasn't aware she had a transplant," Mike told her. "From what I'm hearing now, it wasn't generally known. She had had an aortic valve replaced, and the transplant came so fast after it that even most of her friends didn't realize she'd had a second operation. And apparently she's been very quiet about it."

"I just wish I hadn't mentioned her heart when I blasted her. But, Mike, it doesn't change the fact that I do believe Emily Wallace knows Gregg is innocent."

"You'd never guess that the way she went for his throat on the stand, Alice."

"She was trying to convince herself, not the jury, Mike."

"Alice, honestly, that's taking it pretty far."

"I can understand why it sounds like that. Mike, Richard did talk about filing an appeal. It helped Katie to hear that, but was it just talk?"

Michael Gordon decided that he would not tell her about the phone call from a possible new witness until they met for lunch tomorrow. "Alice, as it stands now, I don't think there are any decent grounds for an appeal. But we're going to establish a reward for any information that could lead to a new trial. I'll tell you all about it tomorrow. Let's leave it at that."

"I agree. Good night, Mike."

Mike snapped off his cell phone. There was something that he couldn't initially discern in Alice Mills's voice. But now he realized what it was: her abiding certainty that Emily Wallace believed that Gregg was innocent.

Shaking his head, he dropped the phone into his pocket, and headed for the door.

At that same moment, alone in the Park Avenue apartment, Alice Mills went into the guest room that was now hers, and where she had sometimes stayed overnight when Gregg and Natalie were married. She opened a drawer and looked at the picture of Emily Wallace that she had cut out of the paper this morning.

Her eyes brimming with fresh tears, with a trembling finger she traced the contour of the heart that had saved Emily's life.

54

The chance meeting with Marion Rhodes on Saturday afternoon had lifted Emily's spirits. For the most part she knew that she was a private person and not given to sharing her problems with others. But she had felt instantly comfortable with Marion, both last week and today, and looked forward to talking to her.

For that reason, when she got home just in time to catch the ringing phone, she was able to sound upbeat.

It was her father calling from Florida. He had e-mailed her yesterday, congratulating her on the verdict and asking her to call him when she got a chance. She had intended to call him last night, but she knew he would detect that she was upset and she didn't want to worry him.

Then this morning, after she had read the paper, she put off calling him again.

"Em, I was so happy for you about the verdict. That's one big feather in your cap. How come you didn't call your old man last night? I figured you must be out celebrating."

"Dad, I'm sorry. I meant to call you last night, but when I got home I didn't have the energy to pick up the phone. I went straight to bed. I would have called you when I was running around today, but I forgot my cell phone. I just walked in the door. How's Joan?"

"Great. But we're both upset about those newspaper articles. We saw them online. We know you have never wanted to talk about the transplant. And the mother of that lady who got killed really wasn't fair to you."

She tried to sound reassuring. "Oh sure, I was a little upset, Dad. But I'm okay about it now and I truly do feel sorry for that poor woman."

"I hope now that this trial is done that you'll relax and maybe even have some fun. And you know you can hop on a plane anytime and come down here. Joan would cook you some decent meals, not that crummy take-out stuff I know you live on."

"I'll definitely get down there for Thanksgiving, Dad, but you wouldn't want to look at my desk right now. It's a disaster. I've got a lot of catching up to do."

"I understand. Em . . ."

I know what's coming, she thought.

"Em, I'm always afraid to ask because I know you miss Mark. But it has been three years. Is there anybody you have any interest in?"

"It's okay to ask, Dad. The answer is no, but I'm not saying it can't happen. Since I was assigned to this trial seven months ago, I've barely even had time to take Bess for a walk."

Emily surprised herself by making an additional comment, but then realized that the sentiment she was expressing was honest. "I know it's been three years, Dad, and I know I have to get on with my own life. I'm beginning to understand that I not only miss Mark, but I very much miss sharing my life. And I want to have that back again."

"That's good to hear, Emily. I really do understand. After your mother died, I never thought I'd ever look at another woman. But after a while it does get very lonely, and when Joan came along, I was sure it was right."

"It was right, Dad. Joan is a doll. And it's a comfort for me that she takes such good care of you."

"That she does, honey. Okay, talk to you in a couple of days."

After Emily hung up, she played back the seven messages that had been left today on her answering machine. One was from her brother, Jack. The others were friends congratulating her on the outcome of the trial. Several were invitations for dinner very soon and one was actually for tonight. A couple of them, in a very caring way, expressed shock that what they had thought had only been valve surgery had ended up in a transplant.

She decided to call Jack and the friend who had invited her for tonight. The rest could wait until tomorrow. She got Jack's voice mail, left a message, then made the second call to Karen Logan, a law school classmate who was married and had two children. "Karen, I really need to veg out tonight," she said. "But let's make a date for next Saturday if you're free."

"Emily, tonight would have been just a plate of pasta at our house. But I really wanted to ask about next Saturday anyway." There was hope and trepidation in her voice. "We'd like to go out to a nice restaurant and bring along someone who very much wants to meet you. He's an orthopedic surgeon, thirty-seven, and, if you can believe it, has never been married. He's brilliant but he's so normal and he's such a nice-looking guy."

Emily knew that Karen was pleasantly surprised by her answer. "Sounds pretty good. I'm up for it."

It was almost six o'clock. Emily took Bess for a ten-minute walk, fed her, and decided to run out to the video store and rent a couple of movies. The last thing I want to watch tonight is *Fugitive Hunt*, she decided. I'd feel as though I were still at the office. And I think I'll get some of that "crummy take-out stuff" that Dad was accusing me of living on, she thought, smiling.

She never did get to watch the second movie. By ten o'clock she couldn't keep her eyes open any longer and went to bed. The movie she did watch had been okay, but not great. She'd kept dozing on and off as it played. She woke up on her own at eight thirty Sunday morning, surprised and grateful that Bess had let her sleep.

It was October 12th and an anniversary of sorts. It was on that day seven years ago that she had met Mark at a tailgate party at Giants Stadium. She had gone there with her date, who had invited some of his fellow alumni from Georgetown to join them. One of them had been Mark.

It was unseasonably cold that day, Emily remembered as she got out of bed and reached for her robe. I wasn't dressed nearly warm enough. My date was so into the game he never noticed that my lips were blue. Mark took off his jacket and told me to put it on. When I tried to refuse, he said, "You must understand, I'm from North Dakota. To me this weather is mild."

It was only later that I found out he spent most of his growing-up years in California. His father, a West Point graduate, had been career army. Like him, Mark was an engineer and when he moved to Manhattan after graduate school had joined the Army Reserve. Mark's parents now lived in Arizona and kept in touch with her regularly.

We were married three years, and he's been gone three years, Emily thought, as she went downstairs for the familiar routine of letting Bess out and turning on the coffeepot. Is that part of the problem, that I've been wanting to have that wonderful feeling of looking forward to the end of the day and being with someone who loves me and whom I love? She answered herself: Yes, it is.

Sunday morning. I haven't gone to church much lately, Emily thought. They had moved to an apartment in Fort Lee after they were married. Mark had volunteered as the leader of song at their church. He had a wonderful voice. That's one of the reasons I've gone so seldom, she acknowledged. When we went together, he was always up there on the altar.

"*I will go unto the altar of God, the God who gave joy to my youth.*"

She was on the verge of tears again.

No way, she thought, resolutely, no crying.

A little more than an hour later, she was at the ten thirty Mass at St. Catharine's. It made it easier that the leader of song was a young woman. The prayers and responses, familiar since she was a child, came back easily to Emily's lips.

It is right to give Him thanks and praise . . .
For Thine is the power and the glory . . .

During Mass she prayed not only for Mark but to him: I'm so glad we had that time together, we were both so blessed.

On the way home, she stopped and did some real shopping at the supermarket. Gladys, her weekly cleaning woman, had left a long list and added an impassioned plea: "Emily, I'm running out of everything."

There's another job I've been putting off that I'm going to do today, Emily decided, as she paid at the checkout counter and then begged some empty boxes from a clerk. I'm going to pack Mark's clothes and give them away. It's wrong to have them go unused when they'd be a godsend to someone else.

Unable to part with anything that had been Mark's when she moved from Fort Lee to the house in Glen Rock, she had put his dresser in the small guest room and hung his suits and coats in the closet there. She thought of all the times that first year when she had buried her face in one of his jackets, trying to find a trace of the scent of his shaving lotion lingering in the fabric.

At home, she changed into jeans and a sweater and

took the boxes to the guest room. As she was folding the jackets and suits she tried not to dwell on the special occasions when Mark had worn them.

When the closet and dresser drawers were emptied, she thought of something else that should not be kept any longer. She went into her own room, opened the bottom drawer, and scooped up the frilly nightgowns that had been her shower presents. She added them to the last box, then, anxious to get away from the sight of the packed clothes, she closed the door of the guest bedroom and went downstairs.

An always-willing Bess jumped up and down when she saw Emily take the leash from the hook on the back porch. Before they went out, Emily took a quick side glance to make sure that Zach was not puttering in his backyard, but there was no sign of him. Even so she crossed the street immediately. A few steps later she was passing the house of Madeline Kirk, the reclusive old lady whom she had only glimpsed at her mailbox or sweeping her walk. She's so alone, Emily mused. I never see any sign of cars in her driveway as if she has company.

And for the two years I've lived here, you could just about say the same for me, she added, ruefully.

"It's clearly time for a change," she told Bess, as they continued down the block. "I don't want to end up like that poor soul."

They walked for almost an hour. Emily felt that her brain was beginning to clear. So what if people know I've had a heart transplant? she asked herself. I'm certainly not ashamed of it. And since it was two and a half years ago, I doubt that anyone will look at me now as if I'm about to keel over.

And as far as Alice Mills telling me that in my heart I know Gregg Aldrich is innocent, I think my problem is that he comes through as a very nice guy and I'm sorry for his daughter. I'll take one more look at his file and put it away. He has absolutely no grounds for an appeal.

That evening as she watched the second movie she had rented and ate lamb chops and a salad on a tray in the living room, she found herself trying to remember what it was that had bothered her when she was packing up the nightgowns she intended to give away.

55

From his front window, Zach had watched Emily cross the street with Bess on Sunday afternoon. He correctly surmised that she had not walked past his house because she didn't want to run into him. Just wait, he warned her silently, just wait.

The satisfaction he had felt when he squeezed the life out of Madeline Kirk had been replaced by the certain knowledge that he was running out of time. She had recognized him. Maybe it had been because she paid attention to the fact that he'd planted mums around his other houses. But even without knowing about the flowers, someone from work or around here might have zeroed in on that computer image that looked like him.

Something else, in the next day or two someone would notice that Kirk's newspaper was still on the porch or that her mail hadn't been taken out of the box. He had thought about trying to buy more time by getting her newspaper and her mail when it was dark but he decided it was too risky. Somebody might notice him.

Or maybe some relatives who were hoping she'd die and leave the house to them might get excited when she didn't answer the phone. Even if they lived on the other side of the country, they still could call the police and ask them to check her out. The minute the cops started nosing around, they'd spot the cut-out screen and the peeling paint on the ground. There was just no way he could make it look as if she had taken off on her own.

After he killed her, he had wrapped her body in garden-sized garbage bags and tied the bundle together with twine. He'd carried her into the kitchen and picked up her car key from a dish on the counter. Then he took her into the attached garage and dropped her in the trunk of her car. After that, he'd gone through her house and found some surprisingly good jewelry and eight hundred dollars in cash hidden in the refrigerator. He'd smirked at the thought of her wrapping her diamonds and money in aluminum foil.

Then, careful to see that no one was outside walking, or no car coming in either direction, he had hurried across the street and back into his house. Before he went to bed, he packed his clothes, his radio, and his television and put them in his car. Instinct kept warning him that he only had a little time. Somebody was bound to come looking for the old lady in the next couple of days, and they'd find her body when they went through her car.

Wherever he had moved, he'd always managed to find a job, and always had a cash reserve. Now, after buying the car, the reserve still added up to almost eighteen thousand dollars, enough to live on until he was settled again. Online, and using yet another phony name, he'd rented a motel cabin near Camelback Mountain in Pennsylvania. Only a few hours away, it would be easy to drive back here in a couple of weeks when the police weren't swarming around here 24/7.

Satisfied with his plans, Zach had slept well. On Sunday morning, he had savored watching Emily in her kitchen, delighting in how unaware she was of his plans for her. When she left her house at about ten fifteen, he'd wondered if she was going back to the office, but then decided that she looked too dressed up for that. Maybe she was going to church? he thought. That would be good. She doesn't know how much she needs to pray. Just before he'd finished off Madeline Kirk she got religion. "Oh . . . God . . . help . . . me . . ."

He knew he should leave right away. He could call the boss in the morning and say his mother had taken a turn for the worse and he had to go to Florida now. He would tell him how much he'd enjoyed working there and would miss everybody. He could call the rental agent and say the same thing, and that he'd leave the key to the house under the mat. They wouldn't care. I'm paid up till the end of the month, and they'll be just as glad to get me out early so they can get the house ready for the next tenant.

Of course, even though he would disappear from this house, he would soon have to make one trip back to take care of Emily. Whether or not anyone who saw *Fugitive Hunt* phoned in a tip, as soon as they find Kirk's body, and realize I'm gone, they'll connect me to everything pretty quick. Charlotte and her family, Wilma and Lou . . .

Emily Wallace was all over the newspapers today.

I didn't know she had a transplant. I would have been very sympathetic if she had confided in me. But she didn't. It's really a shame that her new heart is going to stop beating so soon.

Making a careful inspection of every room in the house to be sure he hadn't forgotten anything except what he intended to leave, Zach left his rented house and closed the door behind him.

As he got into his car, he glanced at the new flowers he had planted along the driveway. In a week they had grown and spread. He started to laugh. If I only had a little more time, I'd dig these up and put in mums again!

What a joke that would be on the amateur detectives around here.

56

On Monday morning, Jimmy Easton's public defender, Luke Byrne, went to the Bergen County Jail to talk to his client. After the Aldrich verdict came in on Friday, Judge Stevens had scheduled Easton's sentencing for today at one thirty. "Jimmy, I just want to go over what we're going to say in court today," he said.

Easton looked at him sourly. "You made a lousy deal for me, and I intend to complain about that to the judge."

Byrne looked at Easton, astonished. "A lousy deal? You can't be serious. They caught you running out of that house carrying the jewelry. What kind of a defense did you expect me to come up with?"

"I'm not talking about beating the charge. I'm talking about the lousy sentence they want to give me. Four years is way too much. I want you to talk to that prosecutor and tell her I'll take five years probation with time served."

"Oh, I'm sure Wallace will jump at that," Byrne snapped. "Jimmy, you made a deal to take four years. Otherwise you'd be getting ten years for being an habitual offender. We're past the point of negotiating. Four years was their bottom line."

"Don't tell me four years was the best you could

do. They needed me to get Aldrich. If you had been tougher, I could have gotten probation. They'd be letting me out today."

"If you want me to ask the judge for probation, I will. But I can guarantee that he will never do that unless the prosecutor consents. And I guarantee she won't. You're going to do four years."

"I don't care what you guarantee," Easton snarled. "You just tell Emily Wallace that if I don't get what I want, she won't be taking any more bows for being such a hotshot prosecutor. Not when they hear what else I have to say."

Not wanting to debate it any further, Luke Byrne signaled to the guard that he was ready to leave.

He walked the couple of blocks back to the courthouse and went directly to Emily's office. "Got a minute?" he asked.

Emily looked up and smiled. Luke was one of the best public defenders in the courthouse. Six foot five, with carrot-red hair and an easygoing manner, he did his level best for his clients, but was always professionally cordial to the prosecutors.

"Come on in, Luke. How are you?" As she spoke she slid her hand over the name on the file she had been reviewing.

"Well, Emily, actually, I could be better. I just saw your star witness at the jail and I'm afraid he is in a foul mood, to put it mildly. He thinks I sold him out with the four-year deal. I'm supposed to deliver a message to you that he wants probation and he wants to get out today."

"Are you *kidding*?" Emily asked, her voice rising.

"I wish I were. And there's more. He's threatening that if he doesn't get what he wants, he'll have more to say and it will somehow hurt you. He didn't give me any more details than that."

Luke Byrne could see that Emily was both shocked and upset.

"Luke, I appreciate the heads-up. He can say whatever he wants, then he'll get his four years. And be out of my sight."

"And mine," Luke said smiling. "See you later."

At one thirty, Jimmy Easton, shackled and dressed in an orange prison jumpsuit, was led from the holding cell into the courtroom. After the attorneys had entered their appearances, Judge Stevens asked Luke Byrne to speak.

"Your Honor, Jimmy Easton's testimony was critical to obtaining a conviction of Gregg Aldrich for the brutal murder of his wife. The jury obviously accepted his testimony as credible. The state agreed that his maximum sentence would be four years. Your Honor, he has already spent eight months in jail, and it has been very difficult for him. Many of the other inmates ostracized him because he cooperated with the prosecutor and he is always in fear of being harmed because of that."

Byrne paused and then continued, "Your Honor, I am asking that Mr. Easton be sentenced to probation and time served. He is willing to be very closely supervised and he is willing to do community service. Thank you."

"Mr. Easton, you have a right to speak on your own behalf," Judge Stevens said. "Is there anything you want to say?"

His face flushed, Jimmy Easton drew in a deep breath. "Your Honor, I'm being railroaded. My lawyer didn't do nothin' for me. If he had called their bluff and kept fighting, they would have given me probation. They needed me for their case. I did what I was supposed to do and now they just want to dump me in the garbage."

Judge Stevens nodded to Emily. "Prosecutor, I'll hear you."

"Your Honor, it is absurd for Mr. Easton to claim that he is being railroaded. Our first plea offer was six years, and after much negotiation, we lowered it to four years. We believe that Mr. Easton, who has a long criminal record, must be sentenced to prison. There was nothing more his attorney could have done to persuade us to offer probation. It was never going to happen."

Judge Stevens turned to Jimmy Easton. "Mr. Easton, your case was assigned to me from the beginning. The proofs against you on this burglary charge were very strong. Your attorney vigorously negotiated with the prosecutor. You received and accepted a plea offer that was much lower than you would have gotten under any other circumstances. The state undoubtedly received a substantial benefit from your testimony and you will now receive a substantial benefit for your cooperation.

But under no circumstances can I accept that you are an appropriate candidate for probation. You will be committed to the Department of Corrections for a period of four years. You have a right to appeal if you are dissatisfied with your sentence."

As the sheriff's officer took his arm to lead him away, Jimmy Easton started screaming, "Dissatisfied? *Dissatisfied?* I'll show everybody what it means to be dissatisfied. Just wait! You'll all hear from me soon.

"And you won't like it."

57

On Monday morning, Phil Bracken, the foreman at the Pine Electronics warehouse on Route 46, was sorry to hear from Zach Lanning that it was necessary for him to leave the job ahead of time because his mother was dying.

"Zach, I couldn't be sorrier, both for your trouble, and because you do such a good job. Anytime you want to come back, you've got a job here."

It was absolutely the truth, Phil thought, as he replaced the phone in his office. Zach never goofed off, never ran out for cigarette breaks, always put the merchandise where it belonged, not on the wrong shelves like some of these dopes who only worked here until they could get a better job.

On the other hand, there was something about Zach that made me uncomfortable, Phil admitted to himself. Maybe it was because he seemed way too smart for the job. I always felt that about him. And he never shot the breeze at the end of his shift or went out for a beer with the other guys. Zach had told him he was divorced and had no kids so it wasn't as though he was rushing home to a family.

Betty Tepper, a forty-something divorcée, worked in

the accounting office. When she had learned that Zach was single, she had invited him to a couple of parties but he'd always made some excuse not to go. He just didn't seem interested in having any friends.

What are you going to do? Phil asked himself. In this economy, there are dozens of guys who'll jump at the chance for a steady job here with good benefits.

And Zach Lanning had been kind of weird, he thought. He never looked me in the eye when I talked to him. It was like he was always checking to see if anyone else was coming near him.

Ralph Cousins, one of the newer guys, stopped in the office after he punched out at four o'clock. "Phil, got a minute?"

"Sure. What's up?" Not another one quitting, Phil hoped. Ralph, a twenty-three-year-old African-American, worked the day shift and was going to college at night. He was smart and dependable.

"Phil, something's been bothering me. It's about that guy Lanning."

"If it's about Lanning, relax. He quit this morning."

"He quit!" Cousins repeated, excitement in his voice.

Surprised at Ralph's reaction, Phil said, "He was planning to leave at the end of the month. Didn't you know that? He was going to move to Florida to take care of his mother. But now she's dying, so he left this morning."

"I knew I should have played my hunch. I hope it's not too late."

"What hunch?"

"I was watching *Fugitive Hunt* the other night and I told my wife that the composite of the guy who's a serial killer looked a lot like Lanning."

"Oh, come on, Ralph, that guy is no more a serial killer than you or me."

"Phil, last May when Mother's Day was coming up, I asked him about his mother. He told me that he never knew her, he'd been raised in a bunch of foster homes. He was lying to you. I bet he's out of here because he's afraid somebody who saw that program will identify him."

"I've seen that program a couple of times myself. I think you're crazy, but if you are right, why didn't you call right away? They're always offering rewards for tips."

"I didn't call because I wasn't sure, and I didn't want to make a fool of myself. And I wanted to talk to you. Because if the police came here to question him and it turned out not to be him, I thought maybe you could be sued if I had given the tip. But I'm going to call them now. I wrote down the number Saturday night."

As Ralph Cousins was dialing his cell phone, Betty Tepper came into Phil's office. "What's this I hear?" she asked. "Is it true that Zach Lanning quit?"

"This morning," Phil snapped. Although trying to digest the mind-boggling fact that he may have been rubbing elbows with a serial killer for two years, he was still able to be irritated that Betty could never learn to knock before she barged into his office.

She did not try to hide her disappointment. "I thought I was wearing him down and he was going to ask me out. He was a plain-looking guy, but I always felt there was something mysterious and exciting about him."

"You may be right, Betty, you may be right," Phil responded, as Ralph Cousins dialed the number of *Fugitive Hunt*.

After his call went through, Ralph began by saying, "I know you get plenty of tips, but I honestly believe that my coworker here is Charley Muir, the serial killer."

58

It was Monday morning in Yonkers. Reeney Sling was arguing with her husband, Rudy, a not uncommon situation. She had been the one who had phoned in the inquiry to the *Courtside* office on Friday night. Rudy had hit the ceiling later when she told him what she had done.

"Sal is my friend," he fumed. "Look at the break he gave us. Moving us up here at a discount and letting us pay two months later. How many people do you think would do that? And this is how you say 'Thank you, Sal'?"

Reeney had heatedly pointed out that Sal had a number of guys working for him off the books who might also remember Jimmy. "Any one of them could pass on the same information, and if there is a reward, they'll be the ones to collect. So if there is one, why shouldn't we get it?"

Rudy took a swig of beer. "I'll tell you why. I'll say it again. Sal is my friend. And I'm not going to be the one to get him in trouble. And neither are you."

The tension between them had lasted over the weekend. Then on Sunday night, Reeney had checked the *Courtside* Web site and learned that Michael Gordon intended to announce on Monday night's show a twenty-five-thousand-dollar reward. It would be paid for information leading to proof that Jimmy Easton had ever had access to Gregg Aldrich's apartment when Aldrich was not present and before Natalie Raines was murdered.

"Twenty-five thousand dollars," Reeney had screamed. "Open your eyes and look around this place. Everything is falling apart. How long have I had to live like this? I'm embarrassed to have our friends come here. Think how nice we could fix it up with that kind of money. And maybe have enough to take a trip like you've been promising me forever."

"Reeney, if we tell them Jimmy Easton worked for Sal, they'll ask to see his books. I doubt if Sal even remembers how much he used him. He only has one full-time guy. The others he pays in cash when he needs them on a job. Sal never delivered to the Aldrich apartment. He told me that himself only last week."

"What did you expect him to say? That he would love to have the IRS all over him?"

On Sunday night they had gone to bed furious at each other. On Monday morning, Rudy's resistance was starting to falter. "I couldn't sleep much last night, Reeney," he said.

"Yes, you did," Reenie snapped. "You were snoring all night. With all the beer you drank, you were out cold."

They were having breakfast in the small dining area off the kitchen. Rudy was using his last piece of toast to mop up the remainder of the fried eggs he had eaten. "What I'm trying to say, if you'll let me talk, is that you've got a point. Anyone who ever worked for Sal and met Easton and hears about this reward will be speed-dialing the tip in to *Courtside*. If Sal is going to get in trouble anyway, why should we miss out on the money? If it turns out that Easton never delivered anything there, then *Courtside* doesn't pay and we don't buy any new furniture."

Reeney jumped up and ran to the phone. "I have the tip number written down."

She snatched up a piece of paper and began to dial.

59

As a convicted murderer, Gregg Aldrich was considered a high security risk and was housed in a tiny cell by himself. The awful reality of what had happened to him did not sink in immediately.

When he had arrived at the jail after the verdict, he was photographed and fingerprinted. He had exchanged his Paul Stuart jacket and slacks for the pale green jumpsuit that was issued to all inmates. His watch and his wallet had been documented in his newly opened file and taken from him.

He was allowed to keep his reading glasses.

He was interviewed by a nurse who questioned him about any mental or physical health issues he might have, or any medications he was taking.

It was about two o'clock on Friday afternoon when, still protected by shock from the full impact of the verdict, he had been taken to his cell. Knowing he had missed lunch, a guard had brought him a baloney sandwich and a soda.

"Thank you. I appreciate it," he said courteously.

* * *

On Monday morning, Gregg awoke at dawn to the realization that he simply could not remember a single moment since he'd started to eat that sandwich on Friday. It was all a complete blur. He stared at his bleak surroundings. How could this happen? Why am I here? Natalie, Natalie, why have you let this happen to me? You know I didn't kill you. You know I understood you better than anyone else.

You know I just wanted you to be happy.

I wish you had wanted that for me.

He stood up, stretched, and now keenly aware that he would probably never again jog in Central Park or, for that matter, jog anywhere, sat down again on the bunk bed and wondered how he could ever survive this. He buried his face in his hands. Wrenching sobs racked his body for several minutes until, sapped of all energy, he lay down on the bed again.

I've got to pull myself together, he thought. If I have any prayer of getting out of this, I have to somehow prove that Easton is a liar. I cannot believe he is housed somewhere in this building. *He* deserves to be here. I don't, he thought bitterly.

After the verdict Richard Moore had spoken to him while he was still in the holding cell adjacent to Judge Stevens's courtroom. Richard tried to console him by promising he would file the appeal immediately after he was sentenced.

"In the meantime will I be under the same roof with that scum?" Gregg remembered asking.

Richard replied that Judge Stevens had just issued a

"keep separate" order so that he would have no contact with Easton at the jail.

"Not that he will be there too long," Richard had assured him. "The judge is going to sentence Jimmy Easton on Monday afternoon. Within a couple of weeks he'll be out of the county jail and assigned to a state prison."

It's a good thing, Gregg thought to himself, enraged at what Easton had taken from him. If I had the chance, I think I would kill him.

He heard the noise of the lock turning. "I've got your breakfast, Aldrich," the guard was saying. "I'm bringing it in."

At two thirty that afternoon, Richard Moore, accompanied by a sheriff's officer, appeared at the door of Gregg's cell. Gregg looked up, surprised. He had not expected to see Richard today. It was immediately evident to him that something positive had happened.

Richard got right to the point. "Gregg, I just got out of watching Easton's sentencing. As I told you, I expected it to be fairly low key. Other than some remarks from his attorney and Emily Wallace, and then inevitably a phony speech from him about how he was going to change his life, I thought it would be pretty routine. It sure didn't turn out that way."

As Gregg listened, almost afraid to allow himself to feel any hope, Richard described what had happened.

"Gregg, I have no doubt that Emily Wallace was very shaken up. When Easton was spouting that he would have a lot more to say, I think I know what was going through her mind. She understands that Easton is despicable and a complete loose cannon. And all the reporters who were there now know that, too. This will be all over the papers tomorrow. If Wallace didn't intend to investigate this further herself, the press coverage will make her do it."

Then, seeing the suffering in Gregg's eyes, he decided to tell him now about the reward Michael Gordon had put on his Web site and the phoned-in tip that had prompted it.

As he watched Richard Moore leave his cell, a transformed Gregg Aldrich was fiercely believing that before too long he might be walking out with him.

60

Ted Wesley was clearly unhappy to witness Jimmy Easton's outburst. When he learned Emily knew in advance that he was demanding probation, he exploded. "What is going on here? Didn't you make it clear to him that he was going to prison? And why didn't you tell me before he was in court?"

"Ted," Emily said quietly. "I made it abundantly clear to him that probation was out of the question. I just learned about it a little while ago and I don't think it's that unusual for a defendant to want a better deal at the last minute."

Her tone became resolute. "But I will tell you one thing. I intend to go back through this case as if it had just been handed to me. I'm going to retrace every step. I knew Easton was bad when we started out, but he's much worse than I thought. He is the worst kind of slime. If it turns out that everything he said on the witness stand is true, then he's just spitting at us because he doesn't want to go to prison. On the other hand, if he was lying we've got an innocent man rotting in a jail cell. And if that's the case, we've also got a murderer on the loose who shot and killed Natalie Raines in our jurisdiction."

"Emily, the murderer who shot and killed Natalie Raines is in that cell two blocks away, and his name is Gregg Aldrich. Thanks to the fact you apparently did not make it clear to Easton that he was going away, the media is going to be ranting about what else he may have to say."

Ted Wesley picked up the phone, a sign that the meeting was over.

Emily went back to her office. The file she had been studying most of the morning contained the initial report of the police in Old Tappan, where Jimmy Easton had been arrested in the burglary. It was brief. The burglary had occurred at nine thirty P.M. last February 20th. As he was being processed in the police station, Easton had volunteered that he had information about the Raines murder.

And that was when Jake Rosen and Billy Tryon rushed over to interview him, Emily thought. It certainly was a break that Easton ended up talking. It had been an embarrassment for this office that Raines's murder was still unsolved after two years. If Easton read the papers at all, he would have known that Aldrich was the only suspect. He had met him at a bar. Could he have pieced together the rest of that story, maybe with some help from Billy Tryon?

Jake would never be part of helping Easton to fabricate evidence, but Tryon might. Jake had said he was there for that first interview in the police station, but he had also said that he arrived there after Billy Tryon did.

I don't care if Ted Wesley fires me while he still

has the chance, Emily thought. I'm going to see this through. Then she said aloud what she had been trying to deny. "Gregg Aldrich is innocent. I did everything I could to convict him and I knew he was innocent while I was doing it."

The words Alice Mills had screamed at her echoed in her mind: *"You know that this is a travesty and in your heart you're ashamed to be part of it."*

I *am* ashamed, Emily thought.

I *am* ashamed.

She was startled by how certain she was.

61

Belle Garcia could not get over the fact that Gregg had been convicted. She had hardly slept on either Friday or Saturday night. Last year she had watched a late-night documentary about prisons, and the thought of Gregg being locked up in a cage was simply awful.

"Even Natalie's mother believed in him, so why did those stupid jurors take the word of that horrible crook? If I had been on that jury, he'd be home with his child," she said not once but over and over again to Sal.

On Saturday evening he finally exploded. "Belle, can't you get it straight? I'm sick of hearing about it. No more. Get it? No more!" Then he stormed out of their apartment to take a long walk.

On the other hand, Belle's eighty-year-old mother, Nona "Nonie" Amoroso, wanted to hear everything about it. On Sunday morning, her cruise ship docked in Red Hook, Brooklyn. Belle picked her up and on the way home that was all they talked about. When Belle dropped her at her apartment, around the corner from theirs, she said, "Mama, I know you're a little tired, but come over to dinner tonight. We've missed you so much. But, remember, don't bring up the trial. Like I said, Sal has gotten downright surly at the mention of it."

Seeing the disappointed look on her mother's face she added, hastily, "I have it all planned. Sal has a big moving job tomorrow. He'll be leaving really early in the morning, so he'll want to go to bed pretty early tonight. I'll call you after he's asleep, probably around ten o'clock. Get comfortable in your bathrobe because I've got a lot to tell you." She did not add that she might be seeking her advice about a big decision that she had to make.

"I can't wait," her mother replied. "I've been dying to hear everything about it."

When she arrived for dinner, Nonie was carrying a bag full of the pictures she and her friends had taken, and since she couldn't talk about the case, she proceeded to fill them in on every detail of every day on the cruise.

"Olga and Gertie got seasick right away and had to wear that patch behind their ears. I got one just in case but I never needed it . . .

"The food was out of this world. We all ate too much . . . They were putting something in front of you all day and all night . . .

"And I really enjoyed going to hear the lectures they had. My favorite was the one about sea life . . . you know . . . the whales, and the penguins, and whatnot . . ."

Sal, normally good-natured about his mother-in-law's agonizingly boring stories, couldn't even pretend to listen. Belle did her best to look interested and even sincerely admired the already framed picture of her beaming mother in her lovely new pants suit posing with the captain.

"You mean that guy has to have his picture taken with every person on the ship?" Sal asked incredulously, momentarily joining in the conversation and thinking that some days the captain must be tempted to jump overboard.

"Uh-huh. Of course when you have a couple or a family group, they pose together. But the girls and I all wanted individual pictures so that our families would have them someday after we're gone," Nonie explained.

I get their drift, Sal thought. None of the "girls" are under seventy-five.

After they finished dessert and a second cup of tea, he suggested, "Nonie, you've got to be tired after your trip. And I've got to get out early tomorrow morning. If you don't mind, I'll walk you home now."

Belle and her mother exchanged satisfied glances.

"That's a good idea, Sal," Nonie agreed. "You really need your rest and I'm ready to call it a day. It'll be good to be back in my own bed."

An hour later, just before ten o'clock, the bedroom door closed and Sal already in a deep sleep, Belle settled in her favorite chair in the living room, pulled the hassock under her feet, and dialed her mother.

For the next hour and a half they conducted a thorough review of all of the evidence. The more they talked and the more Belle heard her mother declare that Gregg had been framed, the more anguished she became. Even though Sal denies it, I am almost sure that Jimmy Easton worked for him, she thought. She finally decided to tell her mother about her suspicions.

"You mean that Jimmy Easton may have worked for Sal?" Nonie exclaimed. "Did Sal ever deliver anything to Gregg's apartment building?"

"Sal used to deliver for some antique shop that went bust. I guess not enough people buy that kind of stuff. I don't particularly like it myself. But I know those deliveries were usually on the East Side to those fancy apartment buildings," Belle answered, her tone worried. "I know that's why Sal is upset if I talk about the case . . .

"He's afraid," she sighed. "Over the years he's hired a lot of different guys when he needs extra help. He always pays them in cash. He doesn't want to get involved in all that extra paperwork he'd have to do if they were on the books."

"To say nothing of the medical plan he would have to have," Nonie agreed. "It would cost a fortune. You know how it is, the rich get richer and the rest of us get squeezed. You know how long it took me to save up for my trip with the girls."

Nonie cleared her throat for several seconds. "Sorry, that's my allergies. There was a musty smell on the ship and I think that's what kicked them off. Anyway, Belle, I don't want to see Sal get in trouble over taxes. But if Jimmy Easton worked for him and went into that apartment on a delivery, it would explain why he knew so much about it."

"That's what's been torturing me." Belle was close to tears.

"Honey, you can't let anyone be locked in prison if by just opening your mouth you can change everything. Besides, if because of you Gregg gets out, I'll bet he'll write a check for Sal's back taxes the next day. Tell Sal that. Tell him he's got to do the right thing and if he won't do it, you will."

"You're absolutely right, Mama," Belle said. "I'm really glad I talked to you about it."

"And I want you to tell Sal he can confide in me. I don't mind saying I have a good head on my shoulders."

Belle knew *that* was never going to happen.

Sal left early Monday morning. Hauling her laundry cart with her, Belle immediately went down to the basement, where the little storage area that came with their apartment was located. It was there that Sal kept cardboard boxes filled with records of his moving company from the last twenty years. She knew that Sal hated paperwork, but at least he marked the boxes with the years that the records covered.

Natalie Raines is dead two and a half years, Belle thought. I want to start at that point and work backward. She hoisted the two boxes containing records for the two years prior to the murder onto the cart and got into the elevator.

Back in her living room she began to go through the first box. Forty-five minutes later she found what she was looking for. Sal had a company receipt for delivering a

marble standing lamp to "G. Aldrich" at the apartment
address that she had heard several times on television.
The receipt was dated March 3rd, thirteen days before
Natalie's death.

Holding the receipt, Belle collapsed into a chair.
With her total recall of all important dates in the case,
she knew that March 3rd was the day Easton had
claimed he had met with Gregg in the apartment and
had received the down payment to kill Natalie.

She shivered as she looked at the clear signature
of the person who had accepted the delivery. Harriet
Krupinsky. She was the Aldrich housekeeper who had
retired a few months later and then passed away suddenly about a year after Natalie's murder.

In her bones Belle was sure that Jimmy Easton had
made that delivery. How could Sal know this and live
with himself? she wondered sadly. What that poor man
and his daughter must be going through.

Continuing her search, she soon found absolute
proof that Easton had worked for Sal. It was in a crumpled pocket telephone book that contained a couple of
dozen names. Some of them Belle recognized as people
who had worked part-time for Sal. There was nothing
under tab E but then she turned to J. Scribbled at the
top of the page was "Jimmy Easton." And a telephone
number for him.

Nearly crushed by disappointment in Sal, and equally
anxious about how revealing this information would
impact on him, Belle repacked the boxes but kept the
receipt and the phone book. She lifted the boxes back

into the laundry cart and returned them to the basement. Then deciding that it would be better for Sal if he was the one to make the call, she slumped back down in the chair and again dialed her mother.

"Mama," she said, her voice breaking, "Sal lied to me. I went through his records. Jimmy Easton did work for him and there's a receipt for a delivery to the Aldrich apartment thirteen days before Natalie died."

"My God, Belle. No wonder Sal has been such a wreck. What are you going to do?"

"As soon as Sal gets home, I'm going to tell him what I know and that we're going to call Michael Gordon's tip line. And you know something, Mama? In a way I bet Sal will be relieved. He's a good man. It's just that he's so frightened. I am, too. Mama, do you think there's any chance they'll put Sal in jail?"

62

Tom Schwartz, the executive producer of *Fugitive Hunt*, called the Bergen County prosecutor's office on Monday, just after four o'clock. He reached the prosecutor's secretary and told her that it was extremely urgent for him to talk to the prosecutor about a serial killer they had recently profiled and who might be living in Bergen County.

Ten seconds later Ted Wesley was on the phone. "Mr. Schwartz, what's this about a serial killer?"

"We have good reason to believe that a tip we have just received may lead to the location of a serial killer. Are you familiar with our program?"

"Yes, but I haven't seen it recently."

"Then if you'll bear with me for a few minutes, I'll give you the background."

As Schwartz rapidly laid out the history of the murderer last known as Charley Muir and why his coworker believed that he and Zach Lanning were the same person, Ted Wesley was already envisioning the positive press coverage that he would get if his office was able to capture this fugitive. "You said this guy lives in Glen Rock. Have you got an address for him?" he asked Schwartz.

"Yes, but remember our tipster said that when Lanning called his boss this morning to quit his job, he told him he was leaving for Florida right away. He may already be gone."

"I'll put my detectives on it right now. We'll get back to you."

Wesley put the phone down and pressed the intercom. "Get Billy Tryon in here. And get the Des Moines prosecutor on the phone."

"Right away."

As he waited impatiently, Wesley tapped his reading glasses on his desk. Glen Rock was a quiet, upscale town. Emily lived there, and so did some other people in the office. He reached behind him and took the office directory from a shelf. The tipster had given Zachary Lanning's address as 624 Colonial Road.

Wesley's eyes widened when he opened the directory and looked up Emily's address. She lived at 622 Colonial. My God, if this is the right guy, she's been living next door to a nut, he thought.

At precisely the same moment, the Des Moines prosecutor's call came through and Billy Tryon rushed into the office.

Twenty minutes later, Tryon, Jake Rosen, and the squad cars from the Glen Rock Police Department were at the house where Zach Lanning had lived for two years. When there was no answer at the door, a Glen Rock officer got the number of the realtor who rented the house to Zach and called him to get permission to enter the house.

"Sure you can go in," the realtor replied. "When Lanning phoned me this morning, he told me he'd hang the keys on a hook in the garage. His rental is over. Why are you looking for him?"

"I'm not at liberty to say why right now, sir," the young officer replied. "Thank you."

They retrieved the key from the garage and, with guns drawn, cautiously went inside, then fanned out, checking every room and closet. They found no one.

Billy Tryon and Jake Rosen then went back through each room to see if there were any clues as to where Lanning had gone but there wasn't so much as a newspaper or magazine in the entire house.

"Get the fingerprint people here right away," Tryon said. "We should be able to get prints and then we can verify that he's our guy."

"I hope we can get prints," Jake Rosen commented. "This guy must be compulsively neat. There isn't a spot of dust anywhere and take a look at the way the glasses are lined up in the cabinet."

"Maybe he went to West Point," Tryon snapped, sarcastically. "Jake, tell the Glen Rock guys to ring the doorbells on this block and see if any of the neighbors know anything about him. Make sure the town cops know that we already put out an APB on his car and license plate."

Tryon looked around. A small device on the sill of the kitchen window caught his eye. Then he was astonished to hear a dog barking as loudly as if it were in the room.

The sound was coming through the device, which was operating as an intercom system.

He looked out the window. Ted Wesley had told him Emily lived next door to Lanning. Right now she was hurrying out of her car and up the walkway to her front door. That's why the dog's barking, he thought.

He watched as she opened the door and went inside. Then he could distinctly hear her call out a greeting to her pet.

"Jake," he yelled, "come in here and look at this. That guy Lanning has some kind of microphone planted in Emily's house and he's been listening to everything she says."

"Come on, Bess," Emily was saying. "I'll let you out quick. There's something going on next door with that crazy guy who used to walk you."

"My God," Jake muttered as he listened to the crystal clear sound of Emily's voice. He tilted the blind. "Look, Billy. He's had a direct view into Emily's kitchen. And you know what I think? Looking at this house, this guy is superorganized. He didn't forget to take this device. He left it for the police to find and for Emily to hear about." They heard the porch door open, then Emily calling the dog back inside.

A Glen Rock detective walked into the kitchen. "We're ninety-nine percent sure Lanning is the guy," he said, trying to control the excitement in his voice. "I watched that program the other night. One of the clues they talked about is that Charley Muir loved to plant yellow mums. We just found three big garbage bags filled with them in the garage. We figure he watched that program, too, and got nervous about them."

Through the window, they could see Emily crossing the driveway. She joined them in the kitchen. "Ted Wesley called me and said you're checking out this guy. He filled me in on some of the details. You were talking about the mums in the garage? Zach planted them a little over a week ago on a Saturday and dug them up and planted new flowers twenty-four hours later. I thought it was very odd, but on the other hand he was always very strange."

"Emily," Jake said, softly, "we're pretty certain now that Zach Lanning is the serial killer Charley Muir. There's something else we have to tell you and I know it's going to be very upsetting."

Emily froze. "It can't be worse than what I'm realizing. Back in April, he offered to walk Bess for me in the afternoons. I keep Bess on the enclosed porch during the day and I gave him a key to that area only, not to the door that opens into the kitchen. But one night when I came home late he was sitting inside the porch and it scared me. I stopped the dog walking immediately. I made up some excuse for ending it, but I could tell that he didn't buy it and he was upset."

Her eyes widened and her face paled. "I'm sure now that he was in my house last week. One night when I came home I noticed that the bottom drawer in one of the dressers in my bedroom had a small piece of a nightgown sticking out of it. I was certain I hadn't left it like that."

She stopped. "Oh, my God. Now I know what was bothering me yesterday when I packed those nightgowns to give away. One of them was missing! Jake, tell me what you have to say."

Jake pointed to the window. "Emily, he's got a listening device planted in your house. We could hear you talking to your dog just now."

The enormity of Zach's invasion into her life made Emily physically ill. She immediately had a sick feeling in the pit of her stomach and her legs felt wobbly.

At that moment a Glen Rock detective rushed in. "Looks like we've got a burglary across the street. There's a screen cut out of a back window and the old lady who lives there isn't answering the door. We're going in."

Tryon, Rosen, and Emily hurried across the street with the police. An officer kicked in the front door. Within a few minutes they knew that Madeline Kirk was not in the house. "Check the garage," Tryon ordered. "There's a car key in a dish by the kitchen door."

Following a few steps behind the officers, Emily observed that Madeline Kirk's afghan was crumpled on the floor in the den. She gasped when she saw the pad on the table next to the chair. The words *Fugitive Hunt* were written on the pad. A pen was lying across it. Now certain that something bad had happened to her neighbor, she followed the detectives into the garage. They were searching the interior of Madeline Kirk's car.

"Open the trunk," Billy Tryon directed.

As the trunk was raised, the odor of death was overpowering. Tryon carefully untied the twine holding the garbage bags together and lifted one of them. The rigor mortis that had set in had preserved the look of terror on the elderly woman's face.

"Oh, my God," Emily moaned. "That poor helpless soul. This man is a monster."

"Emily," Jake said gently. "You're lucky you didn't end up like her."

63

Mike Gordon went directly to his office on Monday afternoon after attending Jimmy Easton's sentencing. Those clips of him threatening the prosecutor and as much as saying that he knows a lot more will make for a great show tonight, he thought. Was he bluffing and just lashing out because he didn't get probation? Or is he about to drop a bombshell? The panel is going to have a field day with this tonight.

His secretary, Liz, followed him into his private office and told him that there had been fifty-one responses phoned to the number on the Web site since the offer of the twenty-five-thousand-dollar reward had been posted Sunday evening.

"Twenty-two were from psychics, Mike," she told him, standing in front of his desk. "Two of them must have the same crystal ball. They both see a man with dark hair and wearing dark clothing watching Natalie Raines as she drove up to her house the morning she was killed."

She smiled. "You won't believe the rest of it. They see him waiting for her with a gun in his hand. That's where the vision stops. Apparently, when they get the reward they'll be able to see his face and describe him fully."

Mike shrugged. "I was positive we'd attract some of those weirdos."

Liz did an informal summary of the calls. "Ten or twelve of them were people who said that Jimmy Easton has cheated or robbed them. None of them could believe that a jury found Gregg Aldrich guilty based on his testimony. Some of them said they'd like to go to court when Aldrich is sentenced and tell the judge that Easton is a pathological liar."

"That's good to know but it doesn't do us much good. How about the woman who called Friday night and asked about a reward? Have we heard from her?"

"I was saving the best for last," Liz told him. "She did call back this morning. Says she absolutely has the proof of where Jimmy worked and why he may have been in the Aldrich apartment. She wants to know if we can put the reward money in some kind of secure account to make sure she isn't cheated out of it."

"Did she give her name and a number where we can contact her?"

"No, she didn't want to do that. She wants to talk directly to you first. Doesn't trust anyone else not to steal her information. Also she wants to know if Gregg Aldrich gets out of jail because of her tip, will you have her as a guest on the show with him. I told her you'd be in around now and that she could call back."

"Liz, if somebody gives us concrete proof, of course I'll have them on the show. I just hope she isn't another kook." Worried, Mike thought of how he had told Alice and Katie about this tip at lunch yesterday, and their ecstatic reaction to it.

"Okay. That's all I have," Liz said, cheerfully. "We'll see what else comes in."

"Hold the calls for a while unless that woman calls back. Put her right through."

Liz was barely at her desk when the phone rang. Through the open door, Mike heard her say, "Yes, he is back, and he will speak with you now. Hold just a moment, please."

Mike's hand was on the phone waiting for the buzzer to sound, indicating that the call had been transferred.

"Mike Gordon," he said. "I've been informed that you may have some information pertinent to the Aldrich case."

"My name is Reeney Sling, Mr. Gordon. It is an honor to speak with you. I very much enjoy your program. I never thought I would be getting involved in one of your cases but. . . ."

"How are you involved, Ms. Sling?" Mike asked.

"I have important information about where Jimmy Easton worked around the time that Natalie Raines got killed. But I want to make sure that nobody steals my reward."

"Ms. Sling, I personally guarantee you, and I will put it in writing, that if you are the first person to give us this important information and it leads to a new trial or a dismissal of his charges, you will get the reward. You should know in advance that if your information combined with someone else's additional information leads to that kind of result, you will split the reward."

"Suppose my information is much more important. What would happen then? Oh, just a moment, please. My husband wants to tell me something."

Mike heard lowered voices but could not discern what they were saying.

"My husband, Rudy, said that we'll trust you to be fair."

"It's a fair question to ask," Mike said. "We will proportion the reward based upon the value of each person's information."

"That sounds good," she said. "Rudy and I will come in to see you whenever you want."

"How about tomorrow morning at nine o'clock?"

"We'll be there."

"And please bring any written materials or documents that would help support what you say."

"Absolutely," Reeney replied enthusiastically, no longer afraid of being cheated out of the reward.

"I'll see you then," Mike said. "Let me give you back to my secretary and she will give you our address and any directions you may need."

64

Jimmy Easton had just arrived back at the Bergen County Jail after his sentencing.

Captain Paul Kraft, the shift commander, was waiting for him. "Jimmy, I have news for you. You're about to leave your home away from home. We're going to transport you to the prison in Newark in a few minutes."

"Why?" Jimmy demanded. He knew from extensive past experience that the administrative transfer to state prison after a sentence normally took from a few days to a few weeks.

"Well, Jimmy, you know you've got some problems with guys here because of your cooperation."

"That's what my lawyer tried to tell the judge in court," Jimmy snapped. "I get no peace. I get hassled all the time because I helped the prosecutor. Like these guys wouldn't do the same thing to get their time cut down!"

"There's more, Jimmy," Kraft told him. "In the last half hour we've had a couple of anonymous calls. We think it was the same guy both times. He said you better keep your mouth shut from now on or else."

Seeing the alarmed look on Easton's face, he added, "Jimmy, it could be anybody. It's probably a nutcase.

What you said at your sentence is already on the radio and the Internet. With the problems you've had here and now these calls, we thought it was better to get you out right away. For your own protection."

It was obvious to Kraft that Easton was genuinely frightened. "Jimmy, be honest. Do yourself a favor. You know who made those calls, don't you?"

"No, no, I don't," Jimmy stuttered. "Some jerk, I guess."

Kraft did not believe him, but didn't push it. "We'll check into the number that came up on the caller ID, and trace it back," he said. "Don't worry."

"Don't worry? Easy for you to say. I guarantee those calls came from a prepaid cell phone. I know all about them. I've had dozens of them myself. You make an important call, then you throw it away. Try it sometime."

"All right, Jimmy. Let's collect your stuff. We've already let them know about this at the prison. They'll make sure you're okay."

But an hour later, handcuffed and shackled in the back of the transport van, Jimmy stared morosely out the window. They were on the Turnpike in Newark in the vicinity of the airport. He could see a departing plane ascending into the sky. What I wouldn't do to be on that plane, no matter where it was going, he thought.

He remembered a song by John Denver. "Leavin' on a jet plane . . ."

I wish I was.

I'd never come back here.

I'd start over somewhere.

As the van arrived at the prison gate and was screened for entry, Jimmy was plotting his next move.

Aldrich's lawyer was pretty nasty to me at the trial but I bet he'll be glad to hear from me tomorrow.

When I'm finished filling his ear, he won't even mind that it was a collect call.

65

When he left the house in Glen Rock early Monday morning, Zach Lanning drove straight to Newark Airport. He found a spot in long-term parking, just a few spaces away from where he had parked the van he had bought from Henry Link. As he switched his belongings from one vehicle to the other, he hoped he was blending in with the airport travelers carrying their suitcases to and from the terminals.

He had a scare when he was taking his television set out of the trunk of the car and a security guard drove past but he didn't seem to pay any attention. Zach finished transferring the last of his gear, then locked his car. By then, his nerves were almost shot. That security guard might suddenly wonder why anybody would have a heavy television set and might think he had broken into a parked car.

He might come back and check it out, Zach worried.

But he got out of the lot without any problem. He got back on the Turnpike and began the drive to Camelback. At 7:45 he pulled into a rest area and made calls to his job and to the rental agent telling them that he wasn't coming back.

There was a lot of traffic on the highway and it was

nearly eleven when he arrived at the lodge and went to the reception desk to check in.

As he waited for the clerk to finish a call, he looked around and felt himself calming down. This was just the kind of place he had wanted. Somewhat run down, in an area far removed from the main roads, it was bound to be quiet. The ski season had not yet started. Anybody here now is just looking for peace and quiet and to take autumn nature walks, he assured himself.

The clerk, a slow-moving guy pushing seventy, had the cabin key in his hand. "I gave you one of our best cabins," he said, amiably. "It's preseason and we're not too busy. In another six weeks, this place is gonna be jumping. We get a lot of skiers, especially on the weekends."

"That's nice," Zach replied as he took the key and started to turn away. The last thing he needed was any more conversation where the man could focus on him.

The clerk squinted his eyes. "You've been here before, haven't you? You look familiar. I know," he said chuckling, "you kind of look like that guy who killed all his wives. They had stuff on him on *Fugitive Hunt* last week. I was just kidding my brother-in-law. He looks even more like him than you do."

The clerk started laughing heartily.

Zach attempted to laugh with him. "I've only had one wife and she's still around. And if her alimony check is a day late, I get a call from her lawyer."

"You, too?" the clerk said loudly. "I pay alimony, too. It really stinks. The guy on *Fugitive Hunt* killed his last wife because she got his house in the divorce. He went overboard, but I still kind of feel sorry for him."

"So do I," Zach mumbled, anxious to get away. "Thank you."

"Just so you know," the clerk called after him, "they start serving lunch in the bar at noon. The food's pretty good."

Zach's cabin was the one nearest to the lodge. It consisted of one large room with two double beds, a dresser, a couch, an armchair, and a night table. A flat-screen television was mounted on the wall above the mantel of a wood-burning fireplace. There was a small bathroom with a plug-in coffeepot on the counter.

Zach knew it was not safe to be here for long. He wondered if anyone had noticed that Madeline Kirk was missing yet. And what about Henry Link? He bought into the story that I was going to file all the paperwork at Motor Vehicles and would send it to him in a few days. But suppose he watched that program Saturday night, too? Suppose he thinks I look like Charley Muir?

Zach closed his eyes. The minute they find Kirk's body there'll be a whole new round of publicity and I'll be the lead story on *Fugitive Hunt* again, he warned himself.

He was suddenly weary. He decided to lie down and try to take a nap. He was astonished when he woke up and realized it was nearly six o'clock. Suddenly panicked, he grabbed the remote from the night table next to the bed and turned on the television so he could watch the news.

He wondered if there would be anything about him or Kirk on a Pennsylvania news station. It's possible, he thought. Camelback is only a couple of hours away from Bergen County.

The news was coming on. The anchor began, "We have a grim story about the murder of an elderly woman in Glen Rock, New Jersey. Police believe that the killer was a neighbor who lived right across the street. They also strongly suspect that this man is the very same person who has allegedly committed at least seven prior murders and who was profiled only last week on the *Fugitive Hunt* program."

The anchor continued: "A tip from a coworker sent police swarming to his home where they discovered that he had apparently just fled. A canvass of the neighborhood led to the discovery of a break-in at eighty-two-year-old widow Madeline Kirk's home. Concerned for her safety, the police pushed in the door of her home and shortly thereafter found her body stuffed in the trunk of her car in her garage."

I knew it, Zach thought. Somebody at work saw the show and recognized me. Kirk recognized me. The jerk who checked me in here noticed that I looked like the guy in the composite. And what if he watches the news tonight? There's bound to be a lot more on about me, and a lot more in the newspapers tomorrow . . .

Zach's mouth went dry as the anchor indicated that after the commercial, he would display the same pictures and age-enhanced composites that had been on *Fugitive Hunt*.

I can't stay here, he thought. If that dope at the desk sees this, he's not going to be thinking about his brother-in-law. Before I get out of here, I've got to find out if the van is still safe to drive. And I've got to know if Henry Link has put two and two together and called the police.

Using one of his stash of prepaid phones, Zach dialed information to get Henry Link's telephone number. After buying the car, he had thrown away the ad with the number in it. Luckily it was listed. Nervously biting his lip, he waited for the connection to be made.

He had used the alias Doug Brown when he was with Henry Link. He had also been careful enough to wear sunglasses and a baseball cap all day Saturday when he was shopping for the car.

The connection went through. "Hello." He recognized Henry's gravelly voice.

"Hello, Henry. This is Doug Brown. Just wanted to say that I took the paperwork to Motor Vehicles this morning. You should be getting everything in the mail in the next few days. The van's running great."

Henry Link's voice did not sound friendly. "My son-in-law gave me a hard time about letting you do all the paperwork. He said that if you had an accident before the what-do-you-call-it, the title, was transferred, I could get sued blind. And what about the license plates? He says it's my job to turn them in. And he wondered why you would pay me in cash."

Zach's nerves were raw. He felt as though a net were closing over him.

"Henry, I had no problem at Motor Vehicles this morning. I turned in the plates and they gave me a new title. You tell your son-in-law I thought I was being a nice guy. I had to go to Motor Vehicles anyway to register the car in my name and I was happy to help you out. I really felt bad that your wife was in a nursing home."

Zach moistened his lips with his tongue. "Henry, I deliberately brought cash so there would be no problem. Do you know how many people won't take a check? Tell that son-in-law of yours that if he was so worried, he should have been there with you when you sold the van."

"Doug, I'm really sorry," Henry said, sounding upset. "I know you're a nice guy. The trouble is since Edith's been in the nursing home my daughter and her husband think I can't take care of myself. We made a fair deal and you put yourself out by taking care of the paperwork and now even checking in with me. Most people aren't that considerate these days. And I'm going to give my son-in-law a piece of my mind."

"Glad to help you, Henry. I'll call you in two or three days and make sure that the records came in the mail."

I'm probably okay with the van for a couple of days, Zach thought as he snapped the cell phone shut. When the paperwork doesn't arrive, the son-in-law's going to go straight to the Motor Vehicles office. And right after that, he's going to go to the police.

My luck may be running out. But before I get caught, if I *do* get caught, I'm going back to take care of Emily.

66

Belle Garcia was desperately unhappy at the prospect of confronting Sal when he got home. The few times in their thirty-five-year marriage that they had had a serious argument, it had been because she had been too stubborn about something. But she knew it wasn't like that this time.

The thought of getting Sal in trouble was anathema to her.

It was five o'clock when she heard his key turning the lock in the front door. He walked in looking exhausted. He works so hard, Belle thought.

"Hi, honey," he said, as he gave her a kiss on the cheek and then headed to the refrigerator to get a beer.

He came into the living room, flipped the can open, sat in his favorite chair, and commented on how tired he was. "After dinner, I'll just watch television for a little while and then pack it in."

"Sal," Belle said, gently, "I know you've had a long day. But I have to tell you what I did this morning. I've been so upset about whether or not Jimmy Easton ever worked for you that I decided to go through the boxes you have downstairs in the storage area."

"Okay, Belle," he said with a tone of resignation. "What did you find?"

"I think you know what I found, Sal. I found a phone book with Easton's name in it and I found a receipt for a delivery to the Aldrich apartment right before Natalie Raines died."

It was disconcerting to Belle that Sal was listening to her but would not look her in the eye.

"Sal, here they are. Look at them. You knew that Jimmy Easton worked for you and did deliveries for you. Tell the truth." Pointing her finger and tapping the receipt, she demanded, "Do you know if he went on this delivery?"

Sal buried his face in his hands. "Yes, I do know, Belle," he said, his voice breaking. "He was with me. We were inside the apartment. And he may have had a chance to check out that drawer."

Belle looked at the chapped and rugged hands of her husband. "Sal," she said gently, "I know why you've been so tormented. I know why you are afraid. But you know that we have to come forward. We'll never have peace of mind until we do."

She got up from her chair, walked across the room, put her arms around Sal, hugged him, then went to the phone. She had written down the phone-in number for *Courtside*. When she was connected, she said, "My name is Belle Garcia. My husband is Sal Garcia. He has a moving company. I can give you proof that on March third, two and a half years ago, the day Jimmy Easton claimed that he met Gregg Aldrich in his apartment, he was actually there delivering an antique lamp with my husband."

The staff member asked her to please hold, then added, "Mrs. Garcia, just in case we're disconnected, may I please have your phone number?"

"Of course," Belle responded and quickly rattled it off.

Less than a minute passed and then a familiar voice came on. "Mrs. Garcia, this is Michael Gordon. I have just been informed that you may have critical information pertaining to the Aldrich case."

"Yes, I do." Belle repeated what she had just told the staff person, then added, "My husband paid Jimmy Easton off the books. That's why he's been afraid to say anything."

A tidal wave of hope swept over Mike. He had to let a few moments pass before he could even speak. "Mrs. Garcia, where do you live?"

"On Twelfth Street between Second and Third."

"Would you and your husband get in a cab and come to my office now?"

Belle looked pleadingly at Sal and repeated Mike's request. He nodded that it was all right to say yes.

"We will be there as soon as we can," she told Mike. "I know my husband will want to shower and change first. He was out all day moving people from Long Island to Connecticut."

"Of course. It's five thirty now. Do you think you could be here by seven?"

"Oh, sure. Sal can shower and dress in ten minutes."

And I'll have to get dressed, too, Belle thought. What should I wear? I'll call Mama and ask what she thinks. Now that she'd actually made the call, the relief she felt was stronger than the apprehension about Sal's possible tax problem.

"Mrs. Garcia, take good care of that receipt. You do know that if this checks out, you may be entitled to the twenty-five-thousand-dollar reward."

"Oh, my God," Belle moaned, "I didn't know anything about a reward."

67

At six o'clock on Monday evening, Emily, holding Bess in her arms, headed for her car. Her immediate neighborhood was cordoned off with yellow tape to protect the physical integrity of the three crime scenes—Madeline Kirk's home, her own home, and Zach's rental house. The large van marked MEDICAL EXAMINER was parked at the curb. Squad cars were posted all along the street.

Totally traumatized by the death of her neighbor and the knowledge that Zach Lanning had been not only spying on her but creeping in and out of her house, she had told Jake Rosen that she had to get out. Walking her to her car, Jake said soothingly, "I'll take care of everything." She completely understood that her home had to be fully processed for fingerprints, any additional electronic devices, and any other evidence that Zach Lanning may have left behind.

"Try to calm down," Jake Rosen told her softly. "It's a good idea for you to get away from this for a couple of hours. When you come back, I will tell you everything that we have found. I promise I will not hold back on you." He smiled. "And I promise we won't leave your house a mess."

"Thanks, Jake. I do insist on knowing right away if he's had cameras or other devices planted anywhere in my house. Don't try to protect me from it." She attempted to return his smile but couldn't manage one. "I'll see you later."

She drove straight to the courthouse. Carrying two folded duffel bags over her arm and holding the leash with Bess excitedly bouncing along beside her, she got into the elevator. There were only a handful of people left in the whole office.

As she walked down the inner hall toward her own office, a couple of young investigators who had heard about the discoveries patted Bess and expressed their outrage at what Lanning had done to her and to the old lady. Then, sympathetically, they asked if there was anything at all that they could do for her.

Emily thanked them. "I'm okay. I am going to stay home the next couple of days. I want to have all my locks changed and I don't have to be convinced that I have to upgrade my alarm system. I'll just be here a few minutes. I have a bunch of files that I need to go through that really got backed up while I was on the Aldrich trial. While the work is being done at my house, I can make some headway on them."

"Can we at least help you carry them out to the car?"

"That would be great. I'll let you know when I'm ready to go."

Emily went to her office and closed the door. There were indeed plenty of files that needed her attention but they would have to wait. She had made the decision to pack up the entire Aldrich file and bring it home. That was the reason for the duffel bags. She didn't want anyone to be able to see what was in them. She intended to go back again through this case and scrutinize every word contained in the hundreds of pages of documents to see if anything had been missed.

It took her about thirty minutes to reorganize the folders and pack them in the duffel bags. One of the thicker folders, which she particularly wanted to scour, contained copies of the New York police reports from the nearly twenty-year-old murder in Central Park of Natalie Raines's then roommate, Jamie Evans.

It had happened so long ago. Maybe that file didn't receive enough of our attention, she thought, as she watched her colleagues lift the duffel bags into her car.

On the way home, Emily wondered if she would be able to fall asleep in her own house tonight, or for that matter, anytime soon. The personal invasion and sense of humiliation is bad enough, she thought with a lump in her throat. But the reality of that psychopath Zach Lanning still on the loose was terrifying.

But there was also a part of her that needed to be in her own home.

As she pulled into her driveway, Jake walked out of her house to meet her. "Emily, we're all finished inside. First let me tell you the good news. There were no cameras or listening devices other than the one you already know about in the kitchen. The bad news is that Lanning's fingerprints are all over your house and they're a match to Charley Muir. We even found his prints in the tool room in the basement."

"Thank God there were no cameras," Emily said, feeling huge relief about that part of it. "I don't know how I would have handled that. The rest of it is bad enough. And I can't believe he was even in the basement handling my father's tools. When I was growing up, Dad was always fixing something. He was so proud of his workshop."

"Emily, we have to talk about something. We both know that Lanning is still out there and that he's a maniac. And he's a maniac who's been obsessed with you. If you are even thinking about staying here, we'll have a police officer outside 24/7 until he's apprehended."

"Jake, I've given that a lot of thought in the last couple of hours and I was pretty torn about what to do. I think I'm going to stay here. But I would like an officer to be outside." She half smiled. "And please ask the officer to watch the back of the house carefully. Lanning liked to go in through the porch."

"Of course, Emily. The Glen Rock police will make sure that any officer assigned continually walks around the house."

"Thanks, Jake. That makes me feel a lot better. I'll have to introduce Bess to the officer on each shift so she doesn't keep barking her head off."

Seeing the duffel bags on the backseat of her car, Jake asked if he could carry them inside.

As much as she trusted Jake, at this point she didn't even want to tell him what was in them. "That would be good. They're kind of heavy. I brought home some files to work on. I won't be back in the office for a couple of days. I want to be here when the locks are changed and when they upgrade my pathetic alarm system that Lanning got around so easily."

68

Detective Billy Tryon returned to the courthouse at eight thirty on Monday evening to drop off some of the physical evidence from the Kirk homicide. He had stayed at the crime scene from the beginning and went back and forth among the three houses, supervising the collection of evidence. Most of his time was spent in the Kirk home and garage.

After he spoke to Emily in Lanning's kitchen, he did not want to encounter her again. When she left around six, he asked Jake Rosen where she was going. Jake told him that Emily only said she had to get out for a while.

Billy was pretty sure she had gone to the office. His cousin Ted had told him that after Easton's outburst in court, Emily had informed him she was going to retrace every step in the case.

Ted heatedly told Billy that he had been a half inch away from forbidding her to spend any more time on it, but was afraid she might end up signing an ethics complaint against him. "If she did that, I can assure you that I won't be the next attorney general," he had railed.

From his vantage point in the Kirk house, Billy waited to see when Emily would come back. She returned about seven thirty and he saw her talking to

Jake Rosen in the driveway again. He didn't like the way they always seemed so cozy. Then he watched as Jake lugged two heavy-looking duffel bags into her house.

When Jake came back out, Billy called him over. "What was in those bags?" he demanded.

"Emily is going to take a couple of days off and she wanted to bring some files home to work on. Why would that bother you?"

"I just don't like her attitude about anything," Tryon snapped. "All right. I'm out of here. I'm going to take the evidence bags back to the office, then go home."

On the drive back to the courthouse, Billy Tryon was in a rage. She's trying to undo that verdict and she's trying to blame me. I'm not going to let that happen.

She's not going to destroy me.

And she's not going to destroy Ted.

69

After he spoke to Belle Garcia, Michael Gordon couldn't dial Richard Moore's number fast enough.

"Hi, Mike." Moore sounded upbeat. "I saw you at the courthouse today, but I never got a chance to talk to you. As soon as Easton's sentence was done, I raced over to the jail to tell Gregg what happened. He needed to hear something positive, and I think for the first time since the verdict he has some semblance of hope."

"Well, he may have a lot more soon," Mike said emphatically. "That's why I'm calling you now. I just got off the phone with a woman who gave me information about Easton. If she's telling the truth, it will blow this case apart."

When he relayed the contents of his conversation with Belle Garcia, Richard's reaction was exactly what he had expected.

"Mike, if this woman is credible, and if she's got a receipt and a telephone book, I think I can get Gregg out on bail while it's investigated further." Richard's voice became increasingly animated. "And if all this is true, I don't think he'll just get a new trial. I don't believe Emily Wallace would seek to try this again. I think she would move before Judge Stevens to vacate the verdict and dismiss the indictment."

"That's the way I see it," Mike agreed. "These people will be here in a little while. We'll know very soon where we're going with this. If they have what they claim they have, I'm putting them on *Courtside* tonight, and I'd like you to be on with them."

"Mike, I'd be glad to, but I have to tell you that I have very mixed feelings towards these people. I don't know if I can be civil to them. Of course, I'm ecstatic for Gregg if this pans out. On the other hand, I am outraged that this guy would sit on this information because he might have to pay some back taxes. It's a disgrace and that's the kindest word I can think of."

"Look, Richard, I completely understand how you feel. They should have come forward sooner and I am sure you will say that tonight. But if you come on the program and just attack them, it's not going to help Gregg. And the last thing you want to do is scare off anybody else out there who's also been afraid to speak up for whatever reason."

"I hear what you're saying. I won't attack them, Mike," Richard answered. "Maybe I'll even kiss them. But I still think it's a disgrace."

"It's an even bigger disgrace if Jimmy Easton was coached by someone to tell that story," Mike reminded him.

"Emily Wallace would never do that," Moore insisted.

"I didn't say she personally did, but look at it this way:

When all this comes out, won't they want to file perjury charges against Easton?"

"I'm sure they will."

"Richard, trust me, if someone in the prosecutor's office or some police officer fed him information to bolster his testimony, he'll turn that person in. Then he'll swear that he was threatened with the maximum sentence on his burglary if he didn't agree to lie on the witness stand."

"That I can't wait to see," Moore said vehemently.

"I'll call you back after I talk to the Garcia couple. God, I hope this is the answer."

At ten minutes of seven, Belle and Sal Garcia arrived at Michael's office. For the next half hour, with a young associate producer sitting in as a witness, he listened to their story.

"It was a heavy marble standing lamp," Sal explained, nervously. "A guy who had a little antique repair shop on Eighty-sixth Street used to have me make deliveries for him. Jimmy Easton was working for me that day. We carried the lamp up together.

"The housekeeper told us to put it in the living room. Then the phone rang. She asked us to wait a minute and went into the kitchen to answer it. I told Jimmy to wait for her to sign the receipt. I remember I didn't want to get a ticket for being double-parked. So I left him alone in the living room. I don't know how long he was in there by himself. Then I got a call last week from my friend Rudy Sling."

Rudy Sling, Mike thought. His wife Reeney is the one who phoned to say she could tell us where Jimmy worked.

"Rudy reminded me that when I moved him up to Yonkers, Easton was on the job, and Rudy's wife, Reeney, caught him going through the dresser drawers. So my guess is that Jimmy may have opened that squeaky drawer looking for anything he could steal while I was on my way to the truck and the housekeeper was in the kitchen on the phone." Sal swallowed nervously and reached for the glass of water Liz had brought in for him.

Reeney Sling and her husband are coming in tomorrow morning, Mike thought. They can back up this story. All the pieces fit. As the welcome information kept sinking in, Mike had the incongruous thought that now Gregg and he could play handball again at the Athletic Club.

Sal gulped the entire glass of water and sighed. "I guess that's it, Mike. Now you know as much as I do about that delivery, except I dug out some receipts for other jobs I did for that antique repair place, to show you that this one isn't a phony."

Mike examined the delivery receipt with the housekeeper's signature, and the pocket phone book with Jimmy Easton's name scrawled in it. Then he glanced at the dozen other receipts Sal had brought him.

It's all here, he thought. It's all here. Barely able to

maintain his professional reserve, he told them that he wanted them to appear on *Courtside* tonight.

"That would be fine," Belle agreed. "Sal, it's a good thing I made you wear your good suit and tie, and Mama told me to wear this outfit!"

Sal shook his head vehemently. "No. Absolutely not. Belle, you convinced me to come here and I did but I don't want to go on that show and have everybody hating me. Forget it. I'm not going!"

"Yes, you are, Sal," Belle said firmly. "You're no different than lots of other people who would have been afraid of getting into trouble by telling the truth. In fact, you're a good example to them. You made a big mistake and now you are correcting it. I made a big mistake, too. I've been sure for over a week that Jimmy Easton worked for you and I should have gone through those boxes sooner. That trial would have ended before Gregg Aldrich had to listen to that guilty verdict if both you and I had done the right thing. Most people will at least try to understand. And I'm going on the show whether you do or not."

"Mr. Garcia," Mike said, "I hope you will reconsider. You were in the Aldrich living room with Easton on exactly the same date that he testified under oath that he met there with Gregg Aldrich to plan the murder of his wife. It is vital that people hear that directly from you."

Sal looked at Belle's worried but determined expression and the tears she was trying to blink back. She was scared to death. They were sitting side by side on the couch in Mike's office. He put his arm around her. "If you can stand the heat you'll get, I can, too," he said, tenderly. "I'm not going to let you go on alone."

"That's great," Mike exclaimed, jumping up to shake their hands. "I'm sure you haven't had dinner yet. I'll have my secretary bring you to the conference room and she'll order some food in for you."

After they left his office, he called Richard Moore. "Come on in as fast as you can get here," he said, enthusiastically. "Richard, these people are telling the truth. The delivery receipt is signed by Gregg's housekeeper, the one who died. I don't mind telling you I'm about to cry."

"Me, too, Mike, me, too." Richard Moore's voice also had a catch in it. "You know something? I just started believing in miracles again. I'll leave in a couple of minutes. It shouldn't take more than an hour to get into the city. I'll be there well before nine." Then his voice broke. "First, I'll send Cole to the jail to tell Gregg what's going on. And I'll call Alice and Katie."

"I only wish I could be there with them when they hear this," Mike said, thinking back to that awful moment in court when the word "guilty" had been repeated twelve times.

"I'm going to make one other important call," Richard said, his tone now quietly firm. "Emily Wallace. And you know what, Mike? I don't think that she's going to be surprised."

70

Zach turned off the television after the segment about him was finished. Seeing the composite again that was so similar to the way he looked now terrified him. He knew it was too dangerous to stay here another minute. He'd noticed that the clerk had a little TV in his office, and it was obvious that he was not all that busy. If he was still there at six o'clock, he could easily have been watching that channel. Or maybe he was at home, sitting in front of his television. Either way, if he saw the composite again, even his slow brain might start working.

The van was in the complimentary parking area next to the lodge. Luckily, the clerk had not asked him for the license plate when he had checked in. If the police ever came here looking for him, somebody might be able to tell them the make and color of the van, but he doubted that anyone would remember the license plate number.

Frantically weighing his options, Zach decided to pull down the shades, turn on some lights, and leave. At least until tomorrow, that would give the impression that he was still here.

Immensely frustrated, he knew that if the clerk hadn't

noticed him, this cabin might have been relatively safe for at least a few weeks. It was better to get down to North Carolina, find a place to stay, and then drive back up to Glen Rock to take care of Emily in a few months, when the heat was off.

But then something told him again that his luck was running out. Wherever he went, he knew that at any moment there could be a police car behind him, with flashing lights and siren blaring, forcing him to the side of the road.

He thought back to Charlotte divorcing him, and getting a judge to decide she should get his house. He thought of Lou and Wilma, and how good he had been to both of them, and yet both of them had left him.

By now Emily must know he had been spying on her and going through her house. He hoped she understood the reason that he had left the intercom system in his kitchen: It was his message to her that he would be back.

He could imagine what was happening there now. Emily's sure to have a guard outside, in case I come back looking for her. But who's to say that I won't find her someplace else? And who's to say I can't sneak back into the neighborhood again?

Zach had not unpacked a single thing from the van. Now as he got into it, having decided that he would drive through northern New Jersey to the New York Thruway and find a motel in one of those sleepy hamlets on the way to Albany, he had a thought that pleased him.

He had taken Emily's fancy nightgown with him last week. It was obvious she'd never worn it. She should wear it, Zach thought.

Maybe it would be nice to tuck it around her after she's dead.

71

Emily pulled down the shades in her kitchen and put on water to boil for pasta. Energy food, she told herself. That's what I need. Bless Gladys for trying to make sure that I don't starve. Her cleaning woman sometimes brought in containers of her homemade pasta sauce or chicken soup and left them frozen in the refrigerator. Now the pasta sauce was defrosting in the microwave oven.

While it was cooking, Emily made a salad and set it on a tray to take into the living room. Tonight was not the night to start on the Aldrich files, she decided. Her nerves were simply too raw. Yesterday afternoon I walked past Madeline Kirk's house and thought how I didn't want to end up a recluse like her. While I was thinking that, she was wrapped in plastic bags in the trunk of her car.

The pleasant autumn day had turned into a sharply cold night. She had changed into pajamas and a robe and turned up the heat, but even so could not get warm. What did Nana used to say? Emily asked herself. I know: "I'm chilled to the bone." I think after all these years I finally know what she meant.

Bess was asleep now on a pillow on the kitchen

floor. As she took warm Italian bread from the oven and poured herself a glass of wine, Emily kept glancing at the dog for reassurance that she was still there. If that guy Zach tries to come back, Bess will warn me, she thought. She'll bark her head off. But of course the police officer is outside guarding the house. My own private bodyguard, she thought. Just what I needed.

Then she wondered if Bess might actually be *glad* to see Zach. She'd probably think he was there to take her for a walk. He even took care of her while I visited Dad and then Jack. My helpful neighbor. Emily shivered at the memory of coming home and finding Zach sitting in near darkness on the porch with Bess on his lap. I was lucky he didn't kill me that night, she thought.

The comforting aroma of the marinara sauce filled the kitchen and the spaghetti was ready. Emily dumped the spaghetti in a strainer, transferred a portion of it into a bowl, took the sauce out of the microwave, and spooned it over the pasta.

She carried the tray into the living room, placed it on the wide tray table in front of her favorite chair, and sat down. Bess, hearing her move, woke up, trotted into the living room, and settled beside her. It was quarter of eight. I'll find something worth watching until *Courtside* comes on, Emily thought. There's bound to be a panel discussion about Jimmy Easton's outburst. After that, I'm sure the news will have plenty of coverage about Zach Lanning.

Jimmy Easton and Zach Lanning. A great combination for my viewing pleasure, she thought as she began

to twirl the spaghetti onto her fork. Michael Gordon
was in the courtroom today. I'm sure he'll show a clip of
Easton's speech. "I did what I was supposed to do." How
much of Easton's testimony had been fed to him?

From where she was sitting she could see the duffel
bags with the Aldrich files stacked against the wall in
the dining room. Tomorrow morning, early, I'll start on
them, she decided.

The phone rang. For a moment Emily was tempted
to let the answering machine pick it up, but then she
realized it might be her father. He's bound to hear about
Madeline Kirk and be worrying about me.

But the caller was Richard Moore, not her father.
"Emily, I heard about that serial killer and that he murdered your neighbor, but Cole just told me he was also
stalking you. I'm so sorry. You've got to be pretty rattled
about that."

"That's a good way of putting it, Richard, and yes, I
am. There's a cop on guard full time at the house."

"I would hope so. Emily, you'd better watch *Courtside*
tonight."

"I was planning to watch it. I'm sure it's all about my
witness, Jimmy Easton."

"It is all about him, Emily, but there's a lot more
than what happened in court. Mike has a guy coming
on the show who has proof that Jimmy made a delivery
to Gregg's apartment the very day he swore he got the
ransom money."

For a long minute Emily simply could not speak.
Then she said quietly, "If that's the case, I want those

people in my office tomorrow morning. I want to see that proof and if it's legitimate, Gregg Aldrich will get out on bail, then we'll take it from there."

"That's what I expected you to say, Emily."

A little more than an hour later, her dinner barely touched, her arm around Bess, Emily watched *Courtside*. When it was over, she went into the dining room, turned on the light, and pulled the first batch of files from the duffel bag.

She did not go to bed at all that night.

72

The inmates at the state prison filed into breakfast on Tuesday morning at seven A.M. Jimmy Easton had not slept well. He had already been hassled by some of the other inmates about being a snitch. "You'd sell out your mother, Jimmy," one of them had shouted to him.

"He already did," another one yelled back.

I'll call Moore this morning as soon as they let me get to a phone, Jimmy thought. When I spill the beans to him, I know they'll try to bring me up on perjury charges. They'll want to bury me, but they still need my testimony. Moore will tell them to give me a good deal. So when I make the prosecutor's office look dumb, the guys here will get a laugh out of it and get off my back.

He wasn't hungry, but he ate breakfast anyhow. Oatmeal, toast, juice, and coffee. He didn't talk to the guys on either side of him at the table. Or they didn't talk to him. No problem.

Back in his cell he started to feel lousy. He lay down on his bunk but the burning feeling in his gut wouldn't go away. He closed his eyes and drew up his knees as the burning became hot coals ripping up his insides. "Guard," he called, feebly. "Guard."

Jimmy Easton realized he had been poisoned.

His final thought was that his prison term had been shortened.

73

On Tuesday morning, a nine o'clock meeting took place in Prosecutor Ted Wesley's office. Richard and Cole Moore had brought along Sal and Belle Garcia to repeat their story. Richard had presented the receipt and the phone book to Wesley and Emily.

"We will also obtain the sworn affidavits of a couple who live in Yonkers, Rudy and Reeney Sling," Richard Moore said. "When Jimmy Easton was helping to move them into their residence in Yonkers nearly three years ago, Mrs. Sling found him going through the dresser drawers, obviously looking for something to steal."

The people on the panel at *Courtside* last night had been so kind, Belle thought, but it had been a shock to learn that Reeney had tried to cash in on the fact they knew Jimmy Easton worked for Sal. Some friends! she sniffed. When I think of how Sal moved them for free when they had to get out of their apartment and couldn't afford to pay him! And Mike told me Reeney will get some of the reward because it's important that Jimmy Easton tried to steal from them. He said that it shows a pattern.

Emily Wallace was even prettier in person than on

television, Belle decided. When you think of all the trouble she's had, poor thing. Being a war widow. The heart transplant. Living next door to a serial killer who was spying on her. She must be very strong. I hope she gets a break. It's not her fault she worked so hard to convict Gregg. That was her job. And she's been so nice to us. Someone else would be furious that all that work she did at the trial was wasted.

But someone is furious about it, she decided: the prosecutor. She didn't like *him* at all. He'd hardly even acknowledged Sal and me when we got here. You'd think we were the criminals. She'd heard that he was going to be appointed attorney general of the whole country. Now he was glaring at Emily when she said she wanted his okay to go to Judge Stevens and get Gregg Aldrich released on bail.

I'd love to meet Gregg, Belle thought. But he'd probably be mad at us, even though we finally spoke up. Maybe I should write him a letter of apology? Or send him one of those nice "Thinking of You" cards?

Prosecutor Wesley was saying, "We will consent to having bail reinstated. However, Richard, even if Jimmy Easton lied about having access to the Aldrich apartment, it doesn't mean that Gregg Aldrich did not solicit him to kill Natalie Raines."

That's ridiculous, Belle thought. She could see that remark made Richard Moore really angry because his face got all red. Then Moore said, "I doubt any thinking person would believe that Jimmy Easton delivered a lamp to the Aldrich apartment at three P.M. and was back an hour later to get a down payment on a murder contract."

"Maybe not," Ted Wesley snapped. "But don't forget that before Easton came forward, Gregg Aldrich was the only suspect in this case, and for my money he still is the only suspect, and the right one."

He's not going to admit how wrong he's been, Belle decided, then watched as Emily Wallace stood up. She's so graceful, Belle thought. That red jacket is so nice with her dark hair. She's wearing a turtleneck under it. I wonder if the heart surgery left a big scar?

Emily looked at Belle and Sal. "I know it took courage for you to come forward. I'm very glad you did."

She turned to Richard. "I'm sure Judge Stevens is in. We can walk down to his chambers and talk to him. I'll call the jail and tell them to bring Mr. Aldrich right over. Then we can go on the record about the bail."

Her tone changed as she addressed the prosecutor. "As you know, I'm taking a couple of days off. I'll be home most of the time if you need to contact me. Or you can always call my cell phone."

Belle noticed that the prosecutor acted as though he hadn't heard her.

Boy, I'd hate to work for *him*, she thought.

74

At ten thirty A.M., Judge Stevens reinstated bail for Gregg Aldrich.

Forty-five minutes later, after phoning Alice and Katie, Gregg was having coffee with Richard Moore in a diner near the courthouse. "How long was I there, Richard? About ninety hours? I don't even remember the weekend, but it was still the longest ninety hours of my life."

"I can understand that. But you won't ever be there again, Gregg. You can count on that."

Gregg looked tired. "Can I? That's the trouble. I'm back to being the chief suspect in Natalie's death. I'll always be the 'person of interest' to the police. What's to keep somebody else from coming up with some wild story? Remember I still can't account for those two hours when I was out jogging the morning Natalie died. I don't have a witness who saw me in the park. Suppose someone in New Jersey comes up with the story that they saw me in Natalie's neighborhood in Closter that morning or in her driveway. What happens then? Another trial?"

Alarmed, Richard Moore stared across the table.

"Gregg, are you suggesting you might have driven to New Jersey that day?"

"No, of course not. My point is that I'm still so vulnerable. I must have seen someone I knew that day when I was jogging, but I was sick with worry about Natalie. I think that's the reason I was so tuned out."

"Gregg, don't torture yourself thinking that someone is going to appear out of the blue and say they saw you around Natalie's house that morning." Richard Moore sounded unconvincing even to his own ears. Not likely, but it could happen, he thought.

"Richard, hear me out. On the witness stand I testified that when I looked in the window of the Cape Cod house I could tell that Natalie was terribly upset. She was practically in a fetal position on the couch. On the drive home I was desperately worried about her even though I had begun to realize that I was ready to let her go. I was tired of the drama. On that drive from the Cape, I was even remembering how much fun I had with Kathleen and thinking I wanted that kind of relationship again."

"Maybe you should have said that on the stand," Richard said quietly.

"How would that have sounded? Richard, I had a lot of time to think sitting in that cell yesterday. Suppose Natalie was afraid of someone? No one ever saw the man she had hinted she was seeing and maybe he doesn't exist. Maybe she said that to get me to stop calling her. But suppose she really was seeing someone, and that someone was lying in wait for her when she got home?"

"Gregg, where are we going with this?"

"I'll tell you where. I'm not made of money, and with all due respect you didn't come cheap. But you have that private investigator, Ben Smith, who works for you, don't you?"

"Yes, I do."

"I'll pay him, or someone else you hire, to open up this case and start from scratch. I've been the 'person of interest' long enough. I'll never be free until Natalie's killer is found and I'm exonerated."

Richard Moore took the last sip of his coffee and signaled for the check. "Gregg, everything you said about being vulnerable is absolutely true. When Ben was investigating to try to find whoever Natalie may have been seeing, he came up blank. But just the way the Garcia couple was sitting out there on this lifesaving information, so may somebody else. We start searching today."

Gregg stretched his hand across the table. "Richard, I'm glad you agree with me. If you hadn't, this would be the last coffee we'd share. And now I want to get home, kiss my kid and Alice, and take the longest shower of my life. I feel as if the smell of that jail cell is sticking to my skin."

75

⌇

I know I should feel tired but I don't, Emily thought as she drove down the West Side Highway in Manhattan. There's probably no connection between Natalie's death and the fact that her roommate, Jamie Evans, was murdered in Central Park nearly twenty years ago. The police believe that Jamie was the victim of the same mugger who assaulted three other women in the park around that time.

But she was the *only* one who was murdered.

Alice Mills has never believed there was even the possibility of a connection between the two murders, and there probably wasn't. Natalie never even met the guy Jamie was dating. She only saw his picture once and wasn't even sure if it was still in Jamie's wallet when she was killed.

Two and a half years ago, in the early stages of the investigation into Natalie's murder, Billy Tryon had gone to the Manhattan District Attorney's Office to review the reports in the Evans case and determine if there could be even a remote connection. He had copied the major reports and had brought them back to New Jersey. Included had been a police artist's sketch of a possible suspect, which had been drawn from Natalie's description of the picture she had seen in Jamie's wallet.

The sketch depicted a white male in his midthirties with longish blond hair. He was attractive in a scholarly way, with thick brows and rimless glasses covering oval-shaped brown eyes.

The District Attorney's Office was located in lower Manhattan at 1 Hogan Place. Emily parked in a garage nearby and walked through the crowded streets to that address. She had phoned ahead to the Captain of Detectives, who had assigned veteran Detective Steve Murphy to retrieve the Jamie Evans file and assist Emily when she arrived.

In the lobby, a clerk called up to Murphy, who verified the appointment. Emily was then permitted to pass through security. The detective was waiting for her when she got off the elevator on the ninth floor. A pleasant-faced man of about fifty with close-cropped hair, he greeted her with a warm smile.

"Haven't you got enough crime in New Jersey without coming over here to solve our twenty-year-old cases?" he asked genially.

Emily liked him immediately. "We've got more than enough crime in New Jersey," she agreed. "Feel free to solve ours anytime."

"I have the Evans file in one of our offices near the squad room."

"Fine."

"I took a look at it while I was waiting for you,"

Murphy said, as they walked down the hall. "We figured it was a robbery gone wrong. She probably resisted giving him anything. Three other women were mugged in the park around that same time. Evans was the only one killed."

"That's what I understand," Emily told him.

"Here we are. Not the most palatial surroundings."

"I assure you, neither are ours." Emily followed Murphy into a small room furnished with only a battered desk, two unsteady-looking chairs, and a file cabinet.

"The Evans file is on the desk. Take your time. We can copy anything you want. I'll be back in a minute. I need to make a couple of calls."

"Of course. I promise I won't be too long."

Emily didn't know quite what she was looking for. I'm like the judge who was trying to decide a pornography case, she thought. He said, "I can't define it, but I know it when I see it."

She read quickly through the stack of detective reports in the file. She had already seen a number of them, since they had been in the packet that Billy Tryon had brought back. Jamie Evans had been attacked early in the morning and strangled. She had been dragged from the jogging path to an area behind thick bushes. Her watch, pendant, and ring were gone. Her wallet was emptied of cash and credit cards, and was discovered on the grass beside her. Her credit cards have never been used.

At the time of her roommate's murder, Natalie Raines

gave the police a physical description of the man in the picture she had seen only once in Jamie's wallet. She told them that Jamie had confided to her that the man she was secretly seeing was married, but had promised to get a divorce. Natalie had indicated that she believed the man, whom she had never met and whose name she didn't even know, was stringing Jamie along.

Natalie had suspected so strongly that Jamie's death may have been caused by this mysterious boyfriend that the detectives had taken her down to the District Attorney's Office so that they could do the sketch.

So far, nothing, Emily thought. I've seen all this before. But then when she got to the police artist's sketch, her mouth went dry. The sketch in the folder Billy Tryon had brought to New Jersey was not the same as the one in the New York file.

This man was handsome, about thirty years old with blue eyes, a straight nose, a firm mouth and a full head of charcoal brown hair.

This was the picture of a man with a distinct resemblance to a younger Billy Tryon. Emily stared at it, stunned. Noted on the sketch was one sentence. "May be known by the nickname 'Jess.' "

Steve Murphy was back. "Find any good clues we can work on?"

Emily tried to keep her voice steady as she pointed to the sketch. "I hate to say it, but my files may have gotten mixed up. This isn't the one I have in my file. I'm sure that the original your artist made is kept somewhere."

"Sure. You know the system. The sketch is made and

copies are rolled off. We can check against the original. No problem. But I have to tell you, my guess is that if there's been a mixup it happened in your office. I was around when that girl was killed. This is definitely the one I remember being in the file. Is there anything else you want to copy?"

"The whole file if you don't mind."

Murphy looked at her. His voice crisp, he asked, "Are you seeing something that might help us to solve this case?"

"I don't know," Emily said. But as she waited for the file to be copied, she wondered what else is in the Evans file that Billy didn't bring back. Could Billy have been the mysterious boyfriend that Natalie suspected of murdering her friend? Had Billy Tryon ever met Natalie Raines?

And if so, was that why he may have been eager to piece together Jimmy Easton's story and have Gregg Aldrich convicted of Natalie's murder?

Everything is beginning to make sense, Emily thought.

It's not a pretty picture but the parts may be falling into place.

76

Where better to hide than in his own house?

On Tuesday morning, the idea struck Zach like a thunderbolt. He knew the routine. The police would have stormed in there like gangbusters looking for him. He could just picture them, guns drawn, afraid for their lives, going from room to room, then disappointed that they didn't reel in the big fish.

If it weren't for the worry over Henry Link's nosy son-in-law going to the police about the van, he could have lasted for a while in this shabby motel thirty miles north of Glen Rock. He'd had a fairly decent sleep last night and he felt pretty safe. The owner, a shuffling old guy with thick glasses, would never connect him with the picture on his small-screen television.

But what good was that when the van got reported and every cop within a hundred miles was looking for it?

He still had the option of driving straight down to North Carolina right now and trying to disappear into the waves of newcomers settling there. But the need to go back to Emily was overwhelming. He'd sleep here tonight, he decided, pay for the next few days and leave the van here. In the morning, he would take a bus to the Port Authority in New York, then another one out to Glen Rock after dark.

He'd slip through the backyards in his neighborhood, and with any luck his extra key to the rental house would still work. He could go in the back door and wait it out. Of course they'd have a guard for Emily. He knew that routine. Of course she would have had her locks changed. But she always opened the door to let Bess out in the backyard for a minute or two before she went to bed.

Of course Bess would bark when she saw him. But he'd buy those treats she loved so much and throw a couple of them on the ground. That's all the time he'd need to force his way in.

It was a good plan.

And he knew he could pull it off.

77

Emily drove directly home after she left the DA's office. I have to be very careful, she thought, and I have to be very sure. Page by page, word by word, I'll compare the reports that Billy brought back two and a half years ago to the entire Jamie Evans homicide file that I have now.

The sketches are completely different. Steve Murphy confirmed that only one sketch had been done during the Evans investigation and that was the one that I saw this morning. What other reports didn't Billy bring back? What else am I going to find?

As she turned onto her block, she saw that the yellow tape was still around Madeline Kirk's home, but it had been completely removed from both the front of Zach's rental and her own house. I can't wait to see who the new tenant will be, she thought wearily. Whoever it is has to be a vast improvement over the last one.

She waved to the police officer in the squad car at the curb, admitting to herself that it was very comforting to see him there. The locksmith and the alarm people were scheduled to come later in the day. Yesterday she had arranged it that way so she would have a few quiet hours with the Aldrich file before they arrived.

Richard's call last night certainly changed all that,

Emily mused as she parked and got out of the car. Before that call I never would have dreamt that I'd be in Ted Wesley's office this morning, then moving to have Gregg Aldrich released on bail. And when I drove to New York, I certainly never thought I'd find out that my detective has been tampering with evidence.

She went into the house and was greeted with a noisy welcome from Bess. "Bark as loud as you want, Bess," she said, as she scooped the little dog up in her arms. "And no, we're not going for a walk. I'll let you out in the back and that's it for now."

She unbolted the door from the porch and stood on the steps as Bess raced around the yard, her paws making scraping sounds on the fallen leaves. The day had started out with brilliant sunshine but now the sky was becoming overcast and there was a feeling of impending rain.

Emily waited for five minutes then called, "Want a treat, Bess?" That does the trick every time, she thought as Bess willingly scampered back inside. After carefully rebolting the door, Emily rewarded Bess with the promised treat and put the kettle on.

She knew that she needed a jolt of coffee. If I don't have some I'll fall asleep standing up. And I'm hungry. I never *did* eat dinner last night. Richard's call took care of that.

Thanks to Sunday's food shopping, the refrigerator was well stocked. She decided on a ham and cheese sandwich. When she'd made it and poured the coffee, she sat at the kitchen table to have a quick lunch. By the time she finished the second cup of coffee, the caffeine had kicked in and she felt clearheaded as she considered what to do next.

She knew what would happen if she confronted Billy with the sketch he had brought back from New York. He would explode and rant that it wasn't the one he had put in the Aldrich file and obviously some stupid clerk had mixed them up. But why would our office have a second sketch from the Manhattan DA with the same date from nearly twenty years ago unless Billy had brought it back?

He could certainly say that the sketch I have now may have a general resemblance to him but also to loads of other people. He would also point out scathingly that the artist had worked from a description given by a woman who had never even met the person she was talking about.

If I go to Ted now, especially since he's so angry about the Jimmy Easton mess, he'll probably tell me that I somehow mixed them up myself.

I have considered every possibility, Emily concluded. For whatever reason, Billy removed the copy of the original sketch when he brought the file back to New Jersey and then managed to get a second one created as a substitute. That's called tampering with evidence. He never expected that I would ever go to New York to look at the file myself. But I did.

However this turns out, when I'm done with it, I am going to go back through every file that he has ever handled where there have been complaints about him. And that's whether his cousin, our about-to-be attorney general, likes it or not.

The front doorbell rang.

Bess began barking frantically. Emily carried her to the door. It was the locksmith, a man in his sixties wearing jeans and a Giants football sweatshirt. "I understand you want me to check everything, ma'am, all the doors and windows."

"Yes, I do. And I want the strongest locks you can give me."

"Don't blame you. People need them these days. That's for sure. Just look at what happened to your neighbor across the street. Poor old lady. Hear the nut who killed her got in a back window, no problem, and she didn't have a security system."

"I'm having a new one put in today," Emily said. "The technician should be here soon. I wanted both of you to meet my dog, Bess, so that she won't bother you while you're working."

The locksmith eyed Bess. "In the old days a barking dog was considered all the protection you needed. He reached down to rub her head. "Hello, Bess. Hey, you don't scare me."

Emily went back into the kitchen and put the dishes she had used in the dishwasher and then, not wanting to be around the locksmith, whom she suspected of being a talker, went up to her bedroom and shut the door. While she changed into slacks and a sweater, she continued to go back and forth in her mind about how deeply

Billy Tryon might be involved, not only with Easton in the Aldrich case but also in the death of Jamie Evans.

Was it possible that Billy Tryon was Jamie's mystery boyfriend? He definitely resembles the man Natalie described to the police artist. He's been divorced twice. The rumor is that both wives got sick of his affairs. Jamie Evans was a young actress. I understand from the scuttlebutt that his girlfriends are usually in some kind of show business. For heaven's sake, I just *met* one of them last week.

Billy was assigned to head the Raines murder investigation from the beginning. And then it came up that her roommate had been murdered many years before. He made sure that he was the one who would go to New York and go through that file.

If he did kill Jamie Evans, he must have been frantic when he saw that sketch. So he decided to replace it before he brought back the file.

The doorbell rang again. This time it was the alarm company team. After making the necessary introductions to Bess, Emily decided that there was no way that she was going to get any work done at home this afternoon. My bones are aching, she thought. Maybe I can get an appointment for a massage.

I'm just not sure what to do next. One thing I can do is try to find out if anyone knows if Billy ever used the nickname "Jess."

And there is one other thing that I can follow up on, she thought. If Natalie Raines was really as frightened as Gregg Aldrich testified she appeared to be when he was looking through the window at the Cape house, could that be why she drove there at midnight after her final performance in *Streetcar*? Not just to get away from it all, but because she was escaping from somebody who terrified her?

There's only one person who might be able to help me find the answer to that question, Emily thought. Natalie's mother. I never really asked her if she was surprised that Natalie had gone to the Cape so suddenly.

Her cell phone rang before she could try to reach Alice Mills. It was Jake Rosen. "Emily, we just got a call from Newark. Jimmy Easton is dead."

"Jimmy Easton dead! Jake, what happened to him?" Emily could hear Jimmy telling the judge only twenty-four hours ago that he was afraid to go back to prison because the other inmates hated a snitch.

"They're pretty sure he was poisoned. The autopsy will tell." Jake paused, then said, "Emily, you know as well as I do that we're going to have a lot of problems over this. Some people will believe it was prison justice for cooperating. Others will think that someone took care of him because he wouldn't keep his mouth shut about the Aldrich case."

"And they'll be right," Emily said. "Plenty of defendants cooperate to get reduced sentences and they don't end up dead. Jake, I'd stake my life that Billy Tryon had something to do with this."

"For God's sake, Emily, be careful. You can't go around making statements like that!" Jake's tone was both shocked and worried.

"All right," Emily answered. "Consider it unsaid. But I'm allowed to think it. Jake, let me know whatever else you hear. I suppose that I should come into my office but I am not going to. I'll get a lot more done here. Bye."

Emily broke the connection and then dialed 411. She knew that Alice's number was in the Manhattan directory and that it was easier to just dial information than to go back downstairs and pull it out of the file. As she was dialing, she thought, Wait a minute, I do remember it. 212-555-4237! She pressed the numbers, thinking that while she usually had a pretty good memory, this was *really* good. But on the other hand, maybe I'll get connected to a dry cleaner.

The phone rang three times and then a message came on. "This is Alice Mills. I can be reached at 212-555-8456." She's probably been staying with Katie at the Aldrich apartment, Emily thought.

Emily's mind was filled with the memory of the day Alice Mills had come to her office and had sat across the table from her in her black suit, heartbroken but composed. I put my arms around her before she left, Emily remembered.

I wanted so much to help her stop hurting.

Realizing the incredible irony of dialing the apartment of a defendant whom she had just prosecuted and whose case was still open, Emily heard the generic voice say that no one was available and to please leave a message. "Alice, it's Emily. I really need to talk to you. On the stand Gregg testified that he thought that Natalie seemed frightened. You never brought that up so maybe you don't agree. It just occurred to me that she went to Cape Cod right after her last night at the theatre. I know that people she worked with gave statements but I want to look into that area again. I think that maybe we will find something important there."

A roundabout way of saying that maybe Billy Tryon was dating an actress in *Streetcar* and had happened to run into Natalie that last night. And maybe she had recognized him from a long time ago.

Her cell phone rang. It was Ted Wesley's secretary. Her voice nervous, she said, "Emily, the prosecutor wants you in his office now.

"And he said to bring back any files that you took from this office."

78

Forty-five minutes later, Emily, Billy Tryon, and Jake Rosen were in Ted Wesley's office. Wesley, white with rage, stared at them with uncontrolled disdain in his expression. "May I say that I have never seen a sloppier, more disorganized, careless, and wasteful series of events than what you three have managed to achieve. Billy, did you in any way help Jimmy Easton to put together the story that he so convincingly delivered on the witness stand?"

"No, Ted, I did not." Billy's tone and manner were subdued. "But wait. Let me be exact. When Easton told me about writing the letter to Aldrich to say he wasn't going to go through with their contract, but he also wasn't going to return the five thousand that Aldrich had already given him, I said something like you must have considered it a nonrefundable advance. He laughed and then he repeated that phrase on the stand."

"That's not what I'm talking about," Wesley snapped. "Are you telling me that he had his whole story ready to spill to you and that all of the details came from him?"

"Absolutely," Billy replied emphatically. "Ted, look at the facts, even if Emily won't. The minute Easton got grabbed coming out of that burglary, he said to the local cops that he had information on the Aldrich case. They called the office and I went right over there. Everything he said later checked out. He met Aldrich at the bar. Aldrich did call him on his phone. He described the interior of the Aldrich apartment. And he even knew about the infamous squeaky drawer."

"That's right, he knew about the squeaky drawer," Emily retorted. "And now Mr. Garcia has come forward to say that he made a delivery with Easton to the Aldrich apartment and that at some point Easton was left alone in the living room. He could have been trying to steal something by pulling out that drawer, then heard the noise.

"And what about the letter that he supposedly sent, the one you just admitted to helping him explain?" Emily asked him. "Was the entire letter your idea? It made Jimmy look better and it strengthened his story."

Before Billy could answer, Wesley looked at Jake Rosen. "You went out when Easton got arrested. What do you have to say?"

"Sir, I was there for most of that first meeting with Easton in the Old Tappan police station," Jake replied. "Billy didn't coach him." Jake looked at Emily. "Emily, I'm going to be frank. You and Billy have always rubbed each other the wrong way. But I really think that you are being unfair to him now."

"That's all I needed to hear, Jake. Thanks. You can go now," Wesley said sharply.

When the door closed behind Jake, Wesley looked at Emily. "I think it's clear Easton didn't need help putting together his story. He didn't need help because he was telling the truth about what he and Aldrich had done. And now, because of your total lack of judgment in responding to his genuine fear about going back to prison after cooperating, he is dead. Not to mention that Aldrich is out on bail and our case is probably wrecked. Why didn't you just agree to time served as his sentence and all of this could have been avoided?"

"Because he is a career criminal and he would have just gone back to breaking into people's homes," Emily replied firmly. "Maybe this time around someone would have gotten hurt."

Emily stiffened her back and continued. "And there's something else you apparently haven't considered. The jury heard he was going to get four years. If I had later agreed to time served as his sentence, Moore would file a motion for a new trial and argue that I knew and Jimmy knew all along he would get time served, and that the jury should have known that when they were evaluating his testimony. Moore would further argue that Easton would have said anything if he knew he would be getting out. There's no way the judge wouldn't grant that motion."

"Then you should have thought about that when you were negotiating with him before trial," Wesley snapped. "You knew he was a loose cannon and that he could turn on you later on. You should have just given him probation from the beginning. There was a lot of corroboration to his story, no matter what sentence he was going to get. Now the integrity of this office will not only be questioned, but actively maligned. The media is going to annihilate us."

Not knowing when she had first come to this meeting whether she would reveal them, Emily had kept the two sketches in a folder. She took them out and placed them in front of Wesley. "Maybe Detective Tryon can satisfactorily explain this. The sketch that I found in the New York file on Jamie Evans, the murdered roommate of Natalie Raines, was not the one that he brought back to this office. It has the same date on it but that's where the similarity ends. It's of an entirely different person."

As Wesley and Tryon angrily glared at her, Emily continued. "I know perfectly well Billy will claim that it was just a mix-up. But the detective at the Manhattan DA's office who showed me this file is sure there was only one sketch. I suggest to you that it was a deliberate attempt by Billy to keep the right sketch out of the Aldrich file."

Emily paused, not immediately knowing if she was going to say what she was thinking. She took a deep breath. "I also want to point out that the original sketch bears a rather obvious resemblance to Billy Tryon, which may be why he desperately wanted it to never reach our file."

Ted Wesley took the sketches and studied them. "Emily, you are now making not only serious accusations, but also scurrilous and even hysterical ones. Do I understand correctly that Natalie Raines never even met this man, and that this sketch was drawn from her recollection of a supposed wallet picture she may have seen once?"

"This is exactly what I expected that you would say," Emily responded defiantly. "It is my position that not only does this sketch strongly resemble Billy, but that there is no question these sketches were deliberately switched by him to hide something terribly important. And I'm not going to stop until I find out what that is."

"I have had enough of this," Wesley shouted. "I've had enough of your attempts to vilify my finest detective. I've had enough of your attempts to destroy the Aldrich case, which you have almost certainly accomplished. And did it ever occur to you that the detective in New York could be wrong about there being only one sketch?

"I am ordering you to leave these files in my office. And don't touch them again! Go home and stay away from this office until I decide the appropriate sanctions for you. If the media calls you at home, you are forbidden to talk to them. Refer the calls directly to my office."

Wesley stood up. "Now get out."

Emily was surprised that he had not already fired her. "I'll get out, Ted. But just one more thought. Ask around and see if Detective Tryon was ever known by the nickname 'Jess.' And think back yourself if you ever heard that. After all, he *is* your cousin."

For several moments they stared at each other, with no words being spoken. Then, ignoring Billy Tryon, Emily left Ted's office and walked out of the courthouse.

79

Zach decided to wait until midafternoon to take a bus to New York. He knew that the Port Authority was filled with undercover cops scanning the crowds for known criminals whose faces they had locked into their brains. Better to get there during rush hour, he decided.

He had lunch at the motel in the dreary little dump they called a grill. As he was finishing, six people came in. From their loud and excited conversation he gathered that they were going to a five o'clock wedding nearby. They've all checked in here, he thought. It's a good thing I'm getting out. He was sure that a couple of them were looking at him when he was paying the check and then leaving the grill.

Then outside he saw that their cars were parked on either side of his van. Another worry. One of them might remember having seen it, when the son-in-law calls the police and they start looking for it.

He was wearing a leather jacket, brown slacks, and a cap. That's the way they would describe him to the police.

When he left, Zach was carrying his money, his phony identifications, his paid-up cell phones, jeans, a hooded sweatshirt, sneakers, and a gray wig tightly wrapped in a small duffel bag.

He arrived at the Port Authority at six fifteen. As he'd expected, it was packed with commuters. He went into the men's room and changed clothes in a stall, then made his way to the platform for the bus to Glen Rock. He noticed that rain was now pelting the windows of the terminal. There won't be anyone strolling the streets, he thought. The people who don't get picked up at the bus station will be hurrying to get home. So will I.

At seven thirty, he got off the bus in Glen Rock. He tightened the hood around his neck. The hair of the gray wig was plastered against his forehead by the rain. It felt good.

Emily. Emily. Ready or not, here I come.

80

I have got to get some sleep, Emily thought. I feel absolutely worn out. I can barely function anymore. I've tipped my hand to Billy. I have proof of nothing. And even Jake believes that I have a vendetta against Billy.

Now that Jimmy Easton has been murdered, Ted is going to have to answer a lot of questions to the media about how we responded to Jimmy's threats in the courtroom. He needs a united front when he's facing the cameras. He certainly doesn't want *me* around.

And now it's Jake's reputation on the line, too. He may have missed more of that first meeting with Easton than he admitted to and is afraid to say so now. I understand him being afraid. Billy *is* his immediate boss and the prosecutor *is* his employer.

She arrived home in time to find the locksmith about to pack up. "Between those new locks and that pit bull of yours, you'll be fine," he said. "Just remember that no lock will do you any good unless you remember to make sure it's turned. And the same goes for that fancy security system those guys are installing. Okay, nice meeting you and good luck."

"Thanks. And thanks for coming so quickly." And thanks for leaving, Emily thought, then feeling momentarily guilty because the guy really was trying to be helpful.

It was quarter past five. As the locksmith was leaving, the alarm system technicians came up from the basement. "We're all set for now," the older one said. "Tomorrow we'll install your cameras. If you'll come to the kitchen I'll show you how to arm and disarm the system. You can also block off zones if you want to open any windows."

Her eyes almost closing, Emily walked with him into the kitchen, then listened and tried to absorb the differences between this system and her old one. After he left with the promise to return tomorrow, she let Bess run outside for a minute. The back door again rebolted, she checked her answering machine. She was disappointed to see that Alice Mills had not returned her call.

She tried again to reach Alice at her home and then at the Aldrich apartment. She left another message at the Aldrich number. "Alice, I would really appreciate it if you would call me back. You may not want to talk to me and I can understand why. I want you to know that the prosecutor has taken me off the case and I expect to be fired."

She knew that her voice was cracking but continued. "I honestly feel that if we knew why Natalie was frightened, we could find the person who murdered her."

Emily went into the living room, sat in her usual chair, and wrapped an afghan around her. I know that I probably won't stay awake, she thought, but I do want to watch *Courtside* when it comes on. She set the alarm on her watch for nine o'clock, closed her eyes, and was instantly asleep.

The alarm did not wake her. It was the persistent ringing of her cell phone that finally dragged her from sleep. When she answered her voice was groggy. "Hello," she whispered.

"Emily, are you all right? I've tried you three times in the last half hour. I was getting so worried. You sounded so upset when you left that last message."

It was Alice Mills. The genuine concern in her voice brought instant tears to Emily's eyes. "No, I'm all right. Alice, I may be crazy, and I know that the prosecutor thinks I am, but I believe that I know who killed Jamie Evans and almost certainly killed Natalie, too."

Hearing Alice gasp, Emily continued. "There must be some people who were close to Natalie, maybe another actor or a makeup person or a wardrobe lady who heard or saw something. Alice, did you think it was unusual for her to rush off to the Cape the way she did?"

"Natalie was stressed because of the divorce and getting a new agent but I never thought of her as being frightened," Alice Mills said. "Emily, it's not just for Natalie that it's so necessary to find the person who did this. It's also for Gregg and Katie's sake. Did you watch *Courtside* tonight?"

"I intended to but I fell asleep."

"Gregg and Katie and I were guests on it. Gregg talked about how horrible it is to live under this cloud, to be the 'person of interest.' But of course he is ecstatic to be out of jail. Katie is going back to school tomorrow and I'll be moving home."

"To your wonderful little apartment just a few blocks from Lincoln Center," Emily said.

"Did I tell you that?" Alice asked, surprised.

"You must have."

"Emily, there is one person I can call right now who will surely be awake. Jeanette Steele is the wardrobe mistress at the new play that opened at the Barrymore. She of all people might know something. She was with Natalie that last night."

"I'd be so grateful. Thank you, Alice."

Now somewhat awake, Emily got up and went back to the kitchen. It's too late to eat anything much, she thought. Maybe just some toast and a glass of wine. That should do me in pretty fast.

Emily looked at the kitchen window that faced the rental house. The shade was only halfway closed. She walked over to it and for a moment looked out. It was raining hard. What a miserable night, she thought as she pulled the shade down. And that place still gives me the creeps.

Before she put the bread in the toaster, she walked into the living room and looked outside to be reassured by the sight of the police car at the curb.

81

In his familiar perch at the kitchen window of the rental house, Zach was treated to the sight of Emily pulling down the shade. Just as he'd expected, it had been so easy to get in here. He knew that no one had seen him run down the driveway of the house behind the rental. He had vaulted over the low fence and then, key in hand, had been inside in the space of seconds.

He had the treats ready for Bess. Now that Emily was pulling down the shades, he was pretty certain that she was getting ready to go to bed. She'll let Bess out that one last time. Her alarm will be off. Bess will start barking when she senses me coming, he thought. That shouldn't scare Emily for the first few seconds. Bess barks at squirrels.

And then I'll be inside. Even if the barking makes the cop check inside the house, it will only take seconds to kill her. If I get away, fine. If I don't, maybe that's okay, too.

I'm tired of running.

82

Alice Mills called back at quarter of eleven. "Emily, I reached my friend Jeanette Steele, the wardrobe mistress. She was with Natalie that night. She said that Natalie was radiantly happy about the final show. She received a standing ovation that lasted for several minutes."

"Was she with Natalie until she left the theatre?" Emily asked.

"Almost till the end. Jeanette said Natalie changed and was ready to leave. Of course she was exhausted and drained by then. She didn't want any visitors in her dressing room and had said so. But then the producer knocked on her door. A very well-known actor, Tim Moynihan, was there with friends and was terribly anxious to meet her. Jeanette said Natalie wasn't happy about it but she let Moynihan and his friends in. That was when Jeanette left."

Moynihan, Emily thought. Tim Moynihan. He's a good friend of Ted's. I wonder how well he knows Billy. "Alice, I met Tim Moynihan only last week. I swear I think this is the link we need. You don't have his phone number, do you?"

"No, but I wouldn't be surprised if Gregg has it, or

could get it fast. I don't know if he knows Moynihan but I bet he knows some of his friends or the people on his television show. Hold on."

A moment later, Alice came back on. "Emily, Gregg is calling someone who can give him Tim Moynihan's number. While we wait for it, I want to tell you that I am worried about you. Please be careful. Please."

"You won't believe how many locks and whistles I have protecting me. To say nothing of having a patrol car sitting outside my door."

"I read about your neighbor being murdered by that serial killer. It's awful to think that he lived on your street."

"Well, he's gone now." Trying not to alarm Alice any more, Emily did her best to sound matter-of-fact.

"Even so, I worry. Oh, wait a minute, Gregg would like to talk to you."

Emily swallowed, her throat suddenly dry.

"Ms. Wallace, this is Gregg Aldrich."

"Mr. Aldrich, I really had no intention of trying to talk to you. I would only do so with your lawyer present or otherwise with his permission. I called to talk to Alice."

"I know that," Gregg replied. "But, at the risk of breaking any of the rules, I just wanted to tell you that I hold no animosity toward you. Jimmy Easton was a very convincing witness and it was your job to go after me when I testified. You were just doing your job. And, if I may say so, very well."

"Thank you. That's very generous of you."

"Do you honestly think that you may have some lead on Natalie's killer?"

"Yes, I do."

"Will you share that information or hunch or whatever it is with me?"

"Mr. Aldrich, it's not right for me to say more now but I promise you, if what I hope to learn works out, I will talk to Richard Moore immediately."

"Okay. You can't blame me for asking. Here's Tim Moynihan's phone number. It's 212-555-3295."

Emily wrote the number down and repeated it. "I promise that you will know soon."

"All right. Good night, Ms. Wallace."

For a long minute Emily held her hand on the phone before she replaced it in the cradle. It was so odd to feel so close to these two people when she spoke to them. So familiar with them. But of course she had liked Alice from the first time that she had met her.

And Gregg Aldrich? How many times did I battle myself because I just didn't face the truth? Maybe it's just as Alice said—that in my heart I knew he was innocent from the start.

Even this borrowed heart knew it, she thought.

She looked at Tim's number. He may very well be in bed and angry if I wake him up. But I can't wait. Taking a deep breath she pushed the numbers.

Tim Moynihan answered on the first ring. Emily could hear voices in the background and assumed that the television was on. At least he hadn't been asleep. When she identified herself, he was obviously surprised to hear her voice.

She got right to the point. "Tim, I know it is terribly late to call but it is very important. I just learned that you had gone to Natalie's dressing room the final night she was in *Streetcar.* How come you didn't mention it at dinner that night? We did talk about the trial."

"Emily, to tell you the truth, Ted had specifically asked us not to talk about the trial and particularly not to talk about having gone to her show or stopping at her dressing room to say hello. He knew you were tired and under a lot of stress. He wanted you to have a night off from all the work you've been doing. If you remember, Natalie's name came up but in a very general way."

Emily could hardly believe what she was hearing. "Are you telling me that Ted Wesley was at that last performance and stopped in at Natalie's dressing room?"

"Yes. He and Nancy came with Barbara and me and a couple of other friends." Tim Moynihan's voice changed. "Emily, is something wrong?"

Something is very wrong, she thought. "Tim, do you know Ted's cousin Billy Tryon?"

"Sure I do. Everyone knows Billy."

"Was he with you that night in Natalie's dressing room?"

"No. He's never been one of Nancy's favorites. You know how high-and-mighty she can be."

"Tim, maybe you know this. Was Billy ever known by the nickname 'Jess'?"

Tim's voice had a smile in it when he answered. "Not Billy. That was Ted's nickname. He's Edward Scott Jessup Wesley. He never uses 'Jessup' professionally but way back about twenty years ago he'd occasionally have a small part on the series I was doing at that time. He used the stage name 'Jess Wilson.'"

Emily took a guess. "That was about the time that he was having trouble with Nancy, wasn't it?"

"Yes, they actually separated for a few months. He was pretty upset about it."

Sure he was, Emily thought. He was running around with Jamie. He had promised her he would get a divorce and then when he dragged his feet, she probably threatened to go to his wife.

I bet he didn't kill her himself. I bet that Billy did the dirty work for him. And I bet that Natalie had recognized him that last night and he knew it. And she realized that he knew it. That's why she was so scared.

And of course he looks a lot like the guy in the sketch, too, Emily thought. The original sketch, not the substitute. He and Billy have a family resemblance. Their mothers are sisters. It just never occurred to me to think about him when I saw it.

She put the phone down and stood, not moving, trying to comprehend the awful reality of what she now knew. The man about to become the attorney general of the United States, the chief law enforcement officer in this country, was responsible for the brutal murders of two women, nearly two decades apart.

Emily heard a nearby house alarm go off. Then someone pounded on her door. It must be the police officer, she thought. He's going to tell me that he will quickly check that alarm and then come right back. She rushed to open it. Billy Tryon burst in, pushed her down, and slammed the door shut.

"Emily," he said as she cowered in terror on the floor, "you're really not as smart as you think."

83

~~

Sure that Emily must be ready to let Bess out, and too impatient to wait any longer, Zach was standing outside the door of the back porch when he heard the nearby alarm go off and then smelled smoke. He could see that the house at the corner was on fire. The neighborhood would soon be swarming with cops and firemen.

From inside, he could hear Bess's frantic barking. There was no more time. The cop outside her house had run up toward the fire. He had to get into her house. He ran to the basement window that he knew was in the tool area and kicked it in. Then, frenetically pushing away as much of the broken glass as possible, he forced his body through the narrow opening and dropped to the floor.

He felt the blood on his face and hands but he didn't care. The fire had been a sign. It was the end of the road. Fumbling in the dark, he reached for the hammer that he had remembered was on the wall, grabbed it, and made his way up the stairs. His plan had been to strangle her slowly, to feel her twitching in his arms, to listen to her trying to pray.

But he wouldn't have time for that. The cop who was stationed outside would come racing back here.

Step by step, Zach ascended the stairs as blood dripped from him onto the floor. He opened the door from the basement into the kitchen. Bess was in the living room, barking and barking. By now, Zach had expected that Bess would be running into the kitchen toward him. But then he heard a man's voice.

Can this be? The insult to him of Emily being with another man as he visited her made him tremble. His feet noiseless in the sneakers, Zach covered the short distance and then stopped. The man in the room was holding a gun to Emily's head as he pushed her down roughly into a chair.

Then he heard Emily scream, "You won't get away with this, Billy. You know that, too. It's over for you, and it's over for Ted."

"You're wrong, Emily. Too bad I had to set a fire to draw that cop away. Everybody will think that the nut Zach came back for you."

"The nut did come back," Zach said smiling as he raised the hammer and smashed it on Billy Tryon's head. The gun went off as the front door was battered open. As Emily slumped, blood spurting from her leg, Zach was tackled by two police officers. After a furious struggle, they wrested the hammer away from him and, as he lay moaning on the floor, they cuffed his hands behind his back.

Barely conscious, Emily heard a shocked voice yelling, "My God, it's Billy Tryon. He's dead."

Then the darkness closed over her.

84

The next day in Hackensack Hospital, Emily was visited by Gregg Aldrich and Alice Mills. She had known they were coming and was sitting in an armchair. Alice rushed across the room and put her arms around Emily. "They could have killed you. Oh, thank God you're all right, thank God."

"Hey, come on, Alice. You're supposed to cheer up the person you visit in the hospital," Gregg Aldrich said smiling. He was carrying a bouquet of long-stemmed roses. "Emily, thank you for giving me my life back," he said. "Richard Moore told me that the prosecutor has been arrested and will be charged with the murders of both Natalie and Jamie Evans."

"That's right," Emily answered, "I only passed out for a few minutes. When I told the cops what happened, they played it smart with Ted Wesley. They told him that Billy had been caught in my house and had admitted to killing Natalie and Jamie for him. He was petrified but that finished him. He broke down and confessed to everything. So I guess I still have my job. And I guess he won't be going to Washington."

Gregg Aldrich shook his head. "I'll never understand

why all of this happened. But it's over." Gregg took Emily's hand and then bent down and kissed her on the cheek. "I have to tell you something. In some ways, you remind me of Natalie. I'm not sure why. I can't put my finger on it. But you do."

"She must have been a wonderful person," Emily said. "I'm glad if I do remind you of her."

"Do you agree, Alice?" Gregg asked tenderly.

"I know what you mean," Alice said softly, pretending to study Emily as she embraced her again. "We'll leave you and let you rest now. I'll call you tomorrow to see how you are feeling."

Dear God, Alice thought. Of course she is like her! Natalie's heart is beating inside of her. She remembered how, sick with grief, she had given her doctor permission to give Natalie's heart to a young war widow who was his patient, and who was probably not going to live if she did not get a heart very quickly.

I didn't need to read about her transplant at the same time and in the same New York hospital where Natalie's heart was taken. I didn't need to know that my doctor had performed Emily's surgery. The minute I sat across from Emily at her desk, I knew that Natalie was there with me.

Her eyes flooding with tears, she turned to say good-bye to Emily. She must never know. Gregg must never know. They must go on with their lives. Alice knew that she could only see Emily once in a while. She knew she had to let go. "Emily, I hope that you're going to take some time off and heal from this and enjoy yourself," she said.

Emily smiled. "You sound like my father, who is flying in to see me as we speak." And then, not quite sure why she was telling Alice, she said, "I get out of here tomorrow and Saturday night I have a date with an orthopedic surgeon. I'm looking forward to it."

I really am, Emily thought when she was alone again. I'm ready now.

THE SHADOW OF YOUR SMILE

Mary Higgins Clark

1

Olivia Morrow sat quietly across the desk from her long-time friend Clay Hadley, absorbing the death sentence he had just pronounced.

For an instant, she looked away from the compassion she saw in his eyes and glanced out the window of his twenty-fourth-floor office on East Seventy-second Street in Manhattan. In the distance she could see a helicopter making its slow journey over the East River on this chilly October morning.

My journey is ending, she thought, then realized that Clay was expecting a response from her.

"Two weeks," she said. It was not a question. She glanced at the antique clock on the bookcase behind Clay's desk. It was ten minutes past nine. The first day of the two weeks—at least it's the start of the day, she thought, glad she had asked for an early appointment.

He was answering her. "Three at the most. I'm sorry, Olivia. I was hoping . . ."

"Don't be sorry," Olivia interrupted briskly. "I'm eighty-three years old. Even though my generation lives so much longer than previous ones, my friends have been dropping like flies lately. Our problem is that we worry we'll live too long and end up in a nursing home, or become a terrible burden to everyone. To know I have a very short time left, but will still be able to think clearly and walk around unassisted is an immeasurable gift." Her voice trailed off.

Clay Hadley's eyes narrowed. He understood the troubled expression that had erased the serenity from Olivia's face. Before she spoke, he knew what she would say. "Clay, only you and I know."

He nodded.

"Do we have the right to continue to hide the truth?" she asked, looking at him intently. "Mother thought she did. She intended to take it to her grave, but at the very end, when only you and I were there, she felt compelled to tell us. It became for her a matter of conscience. Monica Farrell is the rightful heir to the income from that patent. Alex Gannon was her grandfather, and in his will he left everything he had to his issue if any existed and only then to his brother. And with all the enormous good Catherine did in her life as a nun, her reputation has always been compromised by the insinuation that all those years ago, before she entered the convent, she may have had a consensual liaison with a lover."

Hadley studied Olivia Morrow's face. Even the usual signs of age, the wrinkles around her eyes and mouth, the slight tremor of her neck, the way she leaned forward to catch everything he said, did not detract from her finely chiseled features. His father had been her mother's cardiologist, and he had taken over when his father retired. Now in his early fifties, he could not remember a time when the Morrow family had not been part of his life. As a child he had been in awe of Olivia, recognizing even then that she was always beautifully dressed. Later he realized that at that time she had still been working as a salesgirl at B. Altman's, the famous Fifth Avenue department store, and that her style was achieved by buying her clothes at giveaway end-of-the-season sales. Never married, she had retired as an executive and board member of Altman's years ago.

He had met her older cousin Catherine only a few times, and by then she was already a legend, the nun who had started seven hospitals for handicapped children—research hospitals dedicated to finding ways to cure or alleviate the suffering of their damaged bodies or minds.

"Do you know that some doctors are calling the healing of the child in Pennsylvania a miracle and attributing it to Catherine's intercession?" Olivia asked. "They're preparing to present the case for her beatification."

Clay Hadley felt his mouth go dry. "No, I hadn't heard." Not a Catholic, he vaguely understood that that would be the first step for the Church to eventually declare Sister Catherine a saint and worthy of veneration by the faithful.

"Of course that will mean that the subject of her having given birth will be explored, and because of the vicious rumors that will almost certainly finish her chance of her being found worthy," Olivia added, her tone angry.

"Olivia, there was a reason neither Sister Catherine nor your mother ever named the father of her child."

"Catherine didn't. My mother did."

Olivia leaned her hands on the arms of the chair, a signal to Clay that she was about to stand up. He rose and walked around his desk, with quick steps for such a bulky man. He knew that some of his patients referred to him as "Chunky Clay the Cardiologist." His voice humorous, his eyes twinkling, he counseled all of them, "Forget about me and make sure you lose weight. I look at the picture of an ice cream cone and put on five pounds. It's my cross to bear." It was a performance he had perfected. Now he took Olivia's hands in his and kissed her gently.

Involuntarily she drew back from the sensation of his short, graying beard grazing her cheek, then to cover the reaction returned the kiss. "Clay, my own situation remains between us. I will tell my close friends very soon." She paused, then, her tone ironic, she added, "In fact I'd obviously better tell them *very* soon. Perhaps fortunately, I don't have a single family member left." Then she stopped, realizing that what she had just said wasn't true.

On her deathbed her mother had told her that after she realized she was pregnant, Catherine had spent a year in Ireland, where she had given birth to a son. He had been adopted by the Farrells, an American couple from Boston who were selected by the mother superior of the religious order Catherine entered. They had named him Edward, and he had grown up in Boston.

I've followed their lives ever since, Olivia thought. Edward didn't marry until he was forty-two. His wife has been dead a long time and he passed away about five years ago. Their daughter, Monica, is thirty-one now, a pediatrician on the staff of Greenwich Village Hospital. Catherine was my first cousin. Her granddaughter is my cousin. She is my only family, and she doesn't know I exist.

Now, as she withdrew her hands from Clay's grasp, she said, "Monica has turned out to be so like her grand-mother, devoting her life to taking care of babies and little children. Do you realize what all that money would mean to her?"

"Olivia, don't you believe in redemption? Look at what her attacker did with the rest of his life. Think of the lives he saved. And what about his brother's family? They're prominent philanthropists. Think what this will mean to them."

"I am thinking about it, and that's what I have to weigh. I'll call you, Clay."

Clay Hadley waited until the door of his private office closed, then picked up the phone and dialed a private number that was known to very few people. When a familiar voice answered he did not waste time in prelimi-naries. "It's exactly what I was afraid of. I know Olivia . . . She's going to talk."

"We can't let that happen," the person on the other end of the line said matter-of-factly. "You've got to make sure it doesn't. Why didn't you give her something? With her medical condition, no one would question her death."

"Believe it or not, it isn't that simple to kill someone.

And suppose she manages to leave the proof before I can stop her?"

"In that case we take out double insurance. Sad to say, a fatal attack on an attractive young woman in Manhattan is hardly an extraordinary event these days. I'll take care of it immediately."

2

Dr. Monica Farrell shivered as she posed for a picture with Tony and Rosalie Garcia on the steps of Greenwich Village Hospital. Tony was holding Carlos, their two-year-old son, who had just been declared free of the leukemia that had almost claimed his life.

Monica remembered the day when, as she was about to leave her office, Rosalie phoned in a panic. "Doctor, the baby has spots on his stomach." Carlos was then six weeks old. Even before she saw him, Monica had the terrible hunch that what she was going to find was the onset of juvenile leukemia. Diagnostic tests confirmed that hunch and Carlos's chances were calculated to be at best fifty-fifty. Monica had promised his weeping young parents that as far as she was concerned, those were good enough odds and Carlos was already too tough a little guy not to win the fight.

"Now one with you holding Carlos, Dr. Monica," Tony ordered as he took the camera from the passerby who had volunteered to become the acting photographer.

Monica reached for the squirming two-year-old, who had by then decided he'd smiled long enough. This will be some picture, she thought as she waved at the camera, hoping that Carlos could follow her example. Instead he pulled the clip at the nape of her neck and her long dark-blond hair fell loose around her shoulders.

After a flurry of good-byes and "God bless you, Dr. Monica, we wouldn't have made it without you, and we'll see you for his checkup," the Garcias were gone with one final wave from the window of the taxi. As Monica stepped back inside the hospital and walked to the elevator bank, she reached up to gather the strands of her hair and refasten the clip.

"Leave it like that. It looks good." Dr. Ryan Jenner, a neurologist who had been in Georgetown Medical School a few years ahead of Monica, had fallen in step with her. He had recently come on staff at Greenwich Village and had stopped for a moment to chat a few times when they ran into each other. Jenner, wearing scrubs and a plastic bonnet, had obviously been in surgery or was on his way to it.

Monica laughed as she pushed the button for an ascending elevator. "Oh, sure. And maybe I should drop in on your operating room while it's like this."

The door of a descending elevator was opening.

"Maybe I wouldn't mind," Jenner said as he got into it.

And maybe you would. In fact you'd have a heart attack, Monica thought as she stepped into an already crowded elevator. Ryan Jenner, despite his youthful face and ready smile, was already known to be a perfectionist and intolerant of any lapses in patient care. Being in his operating room with uncovered hair was unthinkable.

When she got off on the pediatric floor the wail of a

screaming baby was the first sound Monica heard. She knew it was her patient eleven-month-old Sally Carter, and the lack of visits from her single mother was infuriating. Before she went in to try to comfort the baby, she stopped at the nurse's desk. "Any sign of Mommy dearest?" she asked, then regretted she had been so outspoken.

"Not since yesterday morning," Rita Greenberg, the longtime head nurse on the floor, answered, her tone as annoyed as Monica's. "But she *did* manage to squeeze in a phone call an hour ago to say she was tied up at work and ask if Sally had had a good night. Doctor, I'm telling you, there's something odd about that whole situation. That woman acts no more like a mother than the stuffed animals in the playroom do. Are you going to discharge Sally today?"

"Not until I find out who will be taking care of her when the mother is so busy. Sally had asthma and pneumonia when she was brought to the emergency room. I can't imagine what the mother or the babysitter was thinking waiting so long to get medical attention for her."

Followed by the nurse, Monica went into the small room with the single crib, to which Sally had been moved because her crying was waking up the other babies. Sally was standing, holding on to the railings, her light brown hair curling around her tearstained face.

"She'll work herself into another asthma attack," Monica said angrily, as she reached in and plucked the baby from the crib. As Sally clung to her, the crying immediately lessened, then evolved into subdued sobs and finally began to ease off.

"My God, how she has bonded to you, Doctor, but

then you've got the magic touch," Rita Greenberg said. "There's no one like you with the little ones."

"Sally knows that she and I are pals," Monica said. "Let's give her some warm milk and I'll bet she'll settle down."

As she waited for the nurse to return, Monica rocked the baby in her arms. Your mother should be doing this, she thought. I wonder how much attention she gives you at home? Her tiny hands soft on Monica's neck, Sally's eyes began to close.

Monica laid the sleepy baby back in the crib and changed her wet diaper. Then she turned Sally on her side and covered her with a blanket. Greenberg returned with a bottle of warm milk but before she gave it to the baby, Monica reached for a cotton tip and swabbed inside Sally's cheek.

In the past week, she had noticed that several times when Sally's mother came to visit, she stopped at the large courtesy counter in the lounge area and brought a cup of coffee with her. Invariably she left it half empty on the nightstand by the crib.

It's only a hunch, Monica told herself, and I know I have no right to do it. But I'm going to send word to Ms. Carter that I must meet with her before I will discharge Sally. I'd love to compare the baby's DNA with hers. She swears she's the birth mother, but if she's not, why would she bother to lie about it? Then reminding herself once more that she had no right to secretly compare the DNA, she threw the swab in the wastebasket.

After checking her other patients, Monica went to her office on East Fourteenth Street for her afternoon hours.

It was six thirty when, trying not to conceal her weariness, she said good-bye to her last patient, an eight-year-old boy with an ear infection.

Nan Rhodes, her receptionist-bookkeeper, was closing up at her desk. In her sixties, rotund, and with unfailing patience no matter how hectic the waiting room, Nan asked the question Monica had been hoping to put aside for another day.

"Doctor, what about that inquiry from the bishop's office in New Jersey, asking you to be a witness in the beatification process for that nun?"

"Nan, I don't believe in miracles. You know that. I sent them a copy of the initial X-rays and CAT scan. They speak for themselves."

"But you did believe that with brain cancer that advanced, Michael O'Keefe would never see his fifth birthday, didn't you?"

"Absolutely."

"You suggested his parents take him to the Knowles Clinic in Cincinnati because it's the best research hospital in brain cancer, but you did it knowing full well they'd confirm your diagnosis out there," Nan persisted.

"Nan, we both know what I said and what I believed," Monica said. "Come on, let's not play twenty questions."

"Doctor, you also told me that when you gave them the diagnosis Michael's father was so upset, he almost passed out, but that the mother told you that her son was not going to die because she was going to start a crusade of prayer to Sister Catherine, the nun who founded those hospitals for sick children."

"Nan, how many people refuse to accept that an illness

is terminal? We see it every day at the hospital. They want a second and third opinion. They want more tests. They want to sign up for risky procedures. Sometimes the inevitable is prolonged, but in the end the result is the same."

Nan's expression softened as she looked at the slender young woman whose body posture was so clearly showing her fatigue. . . . She knew Monica had been at the hospital during the night, when one of her little patients had a seizure. "Doctor, I know it isn't my place to badger you, but there are going to be witnesses from the medical staff in Cincinnati to testify that Michael O'Keefe should not have survived. Today he's absolutely cancer free. I think you have a sacred obligation to verify that you had that conversation with the mother the very minute you warned her that he could not recover, because that was the moment she turned to Sister Catherine for help."

"Nan, I saw Carlos Garcia this morning. He's cancer free as well."

"It's not the same and you know it. We have the treatment to beat childhood leukemia. We don't have it for advanced and spreading brain cancer."

Monica realized two facts. It was useless to argue with Nan, and in her heart she knew Nan was right. "I'll go," she said, "but it won't do that would-be saint any good. Where am I supposed to testify about this?"

"A monsignor from the Metuchen diocese in New Jersey is the one you should meet. He suggested next Wednesday afternoon. As it happens, I didn't make any appointments for you after eleven o'clock that day."

"Then so be it," Monica acquiesced. "Call him back

and set it up. Are you ready to go? I'll ring for the elevator."

"Right behind you. I love what you just said."

"That I'll ring for the elevator?"

"No, of course not. I mean you just said 'so be it.'"

"So?"

"As far as the Catholic Church is concerned, 'so be it' is the translation for 'amen.' Kind of fitting in this case, don't you think, Doctor?"

WITHDRAWN